"I loved this brave, hilarious, impossibly tender book with my whole zombie heart."
Becky Albertalli, author of Simon vs. the Homo Sapiens Agenda

"Blisteringly funny, joyous and smart, with such a big, beautiful heart."   Simon James Green, author of Gay Club!

"William Hussey is a powerhouse of LGBT+ fiction and *Broken Hearts* is a triumph."
Calum McSwiggan, author of Straight Expectations

"A hilarious heartbreaker! Everything you could want from a YA book, great characters, zingy one-liners, and a swoony as heck romance. I loved it!"
George Lester, author of Boy Queen

"Yet another triumph from William Hussey, one of the most powerful and important voices we have in YA right now."   Benjamin Dean, author of The King is Dead

"This book has a big old beautiful heart, and is proof that William Hussey is one of our finest writers for teens."
Phil Earle, author of When the Sky Falls

"The zombies might be fake but the heart is very real... Hilarious and poignant in equal measure!"
Lee Newbery, author of The Last Firefox

For Christopher White, from my heart to yours,
with all my love.

And for Mr Ravi De Silva, Dr Stephen Hoole, and
all the wonderful medics and nurses at the Royal Papworth
Hospital who mended my silly heart and saved my life.
Eternal thanks.

First published in the UK in 2023 by Usborne Publishing Limited, Usborne House,
83-85 Saffron Hill, London EC1N 8 RT,England. usborne.com

Usborne Verlag, Usborne Publishing Limited, Prüfeninger Str. 20, 93049 Regensburg,
Deutschland, VK Nr. 17560

Text © William Hussey, 2023

Cover illustration by Ricardo Bessa © Usborne Publishing Limited, 2023

The name Usborne and the Balloon logo are Trade Marks of
Usborne Publishing Limited

A CIP catalogue record for this book is available from the British Library.

ISBN 9781803700038   JFMAMJ ASOND/23 7774/3

Printed and bound using 100% renewable energy at CPI Group (UK) Ltd, Croydon, CR0 4YY.

WILLIAM HUSSEY

BROKEN HEARTS AND ZOMBIE PARTS

USBORNE

Content note:
BROKEN HEARTS AND ZOMBIE PARTS
*includes references to homophobia
and homophobic slurs*

Eighteen hours after the mythic disaster that was prom, here I lie, naked apart from this flimsy gown, a hairy man-mountain leaning over me, caressing my chest. Okay, so that might sound like some weird sex dungeon thing. It really isn't.

A weird sex dungeon wouldn't be this scary.

"All right, Jesse," says Big Si, "take another deep breath and hold it for me."

I obediently gulp down half the oxygen in the room and puff out hamster cheeks. Meanwhile Big Si skates the echocardiogram probe around my left nipple before pressing it hard against my breastbone. The pressure hurts a bit and I wince, whispering that I'm okay when Big Si apologizes for any discomfort.

So, in case you're wondering, I'm lying on my side on a narrow examination table, my face to the wall, the immense Simon seated on a stool behind me.

"Aaaaaaaand breathe," he says.

I exhale and glance down. My skin gleams with the ultrasound gloop that somehow helps the probe see inside my heart. Except you don't need a probe to see how hard it's hammering right now. My chest thrums like a trampoline at a kids' birthday party.

"Everything all right?" Si asks.

"Fabulous." I nod. "Thanks, Big Si… Except." My eyes go wide. "Oh God, wait. I'm sorry, did you ask me to call you 'Big Si' or did I imagine it? I mean, you *are* quite tall. Not freakishly tall or anything. I actually think you're very nicely proportioned."

And I want to die. Except, no! Don't even think that, not while you're wired up to about a million electrodes (actually four, but still) and having your heart examined. I might not be superstitious, and I definitely don't believe in all that tempting fate bullshit, but it's better to be safe than sorry, right? Especially in a situation like this.

Chuckling comes from behind me, so I guess Big Si isn't too offended by my complimenting his dimensions.

"Right, another deep breath, Jesse." The probe nestles back against my ribs. "Here we go."

I'm in hamster-cheek mode again when the monitor attached to the probe starts to whoosh in this weird, rhythmic, *Star Warsy* sort of way. I'm pretty sure that's the sound of blood gushing into – or pumping out of – my heart.

"Those noises are perfectly normal," Si assures me. "You're a bit keyed up right now, but your pulse will settle in a moment or two, I promise. Just try to relax."

Relax? You've got to be fu— No, sure, good advice, relax. Because everything is bound to be all right. I've never had any kind of issue with my heart before, so this is probably just a bizarre one-off thing that they'll sort with a pill or something. Okay. Good. Let's concentrate on something *not* heart related. My thoughts flip back to Cas. What the hell was going on with him last night? Out of our entire school, I would probably have been voted Most Likely to Fuck Up Prom, and I guess I kind of did, clutching my chest and collapsing like a total drama queen into Morgan's arms (cue screaming kids, cue panicked teachers, cue ambulance sirens) but that was entirely my best mate's fault. Finding Cas like that behind the bins with Matilda Chen? That certainly coincided with my heart kicking into a weird high gear. And as for Cas…?

Yeah, it's no good. I can't make any sense of Cas right now, so instead I rewind to ten minutes ago, just before I entered the echocardiogram changing room. Big Si had been checking his clipboard and asking yet another of the pre-scan safety questions. For my part, I'd suddenly become fascinated by his improbable arms. So freaking huge! I mean, even his biceps seemed to have biceps.

"Still with us, Jesse?"

"Sorry," I'd said, blinking, "what?"

He tapped the top of my head gently with the clipboard. "No need to be worried. We're just going to have a little look inside your chest and—"

"If you find an alien spawn growing inside there, you have my permission to shoot me." I grinned. "A nice clean headshot, please. Honestly, I'd prefer that to going through the whole birthing-a-monster melodrama. *Such* a chore."

Si frowned and gave me this all too familiar up-and-down look. People have been giving me this look pretty regularly for the past seventeen years, or at least ever since I've been able to speak.

"So what we need you to do next," he continued, "is to pop off all your clothes and then— WHOA! No, my friend. Not in the corridor. In the changing room."

"Ah, of course," I said, rebuckling my belt. "Sorry about that. As you can probably tell, I'm just a *teeny* bit hyper right now. But seriously, I'm not a naturist or anything. In fact, I am stunningly uncomfortable around all forms of public nudity."

"That's very reassuring." Big Si nodded. "So get undressed, *in* the cubicle, then put on the gown that's provided. Once you're done, head through the other door and I'll be waiting for you in the scanning room. Oh, just one last thing, we have to check – do you have any piercings?"

I stared at him. "Is that a requirement?"

"No." Si ran his palm across his forehead. "No, Jesse, I just… You see, anything metallic can interfere with the equipment."

"Oh, is it a magnetic thing?" I asked. "Because there was this kid at school whose older brother had a piercing, you know, down *there*, and he got into this medical scanner thingy without telling anyone and his penis was almost completely ripped off. True story."

Big Si closed his eyes. "Do you have such an adornment or anything else metallic in or on your person?"

Did I? The prospect of some vital organ dangling from a piece of hospital machinery like a grisly fridge magnet was enough to make me question my entire piercings history. Or lack thereof. Was it feasible that I'd had a nipple or a belly button or a bellend metallically embellished and completely forgotten about it? I was inclined to say… *No.*

"N-ooo," I said out of the side of my mouth.

"You're not sure?"

This was ridiculous. Of course I was sure.

"That's ridiculous," I said, "of course I'm sure."

Si made a note on his clipboard and pointed to the changing-room door. I'm pretty sure he'd written something like *handle with care* rather than *no piercings*.

The monitor gives this dramatic whoosh and I'm back in the craptacular present.

"And breathe normally," Big Si advises.

I breathe – *kind of normally* – and look at the wall a few centimetres from my nose. There's a laminated poster tacked there, and superimposed over a picture of a diseased heart is a side-on reflection of my face: poodle mop of absurdly curly black hair, big apple-green eyes my mum says are cute, thick eyebrows that keep threatening to meet in the middle, and a mouth on the verge of a scream.

Honestly, with Big Si leaning over me it's all starting to get a bit much. One of the safety questions was, *Are you claustrophobic?* I guess because the echocardiogrammer, or whatever they're called, has to get very up close and personal to do their job. But how are you supposed to know what level of claustrophobia they mean? For example, I've had a fairly trouble-free history with things like crowded buses and hide-and-seek cupboards. Although there was that spin-the-bottle game at Julia Odili's Halloween party when Sammy McBride and I ended up kissing in a closet and I developed a never-ending boner and had to walk home still hugging my coat to my groin. But that wasn't anything to do with a fear of enclosed spaces. That was because Sammy looks kind of like a young Chadwick Boseman from *Black Panther*. So, I don't think unscheduled erections are a side effect of claustrophobia.

Unless they are. I make a mental note to google it later.

Which is all an attempt to divert myself from a sense

of mounting panic. Thoughts of last night's prom and Cas's weird behaviour behind the bins have been like a sticking plaster, holding back the horrible freakiness of this whole scan deal and what it might mean. But now that metaphorical plaster is coming loose and I can feel the walls of this tiny room closing in on me, slowly squeezing my lungs, choking the air out of my throat until I just have to—

"And we're done!" Big Si announces. "Great work, Jesse. Give me a sec and I'll get you some paper towels for your chest."

My mouth clamps shut. My shriek vanishes. I feel strangely cheated.

I turn onto my back and find myself blinking up at Big Si's glistening lumberjack beard. In everyday life, you very rarely get to check out the underside of a guy's beard. Unlike me, Big Si is clearly into high-maintenance grooming. I'm almost sure that probably means he's gay, but that is the kind of assumption my friend Morgan would call "just awful".

I take some paper towels and start wiping off the gloop while Big Si unhooks me from the electrodes.

"How was it?" He smiles.

I begin to stand up, some cool comment forming in my brain, when all at once I let loose this random sob. Honestly, it's mortifying! A weird braying sound, like a donkey that's swallowed a half tank of helium. I guess it comes from all the stress and sleeplessness, but it's such a ridiculous noise that I feel the mother of all blushes erupt across my cheeks.

"Wow, so I don't know what that was about." I laugh, swapping out the donkey impression for some kind of maniacal hyena. "Just so you know, I watch a ludicrous number of horror movies, so it actually takes quite a lot to scare me. And even if I was a bit freaked by all this, I'm not really a crier, I'm more likely to start jabbering on and on about nothing, which is what my mum tells me I do whenever I'm nervous, though I think she's talking rubbish because I am in fact a man of very few words."

I stop, a little breathless, and allow Big Si to give my shoulder a friendly pat.

"It's all good," he says, taking back the used paper towels and binning them. "Nothing to be embarrassed about. Now, if you want to get dressed again and return to the waiting room, Dr Myers will call you through once he's reviewed the scans and my report."

"Dr *Myers*?" I beam, my mortification immediately forgotten. "No way! Is his first name Michael?"

"I think it's Julian."

"Oh. So not like the serial killer from John Carpenter's 1978 horror classic *Halloween*?"

"Not entirely."

"Well, that's good. I guess." I'm almost at the changing

room door when I turn back. "But can I just ask – my heart's basically okay, right? That probe thingy didn't pick up anything really sinister? Because, you know, I'm young and reasonably fit, and I've never had any heart problems before, so I'm sure everything must be absolutely fine…"

Big Si makes a final note on his clipboard and throws me a smile from behind his alluring logger's beard.

"Good luck, Jesse Spark," he says. "Meeting you was certainly…an experience."

As soon as I step into the cardiology waiting room, my mum leaps to her feet. Most of the guys sitting nearby spring up after her, all glaring at each other as they try to figure out how best to assist this damsel in distress. Joke's on them. My mum hasn't needed the help of a man since she was five years old and her dad tried to teach her chess one rainy afternoon. I'm not sure Grandpa ever got over being checkmated in eight moves.

The men sink back into their seats (or are dragged back into them by indignant wives and girlfriends) as Mum rushes over to me. So here's the deal – Mum had me when she was seventeen, and she's still very pretty, even for a decrepit thirtysomething. Hence the hopeless alpha males. Hence endless embarrassment at school, where my mother is the mental pin-up for every straight guy in Year Twelve.

"How did it go?" she asks, taking me by the shoulders.

"Dunno." I shrug. "We have to wait to find out what the doctor thinks of the scans. Mother, stop!"

My mum has this professional lawyer's stare that has the power to cut right through my bullshit. A useful superpower for a defence solicitor, not so welcome in a family environment. Being marginally cool, she uses her power sparingly. She knows, she says, that teenagers must have their secrets. After all, she kept the mother of all secrets (quite literally) for nine months when she was about my age. So she releases me from the Stare and I slump down beside her.

"Stop what?" she asks, acting all innocent.

"Your lawyer tricks are pointless," I mutter. "I'm telling you the truth. If you don't believe me, you can go and ask Big Simon and his fabulous beard."

"His fabulous *what*?" But I refuse to elaborate and so we lapse into silence. A handful of seconds go by before her shoulder bumps against mine. "So they really didn't say anything?"

"God. No, all right? We just have to sit and wait. I'm sure it'll be fine."

"Maybe," she says, picking an invisible piece of fluff from my collar. "But I don't like it."

I turn my whole body towards her. "Oh gosh, thanks, that's wonderfully reassuring of you! I'm so glad you decided to come along for moral support today, but maybe I should have invited my arch-enemy instead. You know, sometimes I wonder if you even like me."

"If I didn't like you, Jesse bear, I'd put the parental locks on the Wi-Fi. Then you'd have to think of something else to fill up those three spare hours every night."

A frumpy-looking woman in a gigantic coat sitting on the other side of Mum arches a drawn-on eyebrow, and it suddenly seems important that I set the record straight.

"My mother is exaggerating," I tell her, leaning across to make my point. "It's nowhere near three hours. Ten minutes, maybe. Fifteen max."

"For Christ's sake, Jesse," Mum says out of the corner of her mouth, pushing me back into my chair while simultaneously throwing the eyebrow woman an apologetic glance. "Will you please stop talking and just look at your phone like a normal teenager?"

I grumble but comply, digging my hand into my jeans pocket and bringing out my mobile. I've had it switched off during the scan, and I'm just starting to flick through a gallery of possible filming locations for *Zombie Honeymoon* (a Jesse Spark/Casper Loomis production) when my message alert screeches around the waiting room. Twenty-seven notifications, all from Cas and Morgan. I catch a few snippets:

Morgs: Jess, what is going on? Answer your bloody messages! 😠

Cas: Sparky, I'm SO sorry about last night. Have I accidentally killed you? Pls reply! 😫

My phone is still stabbing out the *EEEE! EEEE! EEEE! EEEE!* shower scene music from classic horror movie *Psycho* when my mum grabs it out of my hand.

"What's the problem now?" I snap. "First you want me to look at my phone, next you—"

She nudges me in the ribs and nods to where a cardiology patient is clutching his chest. I give him a sheepish wave and put my phone away again – I'll have to message Morgan and Cas back later.

"So." I sigh, casting a sweeping glance around the waiting room. "You okay being here?"

Mum frowns. "Me? Of course. Why wouldn't I be?"

"I dunno. This place. I wondered if it reminded you of Dad? Because if it does, and if maybe you want to—"

"Not at all. Like I said, I'm fine," she insists.

I look at her for a moment. Apart from a broken arm from falling out of a tree when I was five (I was never made for anything so nimble and dextrous as scaling trees), we haven't had much to do with hospitals. At least, I haven't. Mum must have spent a lot of time in them when I was a baby. You see, my dad died of testicular cancer not long after I was born. So yeah, Mum went through a hell of a lot when she was still quite young. We never talk about my dad, though; barely even acknowledge he existed. From the few things Mum has let slip over the years, I know this isn't because he was a bad guy or anything.

I'm not really sure why we don't—

"Jesse Spark," a nurse announces, "Dr Myers will see you now."

I jump to my feet, and at least ninety per cent of the waiting room looks relieved. I have this effect on strangers. It's a gift.

We follow the nurse down a corridor and, before we reach the door at the end, Mum grabs my hand and gives it a squeeze.

"Oh, Jesse." She takes out a tissue and wipes her palm. "You're very sweaty."

"Thanks, Mother. Another ego-boost."

"I'm sorry, love. It's just, I've had clients facing life imprisonment that have perspired less. Let's try to stay calm until we know exactly what's going on, agreed?"

I shoot her dagger eyes. In many ways I'm very proud of my mum. She brought me up more or less single-handedly, while at the same time getting her A levels, then putting herself through uni. To Morgan, she's a role model; to Cas, the mother he never had. In fact, Cas is probably the only straight kid at school who doesn't objectify Sabrina Spark as a dominatrix MILF. But I'd be lying if I said our relationship didn't piss me off sometimes. I often feel more like her sidekick than her son, and that's not always what I need.

The nurse knocks on the door.

"Come!"

We step into a dimly lit room with a small, sniffly man sitting behind a desk. My file is placed beside him and, without looking up from his monitor, Dr Myers sniffs us into a couple of chairs.

"Jesse, is it?" He glances at me over half-moon spectacles. "All right, young man, tell me how you came to be here today."

"Oh," I say, staring at the plastic model of a dissected heart on his bookcase, "my mum and I got a taxi. Mum's car is in for its MOT, and we would've taken the bus, except I thought if my heart exploded on public transport that would be slightly traumatic for the other passengers. Although people are more resilient than you think. Have you heard of that football team whose plane crashed in the Andes and they all had to start eating each other's corpses to survive? Well, they just got on with it, didn't they?"

I stop dead. The doctor is giving me the up-and-down look. Of course he is.

"I didn't mean how did you physically arrive at the hospital." *Sniff.* "I meant, what happened medically to land you in that chair?"

"Oh, that's easy," I tell him. "It was our Year Twelve prom. I wasn't even interested in going, but Morgan said we should, as moral support for Cas, which I didn't understand at the time, but then she said Cas and his awful girlfriend Brianna were having relationship issues. Which did surprise me a bit, because I hadn't picked up any vibe that things were off between them. But apparently they were, and Cas was feeling crappy about it, so we went, and it was actually pretty cool, at least for Ferrivale High. I mean it wasn't like an American prom with jocks spiking the punch and choreographed dance routines or anything, but the tunes were okay, and it would've made a great opening scene for our zombie movie. FYI, me and Cas are filming a zombie movie in September, and we're actually looking for investors, and I know doctors are pretty rich, so if you fancy getting involved…?" Monumental sniff. "We're not amateurs!" I insist. "We've actually got tons of experience. Like, we made our first movie, *Spaghetti Monsters from Uranus*, when we were in primary school. And then in Year Seven we made *Bad Dreams on Maple Avenue*, where a demon with sharpened forks for fingers invades the daydreams of these kids and they all—"

Dr Myers frowned. "Doesn't that sound a bit like *A Nightmare on Elm*—"

"It was a homage," I say defensively. "Anyway, we've got about twenty short movies under our belt now, so if you did fancy investing?" The mother of all sniffs. "Or not. Not is cool. Anyway, so back to the prom – I was thinking about heading home to get my GoPro camera when Ross Stanley tells me I'd better take a look outside because Cas was about to enter a whole world of pain. And sure enough, when Morgan and I get there we find this huge crew of footie lads surrounding Cas. And you'll never guess what? They say he's been caught snogging Matilda Chen, Brianna's best friend, *behind the bins*. At first I can't believe it, basically for two reasons. One, Cas's primary fear since childhood has been bin juice. I'm serious. He can watch *The Texas Chain Saw Massacre* without wincing, but the idea of bin spill is his own personal hell. Two, this is Cas. He's like the anti-cheater. Honestly, he's so moral Jesus would tell him to chill. So I was staggered. And Morgan was staggered. But Cas, he just shrugged and held his hands up to it. And Brianna was crying and her twin brother Ethan and his mates from the footie team were getting all macho protective and then—"

Dr Myers turns to Mum. "Is this normal, Mrs Spark?"

"*Miss* Spark. And yes, this is standard Jesse."

"You have my sympathies." The doctor twirls his fountain pen at me. "Proceed."

"Right." I frown. "Where was I?"

"Something about an imminent fight."

"Oh my God, it was totally imminent," I say, diving back in. "We were all out behind the gym and there wasn't a teacher in sight. So Brianna's brother, who is a total psycho anyway and needs no provocation to be an immense dick, he's squaring up to Cas, and I just know my best mate is about to get annihilated, so I sort of get in between them. Not that I'm a fighter. I tried karate once but the *sensei* said teaching me self-defence wouldn't be right because anyone who attacked me would probably have a very legitimate reason."

"Jesse, none of this is relevant," Mum snaps.

"It is to Cas! I bet everybody hates him now. And okay, Dr Myers, I don't know why he snogged Matilda, but I'm sure it was all a misunderstanding. As I say, Brianna *is* just awful, and why he ever got with her is like this huge insoluble mystery. Except breasts, of course. Morgan tells me Brianna has the sort of breasts a lot of shallow straight boys like."

"Jesse!"

"Okay!" I hold up my hands. "Short version – Cas cheats on Brianna, gets threatened by bullies, I try to talk Ethan out of smashing Cas's face in, Ethan pushes me, my heart starts going crazy, the bullies get scared and run, I fall into Morgan's arms and someone calls an ambulance."

"And by 'crazy' you mean you suffered a rapid and irregular heartbeat," Dr Myers says, consulting my notes. "And a rather eager junior doctor in A&E ordered scans. Usually this would be an overreaction, but it turns out he was entirely justified. Now, young man, can you tell me what this is?"

He takes out a notepad and draws a circle, dividing it equally into three segments.

"Looks like the Mercedes Benz logo."

"That," Myers taps the page, "is a cross-section of a normal tricuspid aortic valve. Basically, it is a crucial bit of cardiac machinery that allows blood to be pumped out of the heart and around the body. Now, when blood is pushed out, these three leaflets come together, closing off the passage back into the heart. They fit as an absolute seal. But that isn't what is happening with your heart, Jesse."

"Oh," I say. "Crap."

"Crap indeed." Below the original drawing he sketches a second circle, this one with only two segments. "This is your valve. Because it has two leaflets, we call it a bicuspid aortic valve. As you can see, the edges of the leaflets are curved and so the seal isn't tight. When your heart pumps blood out, some of that blood is draining back and this can be an issue."

My mum looks pale. "But I don't understand. Jesse hasn't had any symptoms before yesterday. How did he develop this condition?"

"He didn't. Like around one per cent of the population, he was born with it. Often this doesn't cause a problem and people can remain symptomless for life, but Jesse's regurgitation – that's the amount of blood flowing backwards – is reaching a critical point. Hence the rapid heartbeat. In the end this could lead to a fatal rupture where the valve basically tears itself apart. And so I'm afraid we need to intervene."

"Right." I slap my knees. "This is all sounding pretty ominous."

I chuckle although, honestly, I feel completely numb. Not scared, not freaking out. Just…numb.

Dr Myers looks at me for a moment. I actually think I prefer the up-and-down look. Then he tears off another sheet from the notepad and starts a third sketch. When he's done, he holds it out to me and I have to force myself to take it.

"This first incision is how we begin," he says. "From there, the surgery gets slightly more complicated…"

Lying on my bed that evening, I hold Doc Myers's third sketch – *the incision diagram* – above my head. Although I can't stop worrying about what this drawing means, I can't throw it away either. Because this is my future, and even if I bury it in a bottom drawer, there's no way to escape it. And so I turn onto my side and glance at the poster on the opposite wall.

"Hello, boys. What do you think of my plan?"

The two horror icons are facing off and don't seem inclined to chat. *Freddy vs Jason.* Even Cas and I have to agree with Morgan's brutal assessment that this is a *really* dumb movie. And yet any film that hosts a smackdown between Freddy Krueger and Jason Voorhees, the two daddies of 1980s horror, can't be all bad.

"All right," I tell them, "I know my plan involves me striving to accomplish the one thing that's guaranteed to get you guys all stabby and slashy, but as I'm going to be cut open next month anyway, maybe you could be cool for once?" I fold the drawing and slip it under my pillow. "Not that it even matters. That part of my plan is about as likely to happen as one of your films winning an Oscar."

I trail my fingertips down my chest, collarbone to the base of my sternum. I am scared of the surgery, of the anaesthetic and the complete blackness I'll be plunged into during the operation, of the pain and discomfort that Dr Myers said I can expect during my recovery. But that isn't the main thing that worries me. It's the scar I'll be left with. It's almost as if I can feel it already, the legacy of that impossibly big incision scissoring its way along this path. A hideous white-hot brand that will mark me for life. I only wish…

Mum shoulders open the door. She gives me this tight smile over the mountain of laundry in her arms and comes to sit on the bed. "How are you feeling, love?"

"Well, I *was* feeling okay. Mum, what have you done to my favourite T-shirt?" I sit bolt upright and grab a tee from the pile in her lap. "John Landis's 1981 cult classic *An American Werewolf in London,* and you've dyed it pink!"

"Oh." She holds up the vandalized shirt. "Well, maybe it can be *An Ameri*-camp *Werewolf in London?*" I roll my eyes. "Aw, come on, grumpy." She plonks down the washing and drags me into a hug. It's faintly embarrassing that my mother can overpower me so easily, but in my defence she does run a boxercise class three times a week. Mum rests her chin on my head. "Big news today, huh?"

"Yeah."

"You know you're going to be okay, don't you?"

"Psshaw." I nod. "No doubt."

"Because Dr Myers, he said the success rate for the operation is very high, even if there are some risks. But then there's risk in everything, isn't there? I mean, you could walk under a bus tomorrow—"

"Or an escaped madman could break in and murder us both in our beds," I say, warming to the subject. "Then he'd have to dispose of our bodies, of course. Eating us would be the best option. Bones are tricky, though. He'd have to boil those first, maybe use it as the base for a Spark family stew—"

"But you are dealing with things?" Mum cuts in. "Because it would be understandable if you weren't. It's a lot to absorb in one go. And it isn't just the operation itself, there's the recovery and the healing. Now, if that's something that's worrying you, I want you to know—"

"Mum, I'm fine," I say, maybe a touch too brightly. "And I've decided that I'm going to keep myself busy over the next couple of weeks. I've got a two-stage plan and everything."

Three-stage, but I'm not telling my mother about that final ambition. Although, honestly, I'm not sure why. So yes, we butt heads sometimes, and very often we avoid apparently sensitive subjects like my dad, but we're never really awkward around each other, especially about this kind of stuff. My mum was the first person I came out to when I was fifteen, and she absolutely freaking loved it. If I'd been bi or straight or trans or pretty much anything, she would have thrown me the same kind of party we had the following night. Only I guess there might have been less of a willy theme if I'd ticked the straight box.

She invited Morgan and Cas over and hovered in the hall while I told them my news. To be honest, she seemed even more nervous than me. Not that it came as a huge revelation to the guys. I think Cas had known ever since we were thirteen and I explained to him in minute detail the gay subtext of *A Nightmare on Elm Street Part 2*.

But now? I don't know. This kick-in-the-balls heart news has changed things. Although I want to tell her what's really worrying me about the surgery, I can't. Because in the grand scheme of things, it sounds so stupid. Although Mum might understand my fears, her lawyer's practicality would lead her to the inevitable conclusion: *Yes, the operation will leave my son with a very big, very brutal, very ugly scar, but what choice does he have?*

And the answer to that is: none.

"Hello!" a voice bellows up the stairs. "Is he dead then? If so, you have our sympathies, Momma Spark!"

"And our congratulations!"

Mum closes her eyes. "Why did I ever give those two keys to the house?"

"Because they're family?"

She throws a pair of boxers over my face. "As good as."

Feet thunder up the stairs and the door bursts open. Despite the jokes, they're scared. I can see it stamped on their faces. They both stop on the threshold, bug-eyed and breathless. I smile and give them a tiny wave and my best friends wave back.

"Don't just stand there, you dopes," Mum orders. "Get in here."

They obey and we all end up crowded on the bed. Cas plucks a Frankenstein bobblehead from my bedside table while Morgan gives my shoulder a rough shake. This is Morgs code for, *You mean the world to me, and I would destroy anyone who tried to hurt you.*

"You're looking especially gorgeous tonight, Morgan." Mum smiles. "You seriously need to give these two some style tips. If I can get Jesse to comb his hair into something that doesn't resemble an electrocuted poodle, that would be a start."

I let it go. The fact is, Morgan does look gorgeous, her eyes as lustrous and dark as her tight coils of hair, that cute band of freckles across her nose standing out against her light brown skin, a hint of burgundy lipstick complementing her outfit. But as soon as my mum speaks, Morgan pulls her black denim jacket across her chest, hunches in on herself, and cuts her gaze to the floor. I think Mum might say something but just then Cas pipes up.

"What about me, Momma S?" He plants the bobblehead against his cheek and pouts. "Me and Frankie are feeling left out."

I take the toy from him and kiss his nose with it. "One of you is very gorgeous," I say, "the other is a misunderstood monster fated to be chased off a cliff by screaming villagers with pitchforks."

Cas grins. "Aw, Sparky, you remembered my ideal death scenario."

Mum groans and heads for the door. "It must be love."

I glance back at Cas. He is objectively gorgeous, though I refuse to picture him that way. Okay, confession time – once, long ago, I did have something of a crush on my best friend. Not that I ever told him. Cas has this warm russet complexion, wavy brown hair and these deep chocolate-drop eyes, plus whenever he sneezes or is just a bit thoughtful, he tends to wrinkle his nose like the most adorable Disney critter you've ever seen. But he is also my bro, my fellow horror hound, my partner in the diabolical arts. The Jason to my Freddy. We've been inseparable since we were four years old, back when we used to freak out our teacher at story time by booing the heroes and cheering on the goblins and wicked witches. Our friendship is what counts. Plus my bestie is spectacularly straight, so there's that.

"By the way," Mum says, turning back to Cas, "you can tell that creep of a brother of yours that I will chin him one of these days. I won't tell you what he said to me in the supermarket last week – it was that disgusting – but I have destroyed better men than Dean Loomis."

Cas blushes hard. "I'm so sorry, Momma S. That's… I'm sorry."

Poor Cas. Apologizing for his older brother doesn't come easy, even though he's had a ton of practice. Taking out his phone he starts flipping it over his hands, unable to look at any of us. It bugs the shit out of me. Mum knows the Loomis family situation; she shouldn't put Cas on the spot like this.

"Well, I better get out of your hair," she says awkwardly, and I'm glad she's at least picked up on the vibe. "Jesse has some big news for you."

The door closes and I slip down to the floor, folding my long legs under me. My friends flop either side and press their shoulders against mine. I feel this warm, nostalgic glow. These moments of us scooting close have got rarer and rarer in recent months.

"So we are hereby gathered for the big news." Morgan nudges my slipper with her Nike. "Don't leave us in suspense."

I take a deep breath…and pull a complete one-eighty. "Hey, Cas, so what in the name of Guillermo del Toro happened last night?"

They both blink at me.

"Oh, you mean after Kissy McKiss-A-Lot here almost got you killed?" Morgan's brows knit together. "Sorry we couldn't come with you in the ambulance, by the way. Mrs Greetwell said that it had to be a teacher."

"But we called your mum," Cas adds.

"It's cool." I nod. "Although Mr Michaels from history farted the whole way there. He's definitely got some kind of nervous gas problem. By the time we arrived, the paramedic was looking enviously at my oxygen mask. But, Cas," I try out Mum's trademark lawyer's Stare, "snogging Matilda Chen? Were you having an aneurism or something? I mean, I guess she's quite attractive..." I refer to Morgan. "She is quite attractive, yes?"

"God, Jesse," she huffs, pulling her jacket even tighter across her chest. "You do ask some stupid questions."

"I screwed up!" Cas says, throwing up his hands. "So yeah, thanks for the whole nearly dying thing, Jess, it certainly distracted Ethan from kicking the crap out of me. And yes, Matilda is very pretty. And yes, Brianna and me are over, so you two don't have to pretend to like her any more."

Morgan leans back and blinks up at the ceiling. "Cas, I told you before, I never had a problem with your girlfriend, so please stop dragging me into your nonsense."

Something about the way she says this... I don't know. There has been this awkwardness between the three of us recently. It all began around Easter, right when Cas and Brianna first got together. It's nothing to do with me, at least I don't think so. The gap seems to sit firmly between Cas and Morgan, although it can't be denied that it's affected all three of us. We're simply not how we used to be. I don't know exactly what happened, whether Morgan resented how Brianna used to treat Cas and how he always seemed to just put up with her crap; maybe Morgan's disapproval of their relationship grated on Cas a bit too. All I do know is that the spaces between us seem to be widening, and I don't like it.

I glance at Cas. He's playing with the Frankenstein bobblehead again, like it's the demonic puzzle box from *Hellraiser* or something equally precious and fascinating. His behaviour at prom makes no sense. Like I said to Dr Myers, Cas is the most principled person I know. In fact, I think it's the universe trying to achieve some kind of cosmic balance, because the rest of the Loomis family aren't exactly model citizens.

"Well," I murmur, "if I'm totally honest, I didn't really like Brianna."

Cas slaps his cheeks with both hands. "Oh, but I am flabbergasted! I mean, you and Morgs hid your revulsion so well! If only you'd dropped the odd subtle hint, like maybe mentioning five million times a day how you couldn't stand the sight of her."

"*But*," I say, "that was still a dick move. Cheating on Brianna with her best friend. And then there's the bin juice factor. That's another thing I don't get."

"Well, he did it," Morgan snaps. "And apparently he's sorry."

"Wait," I stare at her, "you're okay with this? What about the sisterhood?"

"The sisterhood has its limits," she says. "They stop at the outskirts of Brianna Murray."

"Urgh, Jess, enough!" Cas scrabbles his fingers through his hair. "It happened. I was a horny lad being led around by my dick and I did something awful. Enough about my crappy decisions. What's been going on with you? Because if you're hurt now because you stood up for me—"

"What? No way," I reassure him. "This heart thing? It's something I was born with."

I dig out Doc Myers's first two sketches – of the normal Mercedes logo-shaped valve and my distinctly less desirable version. I don't show them the third sketch. The *incision diagram*. The one that will leave me with the mother of all scars. No one needs to see that. Not in sketch form, not in real life.

Not ever.

I fill them in on what the doc told me about my condition and the plan to deal with it. Cas is rubbing his palms up and down his shins. He doesn't seem able to look at me.

Meanwhile Morgan passes the drawings through her hands.

"What kind of surgery do you need to correct this?" she asks.

"Open heart."

"Ah, man." Cas plants his elbows on his knees and hides his face behind his arms. "Ah, Jess."

Morgan reaches over and gives my shoulder another rough shake.

"Hey, it isn't as bad as it sounds," I tell them. "They just crack open my breastbone, then stop my heart so that they can replace my rubbish valve with one from a pig, or maybe a cow. Afterwards they use electric shocks to start everything back up again, and that's that. Job done. It's a shame about the pig, though. Or the cow."

"Jesse," Morgan says. "All we want to know is that you'll be okay."

"I will." I nod. "Definitely. The operation is a biggie but it's got a great success rate."

"When are they going to do it?"

"In about four weeks."

"*Four weeks*?" They both look appalled, and Morgan gives my shoulder a third hard shake. "Well, we'll be here for you. Right, Cas? I'll take you for walks after, help get you fit again. My mum keeps saying I need to do more exercise."

Finally Cas looks up. His eyes are shining but he manages a small watery grin. "And I'll come round and test out your pig valve with some classic franchise marathons. Hey, we haven't watched the *Scream* movies in ages! Perfect old school Ghostface fare!"

I smile and throw my arms around them. Cas bumps heads with me and Morgan stiffens slightly, which is pretty much standard Morgan.

"There is something even more important you can do for me," I say.

Okay. Deep breath. Here we go. The craziest plan in filmmaking history is about to be unveiled.

"Two things I'd like to achieve before I go under the surgeon's blade," I say, and Cas winces, just like that time he splashed aftershave down his pants before a night out. His brother Dean had told him it would make him irresistible to the ladies. The nurse who later treated his rash disagreed.

"Number one," I say. "We all have to go ghost-hunting at Hunter's Lake."

Morgan rolls her eyes. "We haven't done that since we were twelve."

"Exactly! It'll be nostalgic."

Another dramatic eyeroll, and all at once I have this flash of seven-year-old Morgan Adeyemi-Perera when she first joined our primary school, marching straight over to Cas and me as we played zombies in the playground. Claiming us as friends, without question or argument, and immediately reorganizing our game in a way that made it a hundred times more fun. Our brilliant, bossy new friend, whose bossiness was so much a part of her brilliance you could never resent it. I guess she's been in charge ever since.

"If I've told you once I've told you a million times," she says. "That legend about a little girl haunting the lake is total BS. Don't you remember? I got so irritated by you two dragging me down there in the dark, then scaring each other into screaming hysterics, I researched the whole thing. No little kid ever died there."

"And your second request?" Cas jumps in before I can start a full-on debate with Morgs about the existence of the Hunter's Lake ghost.

"We're doing it." I grin at him. "We're making *Zombie freakin' Honeymoon.*"

There is that third part of my pre-op plan, but I'm keeping that to myself. I know my friends wouldn't laugh at me, and in actual fact, I could do with their help – honestly, my record in the romance department doesn't amount to much more than that closet snog with Sammy McBride in Year Nine – but the whole thing feels kind of private and I don't want to make them feel awkward. I mean, I could just see Morgan's face if I announced, *So, guys, I really think I need to find a summer boyfriend, experience love and maybe even lose my virginity before I become a monstrous, scarred freak that no boy in his right mind would think of looking at twice, let alone dating.*

"Yes, we're making *ZomHon*," Cas agrees. "We sorted out the filming schedule last week, remember? We prep in July ready for shooting when school comes back in September."

I lean forward, my palms pressed together. "Right, but what are we actually waiting for? We break up the day after tomorrow and none of us is going anywhere for the summer. Thing is, guys, you know this project was going to be my submission to get into film school? Well, Dr Myers says—"

"Wait." Cas is looking at me like it's Christmas. "Your doctor is called Dr *Myers*?"

"I know." We high-five. "A guy in a mask called Myers is going to cut me open with a knife."

"Dude. That is *so* sweet."

"You two are in need of some serious therapy," Morgan observes drily.

"Anyway," I continue, "Myers says I can probably keep up with schoolwork during my recovery, but being out on location, running around filming stuff? There's just no way. Not for at least three months. So it's now or never. And we're almost there anyway. We've got a pretty decent script."

I leap to my feet and run over to my printer, where the latest three-hundred-page draft of *Zombie Honeymoon*, a Jesse Spark/Casper Loomis Production, lies in the tray. Hefting it up, I pass our masterpiece to Morgan.

"Looks like you've got *six* pretty decent scripts," she says, weighing it in her hands. "Jesse, if you're serious about shooting this thing in four weeks, you're going to have to cut some of this stuff."

I rock back against my bed, arms folded, pouting for England. "Like what?"

She jabs her finger against a page. "Maybe this helicopter rescue scene in the second act? Where are you going to get a helicopter from anyway?"

"And that casino bit in Las Vegas," Cas says, leaning over Morgan's shoulder. "Why is this newly-wed couple in Vegas anyway? Isn't their backstory that they met at a Greenpeace rally? Would eco-warriors really honeymoon in Sin City?"

"We need to get right to the heart of this thing," Morgan says. "Jesse, what is your film actually about?"

"Urrrruhhh." I rake my fingers down my face. "It's about undead monsters eating brains. Why does it have to be about anything? John Carpenter's seminal 1978 horror masterpiece—"

Morgan cuts me off, swatting me with the script. I have to admit, it's bulky enough to dislocate an arm. "I've told you before, stop saying *seminal*. That word has two meanings, and every time you say it, I can't help thinking of the ickier definition."

"In John Carpenter's *seminal* 1978 horror masterpiece *Halloween*," I insist, "there's a creepy-arsed serial killer going around murdering babysitters. That's it. Nothing deep and meaningful. That's why it was originally called, guess what?"

"Ooo! Ooo! Ooo!" Cas bounces up and down, hand raised. "*The Babysitter Murders.*"

We high-five again.

So yeah, I still bless that sleepover when Cas's brother allowed us to stay up late and watch the mini-series adaptation of Stephen King's *IT* on DVD. We were nine years old, much too young for psychotic clowns luring little kids into sewers, but for better or worse, that old movie shaped the people we are today. It's also why, although Dean Loomis now seems to dislike me, he will always hold a special place in my gruesome little heart.

"Except," Cas says, "Morgan is sort of right. The best zombie movies are usually about something more than just the brain-munching. There's always a subtext. For example, George A Romero's *Dawn of the Dead* was set in a shopping mall because the zoms represented the empty-headed hunger of consumerism."

"And didn't Romero cast a Black lead actor in *Night of the Living Dead*?" Morgan asks. "I remember my dad telling me about that movie being made at the height of the civil rights movement in America. White ghouls mindlessly attacking a Black guy? It isn't subtle but it is saying *something.*"

"Yes, right, fine," I mutter, "but those films are classics."

Cas takes off his trainer and boinks me over the head with it. "And there's no reason *Zombie Honeymoon* can't be a classic too. Don't forget, Romero's first film was made lightning-fast and on a zero budget. Have some ambition, dude."

Morgan holds out the script to me. "While you're thinking about your theme, let's get down to business. You want to shoot this in, what, twenty days? Then you have to be realistic. That means working with a maximum of three locations and three main actors. I can get any extras we might need for zombies and victims from drama club."

"You're sure? It's pretty short notice." Suddenly the enormity of what I'm suggesting has come crashing down on me.

But Morgan just shrugs. "You're talking about drama nerds. They'd kill their grandmothers and dance on their graves for a part in a film."

"Okay then." Cas rubs his hands together. "Let's *Blair Witch* the hell out of this thing. Proper hardcore guerrilla filmmaking, flying by the seat of our pants. What could possibly go wrong?"

I beam at both of them. "Right. So obviously you're my Director of Photography, Cas. We've made enough short films together, and you've got the best eye for shot composition I've ever seen."

Cas takes out his phone and snaps a picture of us. "Why, thank you."

"Delete that at once," Morgan insists.

I turn to her. "And you, misery guts. You're my lead. The happily-wedded wife whose honeymoon is about to go horribly, murderously, cannibalistically wrong."

This is followed by a huge, yawning pause during which Morgan and Cas seem to be trying very hard not to look at each other.

"Guys?" I throw the script onto the bed. "What's the problem?"

"I actually talked to Cas about this a while back," Morgan says. "So, here's the thing, Jess, I'll play the hitchhiker that the young couple pick up en route to their isolated cabin in the woods. Despite the fact that she has a million unnecessary lines right now, I like the way you've written her. She's spiky and clever and resourceful and not…"

I shrug. "Not what?"

"Not the eye candy."

I stare at her. My guts twist. I hate this. "Morgs. First, I do not write parts that are *just* eye candy. I'm not Michael freaking Bay. And you played the love interest in the *Little Shop of Horrors* play at Easter."

"That was comedy," she says, hunching over again and

cutting her eyes to the floor. "I can ham up a comedy love interest, no problem. Drama is different and I... Well, I just can't."

"But you *can*," I insist. "And you *are* eye candy. But don't take my dubiously gay word for it. Cas, she's eye candy, yes?"

Cas is fiddling with his laces. He doesn't look up. "We know filmmaking, Morgan knows acting. We should let her do what she's comfortable with."

Okay, this is weird, and if looks could kill right now... Well, Cas wouldn't be dead, but I'm imagining a very stern telling-off. He knows Morgan's issues as well as I do. Shit, we've talked about it enough over the years. Talked and talked and never really come up with a satisfactory way to reassure our friend. I don't understand how someone as kickass as Morgs can be so bothered by how she appears onscreen. Not her acting, which she knows is awesome, but – I hate to even think it – her looks. So here's the deal: Morgan is convinced she's ugly and fat and "bulges in all the wrong places" (her words). She can't even stand looking at herself in the cast photos the drama society put up in the corridors at school. It's so stupid because I know my friend is beautiful, inside and out. I suppose her fitness-obsessed mum doesn't help. Anyway, what Cas and I decided a long while back was that we'd reinforce Morgan's confidence whenever the opportunity arose. Like right now, for instance! So why isn't he pitching in? My gaze switches from one to the other. Maybe this weird rift between them over the past few months explains Cas's reluctance to back me up. Anyway, something about Morgan's expression tells me that it's pointless trying to argue.

"All right." I admit defeat. "Hitchhiker it is. So, out of our three-week shooting schedule, I'm planning a few days for prep. Not ideal, but it's all we have. I'll start work on the script tonight. Cas, if you can storyboard our scenes as soon as I email them over, we can then check out a few possible filming locations. We also need to ask Mr Prentice if we can borrow the equipment we'll need from school."

"That shouldn't be a problem," Cas says. "Prentice's cool."

I nod. "As well as me directing and Cas as DP, we'll need a sound guy, a make-up artist, and maybe those special effects geeks who help out with the school plays."

Morgan stands up, all business. "I'll talk to the SFX geeks. I might also know a make-up guy."

Cas puts his trainer back on and also stands. "Do you remember Stan Shannon, Jess?"

"Oh God." I roll my eyes. "Stan Shan the Cans Man?"

"I know." Cas grins. "But he's the best sound technician we've ever worked with."

"Agreed," I say reluctantly.

We're all standing now, strangely awkward again, grinning at each other. I break the silence.

"Thank you, guys. Seriously. This means so much."

"It's our pleasure," Morgan says. "And anyway, it'll make great content for my audition showreel."

"And my DP portfolio." Cas smiles.

Morgan steps onto her tiptoes and kisses my forehead. "But mostly we're doing it because we love you. Although, please don't get used to all this physical contact. You nearly dying is a special case. Right, I'm off. Catch you douches tomorrow."

Before she goes, she shoots Cas this look I can't read. I actually think I'm pretty good at reading people, though Mum disagrees. She always reminds me of that time in the park when I saw this dad holding his daughter in his arms and saying, *"Oh, sweetheart, no. The ducks won't come."* Naturally, I thought I'd help out by throwing my entire bag of birdseed at his feet. Cue an army of ravenous ducks. Cue kid screaming like someone had set her hair on fire. Ornithophobia, apparently. Fear of freaking birds. How was I to know?

"Well, Sparky," says Cas, heading after Morgan, "you've got a lot of work to do. Soon as you email over the script pages, I'll get started on the storyboards."

"Thanks," I say. "So, uh, Cas, can I ask? How's it been at school today?"

He pauses, his back turned to me. "The worst part was all the idiots who tried to give me high-fives," he eventually says in a small voice. "Like I'm suddenly this big stud or something. But honestly, Jess? I'm ashamed. I can't tell you why I did it. I just… It seemed like a good idea at the time, that's all."

"Okay." I frown. "And what about now?"

"I don't know. I'm still not sure what else I could have done."

"Not kiss your girlfriend's best mate?" I suggest. "Jesus, Cas, this isn't relationship rocket science. It isn't even relationship finger-painting."

He turns. "I don't know what else to tell you." He looks so defeated in that moment, and I want to comfort him – but before I can think of anything to say, he's gone.

I groan and fall back onto my bed. I hate this sense of drifting between the three of us. We used to talk about everything – the stress of school and parents, guys we liked, girls we liked, our huge, impossible plans for the future – but now? I don't know. There's a sort of caution that wasn't there before, like we're walking on eggshells, careful in case we bump up against each other too roughly.

Frustrated, my mind turns to other things, and I pull my laptop onto my chest. My fingers hesitate before typing a few excruciating words into the search bar. I hit return and a dozen angelic twentysomethings from my favourite queer online magazine fill the screen. All toned and chiselled and absolutely perfect in every way. One has a tiny mole between the ladder of his abs but is otherwise blemish-free. I slip my hand under my shirt and press it hard against my breastbone.

Although I am frightened by the idea of the pain to come, I do believe Dr Myers's reassurances – I *will* survive this. And one day that pain will be a memory. The scar will not. And so, for all the silly and unimportant and crucial and wonderful things that could have been and now can't ever be, I feel this stupid rush of tears. I imagine it again – that blazing trail that will soon rip its way down my torso, transforming me, making me the exact opposite of these shining, beautiful people. And I know it's silly. I know – I *know* – but I can't help crying just the same.

I'm sitting at the breakfast table, feeling pretty zombie-ish myself. By 3.30 a.m., I'd finished the script for *ZomHon* and pinged the last changes over to Cas. Bless him, he stayed up with me, chatting on Zoom and plotting out the storyboards we'd need to plan the shoot. We kept the chat strictly business. No more talk of how he'd cheated on Brianna and defied his bin juice phobia, all in the same evening. Although honestly, I remain worried about my best friend and how he'll cope with the fallout after the break-up. Cas isn't as invulnerable as he likes to pretend.

I'm nodding over my cereal while Mum whirls around the kitchen, a stack of case files in her arms. She offered to make me a bacon sarnie as a breakfast treat, but I refused. I'd wondered if the rashers might just come from the same pig who's donating me his heart valve. Eating the poor guy seemed like adding insult to injury.

"So how did Cas and Morgan take the news?" Mum asks, grabbing her keys from the fruit bowl.

"Yeah…" I yawn. "Pretty well. They both want to be part of the whole thing anyway. Cas said he's going to be there with me, right up till the very last cut. I thought that was really sweet of him… Okay, Mother, why are you looking at me like that?"

"Well…" She jangles the house keys from her finger, brow furrowed. "I just don't know what to say. I mean, it's very supportive, I suppose, but I'm not sure Casper will be allowed to do that."

I blink up at her. "What? Why the hell not?"

"Well, for one thing there's probably a hygiene factor," Mum snaps.

I throw out my arms, not realizing I'm still holding the cereal spoon, and a bullet of muesli hits the cat. "The hygiene factor? What does that even mean?" I ask over outraged yowls. "Anyway, Cas is the most hygienic person I know! Much more than me anyway. There, I said it."

I stare at her, confused, as Jacques shoots me the stink-eye and starts rubbing his cereal-stained backside against my schoolbag.

"Jesse, the fact Cas is more hygienic than you is news to no one," Mum says. "In fact, if it weren't for you salivating over every men's deodorant commercial, I'd have serious doubts about you even being gay."

"That's stereotyping," I object. "Not every gay man keeps himself forensically clean."

"You've certainly taught me that," she agrees. "But whether or not Casper systematically disinfects himself every morning, he certainly won't be allowed into an operating theatre to witness your surgery! Why on earth would he want to, anyway? I know you boys are a little twisted about these gruesome horror things, but I never thought it'd go this far."

"Mother." I knead my temples. "What are you talking about?"

"I'm saying Dr Myers will not tolerate—"

"And *I'm* talking about our movie," I interrupt. "*Zombie Honeymoon*? Cas wants in on the director's final *cut* of the film. He doesn't want to see his best friend's heart being dissected. Jesus, we're not that sick."

My mother clasps the case files to her chest. I think I might finally have got the last word in an argument. I ought to know better.

"And that's another thing," she says. "I'm not sure that taking on a huge project like this a few weeks before open-heart surgery is the greatest idea you've ever come up with."

"But Dr Myers said I could do whatever I wanted before the op."

"I doubt he meant go out and shoot an entire feature film." She grabs her bag from the counter and heads for the door, chucking over her shoulder, "Just promise you'll be careful. And clean that bloody cat!"

The door slams. I gather Jacques up into my arms and take him to the sink. The Thing of Evil shrieks as I sponge the muesli out of its fur, clawing my already scratched-to-pieces hand in the process. Funny creature, Jacques (named in honour of Jacques Tourneur, director of horror masterpiece *Cat People*) – the more love he's shown, the more pain he inflicts. Mum says this makes him a pretty typical male.

I receive one final gouging before the monster leaps gracefully off the counter. Washing my wounds under the tap, I catch my reflection in the side of the toaster. I grin, trying out a heroic clenched jaw. I've got the dimpled chin for it, and I guess my nose isn't too bad, but it has to be admitted, those eyebrows are now very close to finally joining forces. The truth is, I never used to get too hung up on my looks. So I was a seventeen-year-old virgin, okay, but I'd had the not unrealistic hope that that status could maybe change in the not too distant future. Now...?

Hideous scar aside, what teenager would even want to take on a boyfriend with all the grown-up baggage of a major heart problem?

"Yo, Sparky, shall we?"

Cas, shouting through the letter box. I wipe my face on a tea towel, plaster on a smile, and grab my bag.

A bag today is all sorts of ridiculous. Not only is it about four thousand degrees outside, but there is literally nothing to carry. School is done. Our proper classes came to an end the day before prom, but Ferrivale High specializes in its own brand of sadism, making students attend the last two days of school even though there are no lessons.

Cas is practically bouncing as we head in. He pulls out his sketchbook, showing me sheet after sheet of storyboard ideas. Cas is a pretty decent artist and his enthusiasm drags me away from the dark reflections of the toaster. I glance up from his illustration of an exploding zombie and notice that he doesn't even look tired. Moisturizer. Must be.

"If we can get the SFX geeks to pull this off," he says, jabbing his finger at a disintegrating head, "that could be our big money shot. Except... Yeah, I don't know. This is also a huge character moment. Our grieving wife has had to dig deep and find the courage to blow her freshly-zombified husband's brains to bits. So do we go for all-out gore or subtle emotion?"

"Can't it be both?" I ask.

Cas looks at me. "I know horror can be emotional for us, dude. Remember how we both cried when those stupid kids killed IT?"

"Rest in peace, Pennywise." I nod.

"Amen. But most people don't think like us. We can't have big swelling, emotional music playing over some poor guy's head exploding."

"Why not? It's called juxtaposition, Cas. Two unexpected

things colliding. It makes the audience sit up and take notice."

He looks at me for a second, and it's another one of those looks. Something about what I've just said? Or perhaps it's nothing to do with me at all. Because glancing up from the storyboard, I realize we've arrived at the gates of Ferrivale High. Catching sight of us, the crowd hanging out in front of the sixth form block has gone eerily quiet. We start moving between them and I can feel a hundred sets of eyes tracking us.

A hand reaches out and pats me on the back. That seems to break the spell as I'm pulled away from Cas and dozens of kids start asking questions about what happened to me at prom. I scan the faces of the boys, quickly deciding that my impossible ambition to find a summer boyfriend before I go under Dr Myers's scalpel will not be achieved here. A host of achingly straight males with only a scattering of out gay lads, all of whom, like the effortlessly adorable Sammy McBride, are already in relationships. I answer their questions as best I can while pivoting up onto my tiptoes. Cas seems to have vanished.

"My sister heard they diagnosed you with arse cancer," says this upper-sixth kid. He's handsome in a dead-eyed serial killer kind of way. "A lot of gays get arse cancer. They overuse their arses, you see?"

"Which is why you'll never get brain cancer," I tell him.

He looks baffled, sort of proving my point.

I garble some vaguely accurate news to a few genuinely concerned classmates and head off in search of my best friend. Usually this would be impossible. Cas is the king of cross country whereas I get out of breath carrying the Christmas decorations down from the loft.

"Hey!" I puff, catching up with him outside the Ellis Bell Memorial Drama Studio. "So that was weird. I saw a couple of kids actually flinch away from you. Cas, I'm so sorry."

"It's the new normal. Because I wouldn't high-five them back yesterday, the creeps have now joined the haters and formed an anti-Cas collective." He shrugs. "Whatever. I deserve it."

This is so strange. Forty-eight hours ago, Cas was one of the more popular kids at our hellmouth of a school. He was stylish enough to be given a nod by the beautiful people, sporty enough to drift through the dinner hall without being tripped by Ethan Murray and the footie crowd, respected enough to steer the younger Mount Pleasant kids away from trouble. Not having many of the natural gifts to be popular in my own right, I used to enjoy riding Cas's popularity train. All right, so he was never exactly part of the in-crowd, even when he started dating Brianna, but he could move between these groups like he had some kind of clique master key. Now, after a single mystifying snog behind the bins, all those doors have been slammed in his face.

"It'll blow over," I say. "By the time we get back in September, no one will remember how you betrayed your awful girlfriend."

Cas doesn't respond. He's staring up at these big glossy posters from our last school musical, *Little Shop of Horrors* (based on the not-quite-seminal-but-still-pretty-decent sixties horror comedy of the same name). Morgan sang and acted the hell out of the main role of Audrey (the love interest, not the man-eating plant) while Brianna slaughtered every song she was given as street urchin Crystal. Honestly, even her parents were tearing up their programmes and plugging their ears.

It was at the *Little Shop* after-show party that Cas and Brianna got together. I was on the other side of Argento's Hollywood Diner, standing by the jukebox and talking to some of the cast while Cas was having this intense-looking chat with Morgan. He'd probably been telling her how brilliant she'd been, and Morgs was most likely rolling her eyes at his every compliment, when Brianna landed on top of them, crying her heart out. Apparently her parents had given her an "honest review". *Eeeesh.* I remember Cas looking furious, more at Morgan than Brianna, because Morgan immediately cut their conversation dead and started comforting her hopeless co-star. Anyway, about an hour later I stumbled out of the diner to find my best mate sucking face with the worst actress ever to grace the Ferrivale High School stage.

If I'm honest, I don't really know how their relationship lasted those twelve gruelling weeks. I guess I'm just glad it's over and that maybe, just maybe, Cas and Morgan can reconcile whatever differences they have and we three can go back to being we three again.

I'm about to suggest we head off in search of Mr Prentice when the double doors at the end of the corridor swing open and Brianna's crew swarm through. The six girls stop dead at the sight of us. Brianna stares and a kind of sickly electricity ripples through the air. I take a breath. Someone needs to break the tension, and that someone might as well be me.

"Oh, hey, Brianna," I say, giving her this unfathomable salute. "So, I just want you to know, based on my intimate knowledge of Cas – I mean friendly-intimate, not *you-know*-intimate – that, despite the evidence of recent events, your ex-boyfriend really isn't a total shit."

Brianna reacts to this by bursting into tears. Maybe I should shut up. Or maybe I need to explain Cas's essential non-shitty-ness a little more clearly. Yeah, why not? Might as well give it a try. What's the worst that could happen?

6

"Oh, uh, please don't cry. I only wanted to explain…" I gulp and try to do battle with the death glare of Brianna's bodyguards. Under their mascara-laced venom, I almost wither. "I get that this is very awkward, but you should know that Cas is genuinely sorry for what he did and, well, I've known him for a really long time and he's honestly the nicest guy. Like, he once followed a bus for six miles on his bike, just because a little old lady dropped a pound on the pavement as she was getting onboard. Okay, so when he finally caught up with her and tried to give her the money back, she thought he was offering her drugs, then seemed really pissed off when she realized he wasn't, but it's the thought that counts, right?"

"Jess?" Cas murmurs.

I look over at my best friend. "Yeah?"

"For the love of God."

"Oh. Right." I shove my hands into my pockets and hiss a breath through my teeth. "Anyway, I'm sorry about him being a dick. He isn't usually. And that's all I wanted to say."

We stand in silence for a second, us wilting, the girls glaring.

While her flunkies fuss around her, handing her tissues, rubbing her back and whispering in her ear, I ask myself a question I've posed lots of times: what kind of person is Brianna Murray? Right now she's doing that Hollywood crying thing – lots of flapping and quick blinking, no actual tears – so it's difficult to tell if she's feeling genuine human emotions. I used to think her personality was pretty hideous, the way she was always so shallow and self-centred and controlling of Cas, but maybe I was prejudiced against her from the start. I never liked the idea of someone coming from outside to split up our little group, mainly because, unlike social butterfly Cas and drama group star Morgan, I don't have anywhere else to go. But Brianna? Everything is such an overblown performance it's difficult to tell who she really is. I wonder if Cas ever got to know.

Cas clears his throat. "I am sorry, Bree. I think you know that."

A forefinger twirls through the air and Jodie Keys takes centre stage.

"Who said you can talk to our girl?" she demands. "You're just a piece of Mount Pleasant rubbish and the other night you proved it to the whole school." Jodie spins on her heel to find four faces nodding in agreement.

Encouraged, she goes on. "Just because your loser brother used to rule this place, you thought you could step up and join the big boys? Nah-ah. So yeah, you are kind of cute, but there are a hundred better looking guys in the vale. Our Queen B felt sorry for you, that's all. And what do you do when her back's turned? Shove your tongue down that bitch Matilda Chen's throat! Well, I for one—"

"Enough!"

Brianna silences her defender with a brutal side-eye. Honestly, it's sort of impressive. Jodie falls back into the ranks where the other girls look at her like she's just turned up at school in a non-ironic charity shop jumper. Meanwhile Queen B's eyes slide away from the Fallen One and glide back to Cas. I have to admit, she looks absolutely fierce – that flawless ivory skin and flame-red hair, like a living inferno.

"I forgave Matilda the night of the prom," she says. "*None* of this is *her* fault. And Casper's choices can't be blamed on him coming from Mount Pleasant or the fact that his brother is a creepy douchebag. You're a big boy, aren't you, Cas? You don't need to blame anyone else for your mistakes."

Cas's jaw twitches, yet all he does is nod. And I'm officially staggered. So yes, he's held up his hands to being a bit of a dick, but I never thought I'd see the day when Casper Loomis didn't defend his big brother. It's almost as if the same psychic powers Brianna uses to control her posse have now extended to my best mate. It's weird and unsettling and I don't like it.

"And as for you, Jesse." I turn from Cas to the undisputed queen of Ferrivale High. "I heard all about your poor heart and I'm so sorry. I hope you know my brother was only 'standing up for me' when he threatened to pound you into the next millennium?" She says this with sardonic air quotes. "Any excuse to get out a little of that toxic masculinity. But you and Morgan were always so nice to me, I just wish…"

Brianna starts flapping again and, taking their cue, the other girls look at me like I'm suddenly an object of pity. Maybe sensing that she could be redeemed, Jodie lets out this high-pitched sob.

"It's a total shame he's gay," she blurts out. "Because I definitely would."

"Enough!" Brianna shrieks again, and with a final pout in my direction, they all swarm back through the swing doors.

"Wow." I puff out my cheeks. "That was… Wow. So Brianna forgave Matilda pretty quickly, then? I thought you'd both be on her top ten enemies list for the rest of your natural lives. Bit weird, huh?" He doesn't answer and so I nudge his foot with mine. "You know, I don't think I actually asked – do you even like Matilda Chen?"

"Christ, will you shut up!"

I bite my lip. "Okay, sorry."

He presses the heels of his hands into his eyes and shakes his head. "No, Sparky, I'm sorry. You shouldn't be having to deal with my crap right now. And Matilda? I don't…" He takes a breath, as if he might be about to lose it, and I grab his elbows and pull his hands away from his face. His eyes are very red.

"Dude. What the hell is going on with you? You know you can tell me anything, right?"

He gives a sharp nod and looks away. "I don't know, okay? About Matilda. Anyway, she's gone away with her family until the end of summer break, so even if I… Ah, mate." He throws his arm around my shoulder. "Let's just go and find Mr Prentice, yeah?"

And so I decide to just be there for Cas, if and when he wants to talk about the break-up. After all, I've got my own crap to concentrate on – *ZomHon* starts shooting in a couple of days, I've a ticking time bomb inside my chest, and then there's that other ridiculous quest to complete before I go under Doc Myers's scalpel. I glance at Cas and wonder what he'd say if I told him about my madcap plan to find my first – and probably *last ever* – boyfriend.

I'm pondering all this when we bump into Mr Prentice coming out of the drama studio. Prentice is pretty cool for a Ferrivale teacher, by which I mean he doesn't actively despise his students. A bit of a movie fan himself, he even helped Cas and I set up the school's film club, dressing as an unfortunately suggestive banana in the town marathon to help raise funds for studio equipment.

"Boys, what's new?" He grins. Today he is wearing a neon green shirt and paisley tie under a brown suede jacket; a fairly boring look for Prentice. "Jesse, I heard your mum called into the office this morning. News about your condition has leaked to the staffroom. Worst gossips in the world, teachers." He leans in and taps me on the shoulder. "Disaster! But I know your heart will go on, as Celine Dion sang over the closing credits of James Cameron's 1997 blockbuster *Titanic*."

Morgan says that I should get Mr Prentice to do a paternity test. Honestly, I don't see the resemblance.

"Thank you, sir," I say. "Just please, if I die on the operating table, don't let them play that at my funeral."

Cas nods. "Jess and I have a pact. I want *Ghostbusters*, he wants the theme from *The Omen*."

Prentice pulls at his lower lip. "Not awful choices."

"Anyway, we've got a favour to ask…" I'm brimming with excitement as I explain. No other member of staff would get this in a million years, but Prentice will be completely onboard. After all, this is the guy who helped us with our shot-for-shot remake of the vomiting scene from *The Exorcist*. Poor Morgan, she was washing pea soup out of her hair for weeks. "So, I know it's an ambitious project," I conclude, "but I really think we can pull it off."

Cas takes out a list from his blazer pocket. "Here's the stuff we'll need to borrow from the club stores – the high-def DSLR camera and a couple of spare memory cards, the tripod, the Manfrotto Steadicam, maybe the dolly tracks too, the redhead lighting kit with the soft boxes, the handheld mic and boom – our sound guy will have his own cans – the laptop with editing software, a couple of hard drives for extra storage. Oh, and it would be cool if we could—"

"Casper, if I could just stop you there." Mr Prentice twines his fingers together and blushes, like a toddler about to confess to stealing biscuits from the cookie jar. "This is very difficult for me to say." He sighs. "Chaubunagungamaug."

I frown. "Chaubu-what?"

"—nagungamaug. It's a lake in Massachusetts. I'm going there for my summer holiday, to commune with nature and maybe discover my animal spirit guide. The area has a long history among the Native American Algonquian people. I'm going to pitch a tent on the shore and maybe fish and perhaps smoke the odd… Well, the point is, I won't be in Ferrivale for the next month."

"And?"

"And I simply can't allow the unsupervised use of thousands of pounds worth of school property. I'm sorry, boys, it's got to be a no."

"But you know us, sir," I object. "We're responsible, aren't we?"

Prentice starts fiddling with his gruesome tie. "Most of the time. Though let's not forget your Year Nine documentary in which you claimed one of the dinner ladies was in fact the mastermind of an international diamond smuggling ring."

"That was a totally legitimate piece of investigative filmmaking," I object. "And Big Cath didn't even call the police when she found out we'd broken into her garage and opened all those boxes stuffed with diamonds. How were we to know she ran an online costume jewellery business?"

"This isn't just about your trustworthiness, Jesse," Prentice says. "Letting you loose with all that equipment would be more than my job's worth."

My stupid leaky heart hits the floor. No hardware, no *ZomHon*, it's as simple as that. I suppose we *could* film it on my GoPro camera, but the sound would suck and without proper lighting...

Cas snaps me out of my gloom. "This is complete bullshit! How many times have you told us that filmmaking is about taking risks? So why won't you take a chance on Jesse, eh? This is his one opportunity to film his project before he goes in for surgery. Life-changing surgery." His face is flushed, his eyes almost scary. "You know how much getting into film school means to him, but all you're worried about is your stupid job. And what is your job anyway, sir? Isn't it supposed to be about inspiring kids to believe in themselves? If not, what are you actually for?"

"Cas," I say quietly, "it's okay."

He throws off my hand. "No, it's not. It's actually really fucked up."

Silence in the drama studio. A heat haze seems to be shimmering around Cas while I squirm in the afterglow of my best friend's loyalty. We're just lucky it's this particular teacher who's standing in front of us. Prentice sways like a human punchbag.

"You might not want to hear this right now," he says at last, his voice a bit unsteady, "but I *am* sorry. And despite what you've just said to me, Casper, I know it's only because you want to support your friend, so we'll take it no further. I hope you both enjoy your summer holiday. And Jesse, good luck with your operation."

"Dude," I murmur, as the studio doors click behind Prentice. "What the hell? I mean, thanks for standing up for me, but I don't want you getting yourself expelled."

Cas looks down at his fists. "Maybe I was a bit harsh."

He grabs one of the metal folding chairs from the studio stage. I think for a second he might throw it through a window, but instead he flips it open one-handed and sits astride the thing. Cas can do stuff like this and make it look Tom Holland cool.

"So I guess that's it." I sigh.

Cas is quiet for a moment, his chin perched on the chair back, his nose wrinkled in that cute Disney-critter style. Then, very slowly, a devilish smile creases his lips.

"Last day of school tomorrow. If we timed it right…" He looks up and gives me a wink that does something strange to my stomach. "Sparky, if I told you I could save this movie, what would you be willing to do?"

"Short of naked snake wrestling?" I shrug. "Pretty much anything. By the way, I don't *totally* rule out naked snake wrestling."

"Famous last words, mate." Cas claps his hands and laughs. "Famous last words."

The pavement tables outside Argento's Hollywood Diner are heaving with Brianna Murray clones, all taking selfies that seem to require immediate filtering. Cas keeps his head down as we hurry past and push through into the restaurant. The bell above the door plays a snippet from the *Jaws* theme, and I'm home.

Zipping past us on roller skates, a tray of Big Kahuna burgers held over his head, Indiana Jones almost collides with Mary Poppins and the Terminator, who are singing "Happy Birthday" to a group of embarrassed tweens while a weedy-looking Captain America trembles under the weight of a gigantic cake. At the bar, I tip a salute to the boss, Signora Argento, dressed today as Ellen Ripley from the *Alien* movies. She's nonchalantly using a flamethrower to glaze a big order of crème brûlées.

We head towards the back and dive into the red leather of our favourite booth. Knowing the menu backwards, Cas shakes his head when an ageing Sandy from *Grease*

68

weaves on over to take our order.

"Just two milky coffees, please, Doreen."

Doreen blows a pink chewing gum bubble and trundles off towards the bar.

I thread my fingers behind my head and sigh contentedly. For the first time since leaving Doc Myers's office, I feel sort of normal. Argento's is pretty much my favourite place on earth. If it were erased from existence tomorrow, I could easily rebuild an exact replica, from the *Jurassic Park* T-Rex behind the counter with its conveyor belt tongue vomiting up burgers and fries from the kitchen, to the cleaning crew's "Wizards of Bogs" uniform.

Our booth is in the horror corner, surrounded by ghoulish props and iconic posters. Waiting for our coffees, I glance up at the grinning head of Jack Nicholson from *The Shining* bursting through the wall above. Jack and his axe have been looking down on us ever since my tenth birthday party – a minor disaster where none of the invited kids turned up due to my request for an extreme *Goosebumps* theme. None, that is, except Casper Loomis.

Okay, I decided I wasn't going to ask him what's up, but it's tough trying to ignore that vaguely miserable face sitting opposite me. *What is going on with you, Cas? Everything at the prom and now losing his shit with Mr Prentice? This just isn't my best friend.*

"No, it's fine, we'll hang on. See you in a bit."

I blink. Lost in my thoughts, I hadn't realized he was on the phone.

"Was that Morgs?" I ask.

"She'll be here in ten." He waggles his eyebrows and his glumness vanishes. "My fiendish master plan is coming together."

Before I can interrogate him about his scheme to save *ZomHon*, Cas distracts me by shuffling up next to me, pulling out his sketchbook and flipping excitedly through a gallery of fresh storyboards.

"What do you think of these new scenes?" he asks. "Pretty cool, eh?"

They're more than pretty cool. They're freaking awesome! Within seconds, we're hard at work on the storyboards, adding a scare here, cutting a scene there, impaling a member of the living dead on that strategically positioned umbrella.

"Yeeeah." I hesitate. "Even I'm not sure about this brolly bit. Maybe's it's a bit too much?"

"No way!" he objects, adding a catapulting lung to his cartoon. "This is our comedy moment to relieve some of the tension. The wife's umbrella goes right through the zombie's back and explodes out of its chest. Then she accidentally pushes the button on the handle, the canopy opens, and she can't pull the umbrella back out again. Cue loads of gory flapping."

I have to laugh. It could be a standout moment, if we get it right.

"I wish I could draw," I mutter, turning over his sketches. "Even my stickmen don't look like stickmen."

"You don't need to draw." Cas taps his pencil against my forehead. "You're our dream-weaver, Sparky. You create all these amazing worlds up there and then we have the privilege of helping you bring them to life."

Because I'm incapable of taking a compliment, I blush and, say, "Pffft. Don't be ridiculous."

Cas shrugs and goes back to his sketching while I decide to do something very rare. Taking out my phone, I check my social media. It's always a humbling experience. Casper Ricardo Loomis currently has 634 followers on Instagram (that's sixteen down on yesterday, including Queen B's posse); Morgan Adeyemi-Perera has 421 (apart from us, mostly drama geeks). I stare at the tally beside my embarrassingly goofy profile pic – thirteen. One of that lucky number is my mum.

Here's the thing – I don't think people actually *dis*like me. The short horror films that Cas and I premiere every year at our Halloween assembly always go down well (although I suspect some of the audience are just excited about ten uninterrupted minutes in the dark). But however much they might enjoy my movies, this never seems to translate into friends, real or virtual. And I've always been okay with that. Making films is very time consuming; I hardly get to see the two mates I *do* have. But I don't know. If I am going to find this pre-surgery boyfriend and experience love, however fleetingly, then I need to start becoming a lot more sociable.

And fast.

Flicking through a couple of stories, I see that the news of my hopeless heart has started to get around. Some people have even inboxed me with messages of support. Elsewhere, Cas has been memed to within an inch of his life. Someone must have taken a video of the betrayal behind the bins, because there's this scene of us all together, Cas with cartoon smoochie lips, Brianna showering everyone with CGI tears, and me, my cardiovascular system leaping out of my chest and splatting against the wall.

"Oh God," Cas mutters, glancing over at my phone. "Sorry again, Jess."

I rock my head against his shoulder and Cas ruffles my hair. Honestly, I sometimes get the feeling he thinks of me more like a little brother who needs protecting rather than a best friend. Part of me resents this. After all, I am twenty-three days, eight hours and forty-six minutes older than Casper Loomis.

Suddenly the jukebox on the other side of the diner whirs into life. We both look up to see Morgan turn away from the machine and start cutting her way through the crowd.

"'Monster Mash'," she says, bumping her fists together as she slides into the booth. "In honour of you two gruesome dorks. Can't stay too long, by the way. Just popped by to check out your progress." She pulls Cas's sketchbook towards her. When she speaks, her tone has the same brittle inflection she's used with Cas ever since he got with Brianna. Hearing it makes my heart ache. "So I heard you had a run-in with the Brianna brigade. I assume you still have the standard number of testicles?"

Cas's answer is interrupted by the arrival of Signora Argento. Still dressed in Ellen Ripley's jumpsuit, her black hair pulled back in a severe bun, the owner of the diner cocks her flamethrower onto her shoulder.

"So tell me." She clicks her fingers an inch from my nose. "Are you going to order three measly coffees and sit there all night like usual?"

Cas and I avert our gaze while Morgan goes into battle. "Maybe. Is that a problem?"

"Is that a problem?" Signora Argento seesaws her hand, then smacks her palm on the table. "Yes, it's a problem! I can't run a business like this! Day after day, you kids come in here and monopolize my most popular booth. And for what? All you ever do is talk and draw your stupid little pictures and," I feel eyes like lasers boring into me, "*tap-tap-tippity-tap* at your idiot computer. Well, now I say, no more! You three are annoying and I hate you."

"You don't hate us." Morgan sighs.

"No," agrees Signora Argento after a moment's consideration. "Hate is maybe too strong a word. But you must understand, if you don't buy at least six coffees a day, I get my son Dario to immediately escort you off the premises."

"Oh, please," Morgan says, rolling her eyes, "Dario is too nice to do any such thing."

The boss casts a glance across her diner to where her gently smiling son stands at the till. "It's true," she concedes. "Dario is very sweet, like a tiny bird with feathers made of crystal."

"Dario's sweetness aside," I say hurriedly, "what if we give you a credit in our new movie? Catering provided by Argento's Hollywood Diner. Sound good?"

"What is this 'movie'?" she asks, her glare cooling a little.

"I've read the script," Morgan shrugs. "And believe it or not, these two morons have actually come up with something fairly decent. We start filming in the next couple of days. So if we could use your beautiful establishment, free of charge, for planning meetings—"

"And maybe auditions," Cas puts in.

"Then we might dedicate *Zombie Honeymoon* to Sofia Argento," I conclude.

The crème brûlée flamethrower swings down from her

shoulder and comes to rest against my chest. And maybe my mum has a point after all. If being threatened by a temperamental restaurateur is part of getting this movie made, the process might not be all that great for my malfunctioning valve.

"Will there be a grand premiere for this love story?"

I stare at the signora. "This what?"

"You said 'honeymoon'. It's a love story, yes? Like *The Notebook*? I enjoy romances."

"Well, um, yes, I'm sure there'll be a premiere," I say. "And of course, you'd be our guest of honour."

"A red-carpet world premiere!" Sofia preens, then turns to her eldest son, dressed today as history's most feeble King Kong. "Dario! Three coffees for the weird kids! On the house!"

"Oh, but it isn't a love— Ow!"

Morgan stabs the back of my hand with a fork as our hostess marches away. "We'll deal with her screeching at us later. So, these new storyboards?" She again starts riffling through Cas's artwork while I rub my almost-skewered hand. "Shot numbers, locations, lighting cues all included. You two are actually quite professional."

"Huh." Cas drops his chin to the gingham tablecloth. "If only Mr Prentice thought so."

"Yes, so you told me on the phone," Morgan snaps. "Well, if you stopped acting like a bratty teenager, Casper, then maybe you wouldn't be treated like one."

Cas stares daggers but says nothing. So many times now I've thought about intervening, asking them outright what the hell is going on between them. But it all feels so fragile. Like if I push too hard, I'll break something that can never be fixed. And so I stay quiet.

Meanwhile Morgan is suddenly on her feet. "Crap. I have to go."

"Why?" I bounce upright, very nearly castrating myself on the table edge.

"I have an appointment. A drama group friend. Completely slipped my mind. She needs some help running her lines." Her eyes track back almost reluctantly to Cas. "By the way, Jess, you'll need to be at my house tomorrow. 4 p.m. sharp."

"What for?"

"I've found our make-up artist. Some kid I linked up with at drama camp last year. Her speciality is severed limbs and decapitations, so you two should get on just fine. Plus, she's part of Cas's plan to get you the equipment from school."

"What?" This is making my brain hurt. "How?"

Morgan doesn't answer, just heads for the door. We watch her pass the window, hunched in on herself, hands stuffed into her dungarees, shouldering aside a knot of Ferrivale's beautiful people.

"Well." I puff out my cheeks. "I must say, everyone is being super-mysterious these days. I'm the one with the imploding heart but you two are hogging all the limelight."

"About that," Cas says, brightening a little, "maybe it's time I let you in on how we're going to get the film equipment. Just promise me one thing?"

"Um. Okay?"

"You will try your very, very hardest *not* to freak out."

"I am officially freaking out!" I announce to the whole forest. "No, Cas, I'm serious, stop laughing. This so-called 'plan' of yours is crazy and deceitful and practically criminal and anyway, I'm the world's worst actor. Why can't Morgan do it?"

We're now on the forest road heading back to my house. Between the towering oaks to our right, Hunter's Lake glints darkly under a neon-pink summer moon. The Loomises' flat in Mount Pleasant is closer to the diner, but Cas always walks me home first. Another example of how he seems to view me as a kid brother that needs looking after.

"Dude," he says, chuckling, "you can't expect Morgs to do this. *ZomHon* is your baby."

"Yes, all right," I concede, "but this is mortifying! And it won't work. There has to be another way."

He picks up a stone from the path and throws it expertly between the trees. Far out in the lake, I glimpse a neat little spume of water. Cas is sometimes like a living, breathing special effect.

"Great art requires great sacrifice," he says, turning back to me. "And *Zombie Honeymoon* could be great art, *if* we can get our hands on the film club equipment."

I pull on the straps of my backpack and kick at a bit of loose gravel. Of course, my stone launches into the air, pings off a "deer crossing" road sign (being Ferrivale, this deer sports spray-painted penises instead of antlers) and smacks Cas right between the eyes.

Clapping a hand to his head, he exclaims, "Jesse!"

"Sorry, sorry, sorry," I gabble, trying to grab his wrists so I can see the damage. "That really wasn't a commentary on your plan. It was an entirely accidental bit of ninja-ism. Oh God, are you really hurt?"

"Jess, seriously, what are you like?" says Cas, rubbing the injured area. I think he's milking it a bit to be honest, so I decide to ham it up a little too.

"Oh my God," I say. "If I've blinded you, I'll never forgive myself. Not only will I have permanently injured my best mate, I'll have robbed the film world of one of its great cinematographers. In which case, I won't even try to become a director. I'll devote my entire life to caring for you. I'll feed you and bathe you and brush your teeth and moisturize you. You are moisturizing now, right?"

He pulls his hand away and bursts out laughing. "Jesus,

you're an idiot. You do know that blind people are able to do all of that stuff for themselves?"

He has the tiniest scratch across his forehead, but of course there could be serious internal injuries.

"It's not bleeding," I observe, "but I don't want to take any chances. How many fingers am I holding up? Are you feeling concussed? Do you think you might slip into a coma? You should stay at my house tonight. I'll sleep on the floor, you can have my bed. It'll be like that time we tried our first beer and then took turns watching each other all night in case we choked to death on our own vomit. That was fun, right?"

I reach up and brush back his hair, just to check that the scratch doesn't end in some deep, devastating wound, which of course, it doesn't. His eyes are different in the moonlight, more burnt umber than chocolate-drop brown. There are also these little yellow flecks around the iris that I've never noticed before.

"Sparky."

Firmness in his voice. Nothing threatening, only a friend insisting on certain parameters. I blush hard and turn away. It's not like we've never addressed this subject. When I first came out, Cas asked what I suppose all straight friends ask their newly unveiled gay best bud: *Have you ever thought about* me *in that way?* Yeah, like gay men are all so sex-obsessed we find it impossible not to lust after every guy in our lives. Except with Cas it wasn't phrased that bluntly. Anyway, I reassured him that I hadn't.

Which was a bit of a white lie. I wonder if Cas has ever guessed about my long-ago crush on him? All in the past now, of course. I don't think of my best friend in that way any more. Not even a little. Not ever.

Suddenly I hear the roar of an engine, glimpse a splash of headlights out of the corner of my eye. A car, hurtling around the bend in the road.

"Oooft!"

Cas has lunged forward and pushed me off the narrow track and down the bank that rolls into the woods. As I tumble into a thicket, Cas tumbling with me (because instinctively I've grabbed hold of his shirtfront) I catch sight of the car speeding along the road above us. A bottle-green vintage VW Beetle. And the driver, his face almost spectral in the dashboard light.

Any kid who's ever been picked on at Ferrivale High knows those sneering, superior features. The last time I was confronted by them was the night my heart fandangoed its way into A&E. Ethan Murray has the same ivory skin and flame-red hair as his twin sister, but whereas with Brianna the effect is kind of striking, Ethan looks like a catastrophic sunburn waiting to happen.

A moment later we're picking ourselves up off the forest floor, the roar of Ethan's souped-up exhaust fading into the distance. Correction: I'm picking myself up off the forest floor. Cas has this almost supernatural hyper-awareness of his surroundings and so, instead of sprawling arse-over-tit *à la* Jesse, he has landed nimbly on his feet. Even Jacques would be impressed with his dexterity.

"You okay, Sparky?" he asks, helping me up and brushing me down.

"Pretty okay for someone who's almost been murdered," I grunt. "Thanks for saving my life, by the way, but what the actual fuck was that all about? Do you think it was deliberate?"

Cas glances towards the road, a swirl of summer-dry dust still lingering above the tarmac. "I don't think so. I doubt he even saw us. Murray's a bully but he isn't a complete psycho."

"You could have fooled me," I mutter.

"You mean all that posturing at prom?" Cas shrugs. "Toxic behaviour, just like Bree said. Believe me, that guy doesn't give a toss about his sister."

And what about you? I almost ask the question but at the last moment pull back. As I decided earlier, Cas will open up if he wants to. My job is to be there for him when and if he does. Anyway, in the faint yellow glow of the moon, I notice that an impish smile has suddenly spread across his face.

"Oh God," I groan. "I know that smile. I should be worried, shouldn't I?"

Cas throws me a wink. "Follow me."

And that is all he'll say.

Blundering in his wake through the undergrowth, it soon occurs to me that I have no idea where we are. There's no sign of any beaten path. Just trees, bramble and shifting shadows. We used to play in this forest when we were kids – monster hunts in which Cas and I would pretend to be cryptozoologists searching for yetis and Bigfoots (Bigfeet? Don't think we ever worked out the plural). Games devised by Morgan, who would leave us clues and snacks along the way. Inevitably we'd become hopelessly lost and she'd have to come and guide us out of the wilderness.

"Cas, please," I splutter, spitting out bits of leaf from the branch that has just swatted me in the face. "Where are we going?"

"Patience." He shoots me another sly grin over his shoulder. "All will be revealed."

At night in a forest, it's difficult to keep track of time. We might have been rattling about for fifteen minutes when I begin to consider the possibility that, if I lose sight of Cas, I could very possibly die here. If not trampled by some penis-antlered deer, then, when I start to wither from hunger pains, poisoned by the first nut or berry I dare to sample. Images of Dr Myers sniffing at the inconvenience of rearranging his surgery schedule pop into my mind. Actually, it's a morbid sort of fun, imagining who would be gathered at my funeral: Morgan, trying to be all brave and stoic but unable to stop the tears; Mum, guilt-ridden for all the times she invaded my privacy with the Stare; Mr Prentice, consumed with remorse for being a jerk over the film equipment.

And a mystery boy, silhouetted against the dying sun, throwing a single red rose onto my coffin…

Then all at once we're emerging from a tangle of thicket and into a big clearing.

"Oh," I gasp, stumbling to a halt. "Bloody hell. I forgot all about this place."

"Me too." Cas twirls on the spot before dragging me into a delighted hug. "Isn't it perfect?"

The old Lester house looms before us – a Victorian pile of mouldering brickwork, all arches and tottering gargoyles and broken, empty-eyed windows. It's like the hotel from *The Shining* and the cursed house from *The Amityville Horror* had a naughty weekend away together and this was the result. It was originally built for Tobias Lester, a local mill owner, who they say went mad and axe-murdered his entire family…or did Cas and I make that up? Sometimes it's difficult to keep track. Anyway, you get the general idea.

"Remember the story Sammy McBride told us in Year Nine?" Cas says. "His uncle's best mate's cousin knew someone who stayed here overnight on a bet. Next morning, they found him curled up in a corner, his hair turned white, and all he could say was, '*Don't go near the rocking horse! Don't go near the rocking horse!*' Kept repeating it, over and over. And do you remember the weirdest part?"

I nod. "A year later he died of a heart attack – *in a toy shop*."

"And there was a rocking horse right next to him," Cas declares triumphantly.

"Hmm." I frown. "Was there, though?"

"The point is," says Cas, "there *could* have been."

I can't help laughing. "Spooky."

"And a perfect location for a horror movie."

I shake my head. "But we settled on the idea of a cabin in the woods. It's such a classic trope and…Cas, what are you doing now?"

All at once he is up the moss-furred steps and at the front door of the ancient house.

"Locked," he grunts, shaking the handle. Then he steps back, taking in the gaunt façade. "Just a sec."

With that, he bounds back down the steps and disappears around the side of the building.

"But what are you—"

"Stay there, Jess. I just wanna see if there's a loose board or something. I'll be right back."

"Dude!" I call after him. "You know the horror-movie rules. You *never* say, 'I'll be right back'!"

I wait. And wait. After a minute or two, during which

the watchful forest shifts and billows behind me, I decide to make a circuit of the house. It doesn't take long. I pace past dank brick walls, woodwork black and bloated with mould. The boards blinding almost every window seem secure. No sign of Cas. Returning to the overgrown courtyard, I see it immediately – the front door is now standing wide open.

"Cas?" No answer. Heart in my mouth, I mount the steps. "Don't be a dick, Cas. Are you…?"

The smell of emptiness and decay almost makes me choke. Silence lies steadily within the hallway of the Lester house. In the far-off gloom I can make out the sweep of a grand staircase, all silvered with dust. There are a few graffiti tags sprayed here and there, but they seem rushed, almost timid, as if the tagger lost their nerve halfway through. I move carefully to the nearest window, pull aside a shred of curtain from the broken glass, look out onto the empty courtyard and forest beyond.

I let go of the breath I hadn't realized I'd been holding and pull out my phone. My thumb hovers over CAS.

It's then that I hear the *rumble-creak* coming from the next room. *Ver-dum-eeek, ver-dum-eeek, ver-dum-eeek.* In my mind, I see wooden rockers rolling on bare floorboards, a carved horse rearing and bowing, its white painted eyes wild in the gloom. There is a shape perched in the leather saddle, small hands gripping the reins, a bloodied axe planted in its back. I don't know why I'm crossing the hall, have no idea what motivates me to grip the handle, push open the door, and step into the empty parlour. Except, of course, I'm Jesse Spark and I can't help acting like that dumbass character in a horror movie we all love to scream at.

Windows curtained with grime; bits of a broken table piled up in the soot-blackened fireplace; a small chandelier shattered on the floor, its rusted arms bent out of shape; and there, in the deepest shadows, not a rocking horse but a rocking chair. It rolls up and down, almost manically, grinding the floorboards. As if someone has just set it in motion and then stepped out of the room.

Because there is no one sitting in the chair.

I swallow hard.

Take a step forward.

Wonder what the hell I am doing.

And then I let out the loudest scream.

Because a hand has landed on my shoulder and there are lips whispering in my ear, "Don't go near the rocking horse! Don't go near the rocking horse!"

9

"You bloody massive bellend!"

I gasp and slap both hands over my heart. Meanwhile Cas's triumphant grin transforms into a look somewhere between stunned guilt and stark horror. As I stagger with Oscar-worthy commitment over to the rocking chair and swoon into the seat, he fully emerges from behind the parlour door and starts fussing around me.

"Oh my God, Sparky, I'm so, so sorry! It's just, I owed you for the time when you put that mannequin head in my backpack. I wasn't even thinking about your heart. I found this little basement window open round the back and I'm, well, I'm an idiot. Please don't say I've nearly killed you twice in the same week?"

So, yeah, pranks. Specifically, horror pranks. Of course Cas and I have been playing them on each other since primary school. And to be honest, I should have seen through this whole haunted rocking chair thing. Anyway, I'm really beginning to enjoy my revenge when I see the agonized expression on his face.

"Hey, c'mon, I'm only kidding." I drop my hands from my chest and reach out to him, shrugging off the dying act. "But you did kinda deserve it."

He drags me out of the chair, hugs me tight, then pushes me away again.

"*So* not funny, Sparky."

"Well, at least this time I'd have understood the reason I ended up in hospital." I shrug. "Unless snogging Matilda behind the bins was part of some elaborate prank I didn't pick up on?"

I mean it playfully, but I see him stiffen.

"Do you know, I think maybe it was fate," he says, switching the subject with uncharacteristic awkwardness. "Ethan running us off the road tonight. Otherwise we might never have thought of this place and..." His gaze, which had been playing around the gloomy parlour, returns to me. Or, more specifically, to my hands. "Bloody hell, Sparky, you're a proper mess, you know?"

He searches inside his jacket and brings out a packet of wet wipes. Didn't I tell you Cas was the crown prince of hygiene? I'm sure I look horribly funky, sweaty and mud-splattered from my tumble down the bank and our trek through the woods, while Cas himself has barely a chestnut lock out of place. He passes me a couple of wipes and I start cleaning off my grubby hands.

Always being a bit of a disaster area myself, it used to fascinate me how tidy and organized Cas was. Even when we were little kids, he'd bring proper cutlery and paper napkins to school in his lunchbox. The reason is obvious, I guess. The Loomis flat is half the size of our house, and together with Dean, their Nanna Laura, and usually at least fifty boxes filled with trainers, handbags, sunglasses, or whatever else Dean is managing to offload that week in order to keep the family afloat, there isn't room to swing a kitten. And yet still Cas maintains their home in immaculate order. With such a chaotic family, I suppose it's his way of hanging on to some sense of control.

"There," he says in a paternal tone. "All clean again."

"Thanks, dear," I say, and boop his nose.

He digs out a little biodegradable bag from his jacket (because of course Cas would never litter, not even in this filthy old ruin), pops the wipes inside and returns the bag to his pocket to dispose of later.

"So I'll admit that part of my stupid idea to scare you out of your wits just now wasn't just revenge for the mannequin prank," he says, beginning to walk around the room. "I wanted to convince you how scary this place is. So what do you think – instead of a cabin in the woods, our honeymoon couple and their hitchhiker friend have to take refuge in this creepy old house?"

"But what if we get caught?" I say, chewing my lip.

"What if someone lives here?"

He laughs. "Pinhead from *Hellraiser* would be too scared to live *here*. And I didn't see any 'private property' or 'no trespassing' signs, did you?"

And so I turn a director's eye on the place. Cas is right, as usual. Now that my terror of possessed rocking chairs has died down, all I can see are possibilities! My friend's brilliant storyboards start to come alive in my head – I can visualize our trio of main characters holed up in this decaying mansion, their only haven from the zombie hordes that are closing in on all sides. Shuffling corpses with huge pale eyes emerging from the forest. With its rotted doors and shattered windows, all vulnerable to any grasping undead hand, this house is the perfect siege location. A fragile place of safety within which the tension between the characters will be pushed to breaking point.

Cas can obviously sense my building enthusiasm. "Yes?" he asks.

"Yes." I grin. "It's perfect."

All the way home we talk about nothing but the filmic possibilities of the Lester house. I'm so caught up in the excitement of the idea that, before I know it, we're at my front door. It's there that I switch the subject back to Ethan Murray.

"I can't pretend I'm not worried about him," I say. "Even if he didn't purposefully try to mow us down with his car tonight, he *did* try to beat you up before – do you think he'll come after us again? He wasn't at school today, but what about tomorrow?"

Cas shakes his head. "Like I said, he doesn't really care about Brianna. And anyway, I overheard him in the common room yesterday. He was inviting a few people to bunk off and go swimming in the Murrays' pool. I heard he's even hired a DJ."

"Right, I forgot the Murrays were gazillionaires. Who would have thought pig farming was so lucrative? I guess we'll just have to avoid him for the rest of the summer. Or else get your big brother to intimidate him a little?"

It was a joke but Cas winces. "Not really our style, is it?"

I blush, ashamed that I've brought up a character trait of Dean's that makes Cas so uncomfortable. Grasping at the first subject I can think of, I blurt out, "Hey, so I was wondering, why didn't you back me up over Morgan last night?"

He blinks. "What do you mean?"

"All that rubbish about her not being eye candy enough for the wife role in *ZomHon*? Don't you remember our deal? Every time she starts getting negative about how she looks on-screen, we rally round. Build her up, reassure her. But you just sort of agreed that she wasn't right for the role. Honestly, Cas, it really pissed me off. You know she'd be perfect."

I watch his Adam's apple bob a couple of times. In the hard sodium glare of the streetlights, I almost think there are tears in his eyes.

"I guess I wasn't thinking," he says.

"No," I agree, "you weren't." But here's the thing – it's very difficult to stay mad at Cas. Especially when he does that hurt Disney critter thing with his face. So I relent. "Never mind. Maybe there's still time to persuade her."

"Maybe," he says uncertainly, which makes me feel angry and a bit mystified all over again.

"Well, if she doesn't reconsider, you'd better hope there's another actor out there with even half Morgan's skills, and that we can find them in the next couple of days, or we are royally screwed. The wife is *the* crucial role in *ZomHon*. If she can't put over the grief and terror of the situation then we don't have a movie."

"I know. I get it." And I swear there *is* a shimmer of tears in his eyes. "I'm really sorry, Jesse."

"Cas." I sigh. "What's really the matter? Is it something more than the break-up?"

"It's nothing," he insists. "I'm a bit stressed out with stuff at home, that's all. Probably overtired."

"Is Nanna okay?" I ask. "No more falls?"

He shakes his head. "She's fine. Been having some really good days, in fact. And the doctor said her new meds seem to be slowing down the dementia a lot. But you know all that."

I do. I always try to go to Nanna Laura's hospital appointments with Cas. Working long hours on the market, Dean is often unavailable during the day, and anyway I seem to have a knack at keeping Nanna calm in stressful situations. Now quite deep into her dementia, Cas's gran only occasionally manages to find her way back to the world. When she does, I seem to be one of the few people she's still able to remember. I make her laugh anyway.

"So what's going on at home?" I ask.

Cas passes a hand across his face, hesitates, then says, "My cousin. He's coming to stay for a few weeks. As if we haven't got enough going on. His name's Louis. Did you ever meet him?"

"Scrawny kid? Permanently runny nose? I think I might have met him a few years ago. Was it at Nanna Laura's seventieth?"

"He's changed a bit since then," Cas says. "Anyway, he called out of the blue and asked if he could come for a visit. No idea why, he's never shown much interest in our side of the family before. Louis's dad is my dad's second cousin or something. I think they're pretty loaded. Fact is, they've always thought of us as the black sheep of the Loomis clan; looked down on us a bit, treated us like dirt. Still, I said yes because... Well, I don't know why."

"Because you can never say no to anyone?"

He tries a smile that doesn't quite reach his eyes. "I

really wish I was as nice as you seem to think I am, Sparky."

"Pffft." I snort. "Of course you're nice. I don't tolerate jerks as friends."

He gives me another sad, watery sort of smile. "Thanks, mate. Anyway, I told Louis I wouldn't be around much because of the film, which he suddenly got very excited about. Apparently he's done some acting and would like to be involved."

"Fair enough," I say. "But he'll have to audition like everyone else. No free pass just because he's my best mate's cousin."

He laughs and grips my shoulder. "You know, you're turning into a real hard-ass director. I like it." He ruffles my curls before his expression becomes serious. "You're sure you're feeling all right? I'm really sorry for scaring you tonight."

"I'm fine," I tell him. "Honestly, you don't have to worry about me."

"'S what I do."

And with that he wanders off down the road, throwing a "Night, Sparky" over his shoulder. I watch until he disappears around the corner, all the while telling myself that he's fine. It's just a break-up, these things happen, there's nothing to worry about. Digging out my key, I turn to the front door, only to find a dark presence waiting for me on the step.

"What exactly is your issue, Jacques?" I ask the Thing of Evil as I carefully step over a swiping paw. "I feed you, care for you, and all I get back is hissing. It's like being in a relationship with a Kardashian."

I leave the door ajar for a few seconds in case the cat wants to come inside. This act of consideration is rewarded with a look that would cause the vainest Instagram influencer to re-examine their entire self-worth. In the hall I shrug off my jacket and head to the kitchen for a late snack. There, looming over a steaming cup of coffee, something even more unsettling than psychopathic cats and possessed rocking chairs awaits me.

My mother and the Stare.

"Where the hell have you been?"

She taps her watch and makes a sweeping gesture around the room, indicating, I guess, that she expects an answer that incorporates both time and space. I feel the Stare boring into me as I pad over to the fridge and pull out one of her protein bars. I know she's annoyed because she doesn't start the whole "protein bars are snacks for people who actually do some exercise" lecture. I also notice that she hasn't changed into her pyjamas and is still in her boxercise gear, so has probably been simmering on that stool since at least eight o'clock.

"Oh, you know, here and there," I say, biting into the inedible chalkiness of the bar. "Urgh. I'd forgotten how bad these are." I hold it at arm's length. "What do they make these things out of, old tyres and puppies' tears? No wonder people lose weight eating them."

She gets up off her stool, snatches the bar out of my

hand and throws it in the pedal bin. Then a finger is pointed between my eyes.

"Answer the question – where have you been? I've been calling your mobile for hours."

I don't tell her I've had her muted for months. This is not the time. Instead I drift to the snack cupboard in search of a bag of crisps.

"Oh, you know, out selling weed and hotwiring cars." I shrug. "Nothing for you to worry about."

"Ha!" She snorts and returns to her stool. "If only you were that normal, I wouldn't worry."

"All right," I say, raising my hands in surrender. "I was with the guys at Argento's planning some film stuff, then Cas and I went location scouting for a bit. Must have lost track of the time. Sorry, it won't happen again."

I thought it best to edit out the whole plan to repeatedly trespass at the old Lester house. With my mum being a lawyer, it would only lead to awkward questions. Sometimes I'm jealous of the Loomis family set-up – Dean is technically the parent figure but he never interrogates Cas about anything. In fact, it's usually the other way around.

"And this explains why you look like you've been dragged through a hedge backwards?"

The Stare is operating at maximum power. I've heard of hardened criminals crumbling under its intensity. My only hope is a partial confession.

"I just fell down a bank and ran into some trees and bushes and stuff; you know, typical me behaviour. That is the truth, the whole truth and nothing but the truth, Your Honour."

Her eyes narrow. "Well, I'm sure Casper isn't in such a godawful state."

"Oh *please*, if you love Cas so much why don't you just adopt him?"

"Don't be childish, Jesse," she says, taking a sip of her coffee. "In any case, adopting a teenager isn't that straightforward, or I might have done it years ago."

I stuff a fistful of crisps into my mouth and roll my eyes. The good news is that the wattage of the Stare has dimmed and she appears to have bought my story.

"I'm still not happy about you making this film only weeks before your surgery," she mutters. "You know how stressed you get when you're working on a new project. So please don't start yelling at me, but I phoned Dr Myers this afternoon to see what he thought—"

"Yuh duh whah?" I say, spraying crumbs in all directions.

"See, this is exactly what I mean! The slightest thing and you fly off the handle. And I know what you get like with your films – running around with a crew, stressing because your actors can't hit their marks, then you and Cas arguing about the edit. And do *not* tell me you never argue – I've heard you up there, bickering away like an old married couple." Her expression softens for a moment. "Anyway, I told Dr Myers, all that pressure can't be good for you leading up to the op."

"And what did Doc Myers say?"

I can feel my stupid, inadequate heart already sinking through the floor. If Myers vetoes *ZomHon* then there's no way it will go ahead. I'm prepared to tell my mum a few little white lies here and there, but I wouldn't carry on with the film behind her back. Although we occasionally butt heads, we're a team. It's been that way for as long as I can remember.

"He said he thought it was a wonderful idea," Mum says flatly.

"Are you being serious?"

"Unfortunately, yes. He thinks making the film will keep you focused on other things and actually *decrease* your stress levels. He said that up until the surgery date, you should carry on enjoying your life as normal. You know…" She pauses, as if she can't quite believe what she's saying. "I think he likes you."

"Well, he's obviously a fabulous judge of character," I say, trying to keep the surprise out of my voice. "And so, unless Miss Spark has any further questions for the witness, I think that's case closed."

I don't exactly strut towards the door but let's say there's a soupçon of swagger. After all, it's not every day a cardiac surgeon gives you the green light to direct a zombie movie. But I should have known that I wouldn't be allowed total victory. I'm called back into the kitchen where a dustpan and brush are thrust into my hands. Only when every particle of crisp has been tidied away am I allowed to head upstairs to bed.

On the landing I'm stopped in my tracks by her calling my name again.

"What now?" I yawn. "C'mon, Mum, I thought you wanted me to get some rest."

I glance back to find her hovering at the bottom of the stairs. Whatever the opposite of the Stare might be, that's the expression on her face.

"You are all right, aren't you, Jesse bear?" she asks, her fingers pulling at the drawstrings of her hoodie. "Because we haven't really talked. About the operation and what comes next. About anything that might be worrying you."

I try out a carefree shrug. I'm not sure it's one hundred per cent convincing. "But we don't talk," I tell her. "Not about anything important. It works for us."

"Yes, all right," she concedes. "But maybe that's something I've been getting wrong… Look, I'm not saying it has to be anything deep and meaningful, and we don't have to launch into it right at this very moment, but I need you to know, you *can* talk to me about anything. I promise, I'd understand. At least, I promise I'd try."

And she would. I know she would. So why do I shrug and tell her there's nothing to worry about? Why can't I tell any of them – Cas, Morgan, Mum – that I'm terrified? Not only of the pain I'll experience as my chest and ribs begin to heal; that pain isn't even my major worry. But that, when it's all over, when my heart's been repaired and I've been stitched back together, I just can't imagine summoning the courage to take that first look at myself in the mirror. And that, if I can't bring myself to like what I see, how can I expect anyone else to either?

I brush my teeth, batting away these thoughts and thinking instead of Cas's plan to get hold of the film club equipment. I can feel my toes squirming in my slippers. It's completely mortifying, and probably impossible to pull off, but what else can we do? I certainly can't come up with an alternative.

My phone bleeps as I'm heading to my room. Morgan – she's put out a casting call for Friday afternoon at Argento's. All her theatre contacts are on the list. I honestly don't think we'll get much interest, but she seems optimistic. Optimism from Morgs is a rare thing so I suppose I should take some encouragement from that. I collapse onto the bed and hold my phone above my head, texting her back.

The screen goes dark after the message sends and I see myself in the reflection – there's still a stray twig caught in my curls. I can hardly be bothered to pick it out. Instead, I bring up Morgan's Instagram and start scrolling through some of her posts from the productions she's been in. Not only those at school but from the local drama club. Cas and I have gone to every show, cheering her on, and I recognize a few of the boys from other schools and colleges who have starred with her. They all look intimidatingly gorgeous and self-confident. Even if Morgs was willing to set me up on a date with one of them, I'm certain they'd never look twice at me.

But the clock is ticking. Only four weeks to go before I'm hideously scarred and out of the dating game for ever. I need to make something happen.

Idly, I flick over to Cas's account. And smile. Before we left the Lester house, he'd taken a few reference photos of the parlour and staircase. It's the sort of research cinematographers like him do so that they can start visualizing shots ahead of actual filming. In one of them he has caught a candid picture of me standing by the marble fireplace in the parlour. I don't look too bad. A bit scuffed up from the trek through the forest, sure, but my hair is tumbly and kinda cute, and he must have done something with a filter because my eyes are somehow really striking.

Someone called LouisActs17 has left a comment: *Great pic!!! Don't tell me that is Ferrivale's very own Steven Spielberg?! Looking cute, Emerald Eyes x*

Because I'm tired, or dense, or both, it takes a moment

for me to realize that LouisActs17 is in fact Cas's cousin, Louis Loomis. Nice alliteration, I muse, not a bad secret identity for a superhero. I click on his profile pic and his page pops up…

And suddenly the idea that this Greek god of a teenager might actually be a real-life caped crusader isn't all that unbelievable. I sit up straight, banging my head on the shelf above my bed. This is definitely *not* the snotty-nosed eleven-year-old I remember from Nanna Laura's seventieth birthday party. I scroll through dozens of posts – candids of Louis in coffee shops and at music festivals, his toned, tanned arms, threaded with beads and bracelets, thrown loosely around friends' shoulders; stills from theatrical performances and short films, a blazing intensity in those denim-dark eyes; studio headshots in which endless cheekbones and an easy, sultry smile seem to radiate through the lens.

And one glorious picture taken in front of Big Ben at what must have been last year's London Pride. One hand raking through his wavy, golden hair while the other holds a rainbow flag aloft. The caption: *Proud of who I am. Today, tomorrow, and always!*

I rest my palm against my chest and flick back to his comment on Cas's post.

Looking cute, Emerald Eyes x

I let my finger hover over the screen for a moment before taking a big breath and, finally, clicking the little ♥.

11

A hard sun blazes in every window of Ferrivale High. Today it's felt like our school has become the set of some kind of sadistic reality game show, students and teachers cast as contestants to see if we can survive eight sweltering hours in this place without losing our minds. We have done nothing, learned nothing, yet attendance on the last day before summer break is compulsory. To add insult to injury, final period has been an hour of the head droning on in the main hall. At one stage Miss Manders was looking at him so murderously I thought the entire staff might have to hold her back.

But now it's over and I am waiting for Cas at the gate. Not that we're done here just yet. I puff out my cheeks and exhale a long breath. I really don't want to think about what the next hour might bring, so my mind turns back to this morning and an unusually quiet breakfast table.

Even before the post arrived, the mood was off. Mum picking at her muesli while I fed bits of toast to an ungrateful

Jacques. She was obviously still worried that I was holding something back. You don't become a successful defence lawyer without knowing when someone isn't telling you the whole truth.

"I'll be home a bit late today," I said. "Film prep stuff with Cas and Morgan."

She looked up from her bowl and fixed me with her eyes. Not the Stare this time, but a sad, concerned look that was somehow even worse.

"Okay, love. Do you want me to leave your tea in the oven?"

I nodded. "Thanks."

The clock on the kitchen wall ticking out the seconds sounded louder than I'd ever known it. Even Jacques seemed subdued. I watched my mum's gaze drift to the windowsill above the sink and the framed photograph that sits there. It's a picture of a pair of very young parents holding a red-faced, screaming baby between them. My mum looks tired, overwhelmed, and my dad...? Well, Dad died before I could form any real memories of him, so I'm not sure if that warm, slightly crooked smile was one he wore all the time. There's no point in asking Mum, she'd just change the subject.

"Hey?" She jumped at my voice, snatching her gaze away from the photo. "So I should be back home around—"

At that moment Jacques yowled, leaped down from the

breakfast table, and started stalking towards the front door. His mortal enemy had arrived.

"Quick," Mum said. "The Post Office say they'll sue if he mauls another one."

I shot out into the hall and gathered up the Thing of Evil before it could launch an attack on the hand poking through the letter box. The postie's fingers were only there a second before being hurriedly withdrawn, but a second is an hour in cat-time. Anyway, Jacques was not pleased with being denied his prey, so I shooed him out the back door before he could take his revenge on my own fingers.

"Right," I said, straightening up. "I better get moving. Hope you have a nice... What?"

She was standing in the kitchen doorway, an envelope held out towards me. "It's from the hospital."

Now, my back resting against the school gate, I reach tentatively inside my blazer pocket. The letter feels scalpel-sharp against my fingertips. It's from Dr Myers, confirming my surgery date. Included were the consent forms Mum and I needed to sign so that they could perform the operation. My mum had watched as I scrawled a messy signature at the bottom of each page. There were information pamphlets too, detailing what I can expect during my recovery in terms of pain management and rehab exercises, as well as yet more diagrams I didn't want to look at.

I pull my hand back. No need to even think about all that. Not yet anyway.

"Hey, Jesse!"

"See you tomorrow!"

"We can't wait!"

A group of drama kids bustling past. I throw them a small smile. So it seems Morgan's optimism about her casting call was justified. All day I've had a constant stream of amateur actors badgering me with questions and trying to launch into their best audition pieces. Luckily, Morgs has been on hand, like some kind of stern shepherd, steering away her eager flock.

I check my watch and crane onto my tiptoes. There's now a big crowd of freshly liberated teenagers all making for the exit. But no sign of Cas. I'm not too worried. As predicted, Ethan seems to have bunked off the last day. Still Cas has continued to get snide comments and filthy looks thrown at him. His betrayal behind the bins has not yet been forgiven by the in-crowd. Strangely, only Brianna seems to have come to terms with it. Orbited by her entourage, she swept past her ex in the dinner hall without so much as a sideways sneer.

Finally my best friend emerges from the sixth form block and comes jogging over.

"Sorry, sorry," he says. "Thought I'd give Mr Prentice one last try before we embark on this craziness."

"And?" I can't keep the ring of desperation out of my voice.

Cas shakes his head, and my final scrap of hope is snatched away. "He won't budge. Kept saying it wasn't anything personal, that he thinks we're great filmmakers, but that it's more than his job's worth. I suppose I can see his point of view."

"You've changed your tune," I say. "Where's the scary, hulking-out Cas from yesterday?"

"Yeah." He grimaces. "Maybe I overreacted?"

"You think?" I sigh. "So we're really going ahead with this dumbass plan?"

Cas nods. "C'mon, Jesse. Screw your courage—"

"What?"

"To the sticking place. It's a Shakespeare quote. It means be brave."

"Does it?" We both head out through the gate. "Why was Shakespeare incapable of writing anything that a normal person might say? Like, even in the sixteenth century, did anyone really know what the hell he was going on about?"

We wander together down the hill and into town. People are floating listlessly between the shops, wilting under the merciless heat. We pass a toddler on a bench, licking an ice lolly like their life depends on it, while in the town square a man looks on enviously as a dog manages to plunge its backside into the ornamental fountain. Pretty soon we reach the junction where we have to part ways, Cas to head back to the Loomis flat while I continue on to Morgan's.

"Right then," he says, checking the time on his phone. "Morgan's make-up artist friend should be arriving at her place pretty soon. So I'll see you in an hour, okay?"

"Great." I nod, then impulsively catch hold of his sleeve as he starts to move away. "Um, has... Um... Has your cousin arrived yet?"

He turns, brow knitted. "Not yet. Why?"

"No reason."

I wonder if Cas has noticed that I liked Louis's comment on his Insta post. *Looking cute, Emerald Eyes.* I must have spent an hour umming and ahhing about whether to undo that like, and then another hour wondering if I should reply or even send him a DM. I drafted a few casual-sounding responses before deleting all of them. For now, the like alone seems enough... Except, is it? Because this time bomb in my chest is ticking away, and Louis is gorgeous, and gay, and was flirting with me...wasn't he? I don't have a ton of experience of being flirted with, so who knows?

"Sparky?" Cas's frown deepens. "Everything okay? You were going a bit cross-eyed for a minute there."

"Yes, I'm fine. Incredibly...fine," I say, flustered. "See you later then."

I hurry off before he can ask me any more questions.

Morgan lives in the posh new development at the top of town. All big expensive houses with exposed timber beams, built to look like humble barns from the days of yore. Only you don't see that many humble barns with wraparound windows and brand-new Beemers in the driveway. Morgan's dad is a product designer for exercise equipment and her mum, Jenue, owns a string of fitness centres. For some reason she seems to think the name of her mini empire, "Jen's Gyms", is a pun, and laughs hysterically whenever she says it.

I'm slogging uphill to the Adeyemi-Perera home, trying to ignore the sweat flooding down my back and soaking my school shirt, when I jolt to a stop. I had been staring at my phone. More specifically at Louis's Insta page. By this point, every image of him is already seared into my brain, but still, I thought a little refresh wouldn't hurt. Now, due to me slamming on the brakes so abruptly, the phone flies out of my hand and bounces at the sandal-clad toes of the girl standing in my path.

"Oh, hey, Brianna, I didn't see you there," I say, addressing ten diamanté-encrusted toenails.

"Clearly." She bends down and smoothly picks up the mobile that I have been clumsily trying to retrieve from the pavement. She swipes the screen and reads, "LouisActs17. Looks cute." Handing back the phone, she pouts. "Good for you, Jesse. Reach for those stars."

It's something like a miracle, really – while the rest of Ferrivale is busy melting into human-shaped puddles, Brianna Murray looks like she's just walked out of an air-conditioned salon. My guess is that even her sweat glands are a little intimidated by her, so not even a trace of perspiration dares disturb that perfect make-up.

"Oh. Ha. This?" I waggle the phone. "No, that's not what I was… So I wasn't checking him out. Not *out* out, if you know what I mean? Not in a 'I really fancy him' kind of way."

Brianna twirls her finger, signalling, *Bored now, skip to the end.*

"He might be auditioning for the movie, so I thought I should—"

"The movie, yes," she says, laser-focused and re-engaged. "That's what I need to talk to you about. My brother's just picked me up from school, and then I saw you trudging up this ridiculous hill…" She gestures towards a bottle-green Beetle, idling at the kerb. The same car that almost ran Cas and me down in the woods last night. I swallow hard and stare at the pale face behind the driver's window. Ethan's attention is fixed on his phone and he doesn't appear to have noticed me. "Earth to Jesse?"

"Oh right," I say, looking back at Brianna. "Sorry."

"Why are you always apologizing? It's so very…*very*." She sighs. "Anyway, as I was saying, I thought this might be the perfect opportunity to talk about my part in…"

She looks at me expectantly.

"*Zombie Honeymoon*?"

"Really?" A lip is curled. "You're going with that title? Well, if you must. But look, I only wanted to say that I… Well, I wanted to check with you about whether I needed to…"

It's difficult to describe what happens next. It's almost as if another person has taken control of the girl in front of me. A person less forceful, less confident, less…well, less Brianna. She cuts her gaze to those sparkly toenails, long dark lashes hiding her eyes.

"The auditions, they're tomorrow, yes? What time exactly?"

"From five o'clock," I say, a bit baffled.

"And that's at Argento's? Great, I thought so. And what do I need to bring?"

"Um, didn't Morgan put the details in the casting call? A headshot, any acting credits, and your contact details. That's it."

"Yes. I remember now. I just don't want to get anything wrong and screw up my chance." She says all this in the most unBrianna-ish tone I've ever heard. "Is there anything you think I should do to prepare?"

I stare at her. I'd have thought, if Brianna wanted a main role in the movie, she'd simply have assumed she'd get it. Who is this girl?

And then it hits me. I have seen her like this once before.

The endless three months that followed Brianna and Cas getting together almost wiped it from my mind. She had soon fallen into her usual domineering ways, ordering him about, treating his friends as an afterthought, but when they first got together, things had been different. I flash back to the night of the *Little Shop of Horrors* after-show party: Cas and Morgan having their intense conversation at one of Argento's booths, Morgs rolling her eyes while Cas looked increasingly frustrated as he no doubt tried to insist how great she'd been. Then Brianna had landed on top of them, distraught because her parents had told her exactly what they thought of her performance. Not long after, I'd found Cas outside, sucking face with the worst actress in stage history, but before that, I had seen *this* girl. Full of doubt and uncertainty.

I suddenly experience a strange new sensation. I feel sorry for Brianna Murray.

"There's nothing you need to prepare," I tell her gently. "All we'll ask is for you to read a passage from the script. I'm sure you'll do great." I sneak a look at my watch. "I'm sorry but I really have to be somewhere."

"Not a problem," Brianna says with a flick of her hair. "You hurry along."

I am dismissed, and all at once we're back to normal service. The queen of Ferrivale High turns on her heel and strides to the waiting car.

At that moment, the driver's window whirs down and Ethan pokes out his head, fixing me with a malicious stare.

"Is that little Jesse Spark?" he says, a grin spreading across his face. "Jesus, sis, what are you doing talking to that absolute freak? Hey, Jesse, where's your mate Casper? I've still got shit to settle with him."

"Just leave it, Ethan," Brianna pleads. Then, turning back to me, she says, "If I *am* lucky enough to be cast... Well, I want you to know, however it happens, I won't let you down. I promise."

And with that she steps into the car and the Murrays roar away over the lip of the hill.

12

I'm still mulling over Brianna's brief personality switch when Morgan's mum answers the door and ushers me into the house. I honestly think the vulnerability I glimpsed just now was genuine. A fragility beneath the outer shell of the high school queen. But there's also the fact that Brianna seems to have already forgiven Cas for cheating on her. Which is just weird; I thought she'd play on that drama for all she was worth. But perhaps it makes sense. She knows Cas is my cinematographer, and if she thinks she'll nab a big part in *ZomHon* (some chance!), then she'll want him to shoot her in the best light and from the most flattering angles.

"Goodness, Jesse, you're sweating like you've just come out of one of my spin classes." Mrs Adeyemi-Perera laughs as she leads me through the big, glazed hallway, up the spiral staircase, past a wall of Mr Adeyemi-Perera's rather ferocious-looking Sri Lankan Raksha masks, to Morgan's room. "But as I always say, sweatiness is next to godliness.

That's the motto of Jen's Gyms, forgive the pun!"

"Not a pun," I whisper to myself.

"What's that, hon? Oh! And Morgan told me about your poor, dear heart. I want you to know, we run a fantastic cardiac rehabilitation programme at our Ferrivale branch. I'll send you a coupon for ten per cent off, as you're Morgan's very special gay BFF."

She doesn't miss a beat as she skips to the landing like a Lycra-clad mountain goat. I don't think I've ever seen Morgan's mum in anything other than gym gear. Even when she bursts in late to one of her daughter's plays, refocusing the audience's attention as she sidles to her seat (*"No, don't get up, I can squeeze past, I've only a little bum-bum!"*) she's always in the branded sportswear designed by her husband. I tell Jenue that my mum recently said something similar about my sweatiness and she spins around, framing my face with her hands.

"Poor Sabrina, how is she coping with the news? I bet she's worried sick."

I picture that quiet breakfast table again, Mum's gaze drifting to the framed photo on the windowsill.

"She's fine," I say. "You know Mum."

"Hmmm." Mrs Adeyemi-Perera purses her lips. "Her boxercise will help, of course. Great way to work out any unwanted tension. And you." She waggles my head and I feel myself flap like one of those inflatable tube men you see outside car salesrooms. "Not an ounce of fat on you. That should help with your recovery."

"Um. Thanks?"

Releasing me, she throws open Morgan's door. "Look who's here, darling! Our very special poorly boy and… Oh, sweetheart, no!"

Morgan sits up on her bed, carefully placing a bookmark in her play script and brushing biscuit crumbs from her jumper. She takes another cookie from the packet lying beside her and gives her mother an arctic glare.

"Problem?"

Mrs Adeyemi-Perera looks at me with exasperation. "Snacks before dinner again. And yet she expects people like casting directors to take her seriously." I feel my blood start to simmer as Mrs Adeyemi-Perera turns back to her daughter. "You should take a leaf out of Jesse's book. His people always keep themselves so beautifully trim."

"*His* people?" Morgan stares at her. "Can you even hear yourself?"

Morgan's mum grasps my wrist. "I meant that as a compliment, as I'm sure Jesse knows. Most gay people are super-conscious of their bodies and try to keep them in tip-top condition."

I can feel my free hand itching to steal up to my chest, to press against the still unmarked skin and trace the path of future devastation. It occurs to me that, for the first time since we've known each other, I might have some kind of insight into how Morgan feels about her appearance. The looming spectre of my scar – the way people will react to me once the surgery is done – I wonder if this is how Morgan sometimes feels? The self-consciousness, the sickening sense of apprehension? Not that she has any reason to feel this way. My friend is beautiful. I only wish she could see it herself.

I pull myself free of Mrs Adeyemi-Perera and go to join Morgan on the bed, tucking my gangly legs under me and bumping her shoulder with mine.

"Hey, gorgeous, how're things?"

Morgan gives me a rare, full-on smile. "You know, eating cookies, living my best life."

She shrugs and pops the cookie into her mouth. And right now, this is the perfect retort to Morgan's mother's bullshit – to simply ignore the silly woman entirely. Out of the corner of my eye, I see Mrs Adeyemi-Perera folding and refolding her arms, her mouth opening and closing as she tries to formulate a response to her complete irrelevancy. In the end she simply tuts and leaves the room.

"Sorry about that," Morgan says as the door clicks shut. "*Your people?* What century is she living in?"

"Hey, it's not your fault," I say, grabbing a cookie for myself. "My mum can be awful too."

"Your mum is a goddess," Morgan insists.

"Maybe," I concede. "A bit. Anyway, yours is completely out of order."

"I'm used to her nonsense." Morgan shrugs. She drags a cushion into her lap, hugging it to her stomach. She doesn't look upset, exactly – Morgan hardly ever looks upset – but there is something in her eyes and perhaps the tiniest tremor in her voice. "Anyway, I suppose she's right. One of us has a showbiz figure, but the other? Not so much. You wouldn't even think we're related, would you?"

"Morgs…" I begin, but she waves my words away.

Her defences are back up, and so I munch on my cookie and take a look around the room. I can't remember the last time I had Morgs all to myself. Recently Brianna and Cas have always been in tow; it seems ages since we've sat here, just the two of us, chilling out and chatting plays and drama. Cas is all about the visuals of filmmaking, but personally I'm almost as interested in the acting side of things as Morgan. I think a good director has to be.

For all of five seconds I consider talking to her about my scar. About the revelation I just experienced – that we might share similar feelings regarding how we look. It might be good to acknowledge the anxiety. But Morgan is such a private person, so closed off when it comes to discussing her emotions. I can't bring myself to raise the subject so directly. And, if I'm honest, I'm not sure I want to expose my own insecurities just yet. So I sit here in silence, letting my gaze play around the room.

The walls are papered with posters from famous plays and headshots of actors Morgs admires. Mainly character actors rather than conventional Hollywood stars. A small portion of one wall next to her desk is taken up with some of the local productions Morgan herself has appeared in. Not for the first time I notice how this collection is tucked away, right in the dimmest corner of the room.

"Hey, what's this?" I ask, my gaze landing on her bedside table. Leaning over, I pick up what looks like a shooting script. "Are you cheating on me with other directors?"

She grabs the script out of my hand and shoves it under her pillow. "What is it with you and invading other people's space?"

"I suffer from territorial blindness, you know that." I try to draw her in to a hug and she twists my arm behind my back.

"Submit?" she asks coolly.

"Never!" I try to wriggle free. "Yes."

I'm released and flop back against the headboard, nursing my wrist. "You Adeyemi-Perera women are a menace to fragile joints."

"And you're a hygiene-hazard," she says. "Please get your sweaty body off my bed."

I slump very grumpily off the mattress and over to her desk chair, where I twirl in disconsolate circles.

"I'm very happy for you to be seeing other creatives," I say. "In fact, I'm ecstatic. Because hopefully it means you're not taking any notice of the stupid things your mum keeps saying." I cast a narrow look at the door. "Honestly, Morgs, you would be absolutely incredible in the main role for *ZomHon*, so please will you reconsider?"

"Urgh, not this again," she groans. "Look, I know you and Cas think you're being oh-so-subtle with this campaign you've been waging, but really, you might as well get matching T-shirts printed saying *Let's All Boost Morgan's Self-Confidence*. I suppose it's sweet in a nauseating sort of way. It's also unnecessary. I am fully aware that I will never be the eye candy, onstage or onscreen—"

"Morgan, that is complete bullsh—"

She waves her hand. "It is also what I *want*. Please name me one eye-candy actor who ever got the really interesting roles?"

I'm stumped, mainly because what I considered to be our covert plan has been so easily seen through. But also, if Morgan is really only worried about getting the most interesting roles, why has she insisted on the smaller part of the hitchhiker in *ZomHon*?

"So you're basically telling me that the wife character in my movie – the one I think is *the* crucial part – *isn't* interesting?" I say.

For once Morgan seems lost for an answer. Her eyes

skate around the walls as if one of her acting idols might be able to help her out. "I am not saying that," she says finally. "Not at all. In fact, I agree with you. She is the most challenging role. But she also isn't the right part for me. I can't really explain why, but maybe one day I'll be able to make you understand."

I throw up my hands. "Okay. Fine. You know, I'm going to give up trying to understand both you and Cas. One of my best friends doesn't want the most awesome part in my film and my other best friend behaves completely out of character, snogging random girls and going ballistic at Mr Prentice. Urgh." I rock back in the chair. "Seriously, Morgan, this whole break-up thing – do you think Cas is all right?"

"I don't know why you're making such a big deal out of it." She shrugs. "Cas made a mistake, so what? Nobody's perfect."

I roll my eyes to the ceiling. "I know Cas isn't perfect, Morgan."

"Do you?"

"What's that supposed to mean?"

"Don't get all stroppy, okay, but I think maybe you idolize him, just a little."

"I do not idolize him!" *Do I?* No. That's ridiculous. Isn't it? "Anyway," I say. "What's up with you guys? You seem more than usually snappy around him lately."

She looks a bit taken aback. "I don't… What do you mean, snappy? I'm never snappy with anyone."

"Morgan, there are starving piranhas out there who think you should occasionally dial back the snappiness. But these days it seems that Cas gets more than his fair share. I don't understand what's happening between the two of you."

She slides off the bed and goes to stand at one of the wide windows. She seems to be weighing her words.

"Some people grow apart as they get older, Jess," she says at last. "I know that's not what you want to hear, but it's the truth. Not everyone we're friends with when we're kids remains close for life. It's not anyone's fault. Sometimes we just drift."

This chimes so much with what I've been thinking about the three of us – that we've started pulling away from each other for some unknown reason – that I immediately feel defensive.

"But that's not it," I say. "When people drift apart like that, often they can't look back and tell you when it all started. There isn't a fixed point, it just happens gradually. I don't know why it's going on with us, but I do know we were fine, right up until that night at Argento's."

I see her flinch, then try to cover it. "Which night?"

"The *Little Shop* after-show party. When Cas got together with Brianna." Suddenly a thought occurs to me, and it's so obvious I can't believe I never considered it before. But then the idea of Morgan and Cas ever being anything more than friends is just...well. *They're Morgan and Cas.* Nevertheless, because I'm me, I can't help blurting it out. "Morgs, do you have a thing for Cas? Is that why you've been ratty with him all this time? Because he went off with Brianna that night?"

It makes a kind of sense, doesn't it? That intense, almost passionate conversation in the booth. Maybe Morgan rejected Cas and that's why he got with Brianna, to spite her? But perhaps Morgan really did have feelings for him, so cue all these months of snapping and drifting apart and...

No, that still doesn't explain Cas's betrayal behind the bins with Matilda. And honestly, this version of Cas as a cheater doesn't sit right with me. And then I remember what he said last night – *I really wish I was as nice as you seem to think I am, Sparky* – and I'm confused all over again.

I look over at Morgan, who is still staring fixedly out of the window.

"I've never thought of Cas in that way," she insists, seemingly unsurprised by my question. "Not ever. But we're also not the friends we used to be. And I haven't told you that because I knew it would hurt you, Jesse. Because you want everyone to love each other in the same big-hearted way that you love them. But there's only one problem with that."

I knit my fingers tightly together. I hate this. I hate it. "Oh?" I murmur.

She places her hand flat against the glass. "We don't all have your heart."

I think Morgan is telling the truth. I've never got any vibe off either her or Cas that they might be interested in each other romantically. I also know it's pointless trying to ask her any further questions, about why she genuinely doesn't want the main role in *ZomHon* and what her real beef is with Cas. What I do know is that they are both hiding things from me. None of their explanations for anything ring true.

Again, I keep coming back to the night of the *Little Shop* after-show party. Something big happened that night, I can feel it in my bones. Whatever it is, I'm not sure how all this makes me feel. I want to hold onto my friends. Perhaps even more so because I'm an obstinate little git (© Sabrina Spark) and if I'm told by Morgan our friendship group is falling apart, I want to prove her wrong. At the same time, I am infuriated and hurt by all the mystery and weak explanations.

Mostly though, I'm just worried that if I push things

too hard, ask too many questions, then this fracture between us will crack apart even further. Everything feels so raw and delicate right now, it scares me. And so I change the subject.

"Hey, so I was ambushed by Brianna on the way over here," I say, putting as much carefree-Jesse into my tone as I can. "You know she's coming to the auditions tomorrow? Actually thinks she's going to land a big part in the movie." I start to chuckle then stop myself. I suddenly picture that other Brianna Murray I saw this afternoon – a girl whose outer confidence had been stripped away. "You know," I say after a moment, "this'll sound mad, especially after the past few months with her and Cas driving us both crazy, but I felt a bit sorry for her. Just for a second there, it was like she was a real human being…"

Morgan bristles. "Of course she's a real human being."

"Yes, I…I know," I stutter. "I didn't mean it like that."

"Then how did you mean it?"

"Well, just that…" I throw out my arms. "Oh, come on, Morgan, we've spent three months moaning about her, saying how awful she is, wondering what the hell Cas is doing with her—"

"You wondered. I said he was an idiot."

"What?" When she shrugs in response, I plunge on. "You can't stand there now and tell me you didn't think she was the most irritating, self-obsessed person you'd ever met? Morgan, I remember what you said about her. I have the WhatsApp receipts! And what happened to 'the sisterhood stops at the outskirts of Brianna Murray'?"

"She is…challenging," Morgan admits slowly. "But that doesn't mean she can't have dreams and ambitions, like any normal human being. She's not the villain in our story, Jess. And if you want my opinion, I don't think she's all that bad an actress."

I stare at her open-mouthed. "You've got to be kidding?"

"Have I?" Her words crackle with irritation. "You say all the time that you trust my judgement as an actor. Well, I've seen more of her in auditions and rehearsals than you ever have, and I'm telling you, she's a better performer than you think. Better than any of us thought, maybe."

I'm just processing this when the bedroom door is flung open and a whirlwind in human form blows in. Seemingly frozen to the spot, Morgan's mum still has her hand raised, as if about to knock on the door that is no longer in front of her. Meanwhile, the whirlwind sweeps over to Morgan's bed and puts down something that looks like a battered toolbox. She then tornadoes her way back to the stunned mother.

"Thanks for showing me up," she says, and shuts the door in Mrs Adeyemi-Perera's face.

Morgan chuckles and goes to greet the newcomer. She's a girl of about our age, small, almost elfin, and full of a kind of frantic energy. Even for the few seconds when she's returning Morgan's hug, she seems barely able to contain herself. Once released, her eyes are everywhere, taking in the room, Morgan, me – it kinda feels like we're items on a supermarket conveyor belt, all being scanned and processed at superhuman speed.

"Róisín, this is Jesse," Morgan says.

Before I can even think of getting out of the chair, my hand is grabbed and given a single efficient shake.

"Director, right?" Róisín says. "Heard about the heart. That sucks. So Morgan says you want a make-up artist. Here's my portfolio. Take a look. If you like, cool, if not, also cool."

I'm not entirely sure where the ring binder appears from, but it's suddenly open in my lap and the whirlwind has gusted away again. For a while I just stare back at Róisín as she pulls apart the folding trays of her toolbox – or what I now realize is her make-up kit – and starts organizing the contents. Her hair is a tufted shock of purple, her dungarees and retro Spice Girls T-shirt dotted with smudges of lipstick and mascara. She looks up, an eyeliner pencil caught between her teeth.

"Look or don't look, JS," she says out of the corner of her mouth. "I haven't got all day."

"JS?" I ask.

This receives the classic up-and-down treatment. "You

do know they're your initials, right? Generally prefer using initials. More…"

She clicks her fingers at me, demanding an answer.

"Timesaving?"

"Are you sure it's the heart he's got issues with?" she says, turning to Morgan and tapping her temple. "Not anything else?"

Morgan smiles indulgently. "Take it easy, Róis."

I puff out my cheeks and glance down at the laminated photos in front of me. And suddenly Morgan and the human tornado and the room fall away. I start flicking through the portfolio, my excitement mounting with each brilliant new creation – everything's here, from the grisliest battle wounds to the most hellish monsters, from the subtlest ageing effects to the boldest creature design. Up until now Cas and I have had to rely on YouTube tutorials to do our own make-up effects, but if we could get Róisín onboard? Well, our zombies could really fly. Or at least stagger about with added confidence.

"These are incredible," I say, flicking back through the binder. "This fake autopsy body, wow! And this mangled solider! And this vampire surgeon! Even this kid with the bruised arm – it all looks so realistic."

"Oh that." Róisín sniffs, and I jump. Somehow she seems to have teleported herself from the bed to the desk without me noticing. "No, that last one's real. My older brother,

Jacob. Fell down a well one day. Broke his arm. I use it as a reference pic for contusions."

"Okay," I breathe. "So, you are both scary *and* hired."

"Nice." She nods. "And just so you know, I don't work for free. Tenner an hour. And that's a discount because Morgan is a buddy and I think you're funny."

"Well, I have been known to crack the odd joke," I admit.

Róisín shakes her head. "Not deliberately funny. You know." She waves her hand in my general direction. "*Funny.*"

"Right. Well. Thanks. And on the money issue, I'm sure we can—"

"Great," Róisín cuts in. "Nice to be working with you."

I shoot Morgan a panicked look. There is no way I can afford to pay this talented, terrifying girl ten pounds an hour. Truth be told, I couldn't afford to pay her ten pence an hour. That's why we're about to embark on a plan to "borrow" the film club equipment from school rather than hire it from a private production company. As *ZomHon* has literally no budget, I was hoping everyone would work for free. But then I glance back at the portfolio open in my lap and I know we must have Róisín onboard, no matter the cost.

A hand grips my shoulder. I glance up to find Morgan giving me the kind of look an executioner might offer a condemned man just before she throws the switch.

"So, Róis, if this thing is going to get off the ground, we need a favour," she says. "Call it your audition, if you like."

Róisín thumbs the straps of her dungarees. "I don't audition. JS liked my work, said I was hired. Deal's done."

Okay, so this girl might be a force of nature but even a human whirlwind can meet its match. For years, Morgan has claimed my mum as her role model, and in this moment, I realize she wasn't joking. Not one little bit. My jaw almost hits the floor as I see the Stare. Yes, the full-beam trademark Sabrina Spark Stare. It's uncanny, almost an exact match for the one which has put the most bullying of magistrates in their place. And it seems the effect is just as devastating. I watch Róisín's resolve crumble under its magnificence.

"Okay, all right," she mutters, her gaze dropping. "What do you need?"

Morgan turns back to me. The Stare is gone; she actually looks a little sorry for me.

"Are you ready, Jesse?"

"No," I say miserably.

She nods. "Then let's get this crazy show on the road."

14

"I mean, come on," I say, staring at myself in the full-length mirror. "Who even wears a moustache these days? Only incredibly hot retro gay guys and very old women."

"Don't worry," Morgan deadpans. "No one is going to mistake you for either of those."

I ignore her and continue checking out my reflection. I have to admit, Róisín has done a stunning job. By some dark arts she has tamed my permanently messy curls, pulled back my hairline into something like a widow's peak, and streaked it all with hints of grey that match the salt-and-pepper 'tache currently perched under my nose. In fact, everything has been done very subtly – the crow's feet around my eyes, the frown lines on my brow, the just-starting-to-sag latex skin under my jaw. With a suit borrowed from Mr Adeyemi-Perera's wardrobe, I really do look like an ancient forty-year-old!

Still, I grumble, "This is a terrible plan."

"Agreed." Morgs adjusts the tie around my neck until it

feels like she's trying to throttle me. "But I'd hate myself for ever if I put a stop to it now."

"Oh, and why's that?" I ask, batting her away.

She shrugs. "I can't think of another way you'll get your hands on the film gear. Plus, whatever happens next, it's bound to be classic Jesse Spark."

"Stop fiddling with it," Róisín commands as she leans around and adds a touch of glue to the edge of the fake 'tache. "And do you have to sweat so much, JS? I can't keep reapplying this latex mask effect all afternoon."

"Will everyone stop going on about my perspiration issues?" My gaze flits to the bed and to the mobile I'd flung there before my transformation began. It's time. "Oh God, let's just get this thing over and done with. Morgan, will you pass me my phone?"

She hands it to me and, when I unlock the screen, glances over my shoulder, her attention immediately snared by LouisActs17's Insta page.

"And who is this angelic creature?" she asks, taking back the phone and stepping away from me.

I practically launch myself across the room and grab it from her. "That? I mean, him? Him's Cas's cousin." I shake my head. "*He's* Cas's cousin. Louis. He's an actor and he's coming to stay with them for a few weeks, and he might possibly want to audition for *ZomHon*, so I thought I'd check his social media to see if I fancied any of his parts."

Under layers of latex, I feel my cheeks erupt. "I mean, *liked him for any of the parts*. In the film. Film parts, you know? Not *parts*-parts."

"Uh-huh," Morgan says, exchanging a look with Róisín that practically screams, *We both call bullshit*. "Anyway, before we do this thing, Jesse, it might be a good idea to have a little rehearsal. Build up a history for this character you're going to play – his background, where he comes from, make him as believable as poss— And he's already calling the school. That's just perfect."

Desperate to put the brakes on Morgan interrogating me any further about Louis, I had skipped straight to stage two of the plan: phone Miss Hendricks. It's only now, as the slightly eccentric secretary of Ferrivale High picks up, that I realize I've no idea what I'm going to say. The moustachioed stranger in the mirror looks back at me. Who is this guy? What's his motivation? Most importantly, what the hell does he sound like?

"Hello, Ferrivale High, how may I help you?"

I picture the scatty middle-aged woman who greets us every morning as we file past reception – the eternal pencil poking out of her bouffant hair; the fluffy cat cardigans always buttoned up wrong; the bracelet pendants, featuring every religious symbol under the sun, because Miss Hendricks is an "equal opportunities believer". It feels mean to be deceiving someone so sweet and innocent, but this part of the plan is crucial.

"G'day," I say very heartily. "I hope you're having a...fair dinkum afternoon?"

Morgan goggles at me in disbelief and mouths, "*You're Australian?!*"

I goggle back. "*Apparently?*"

Miss Hendricks is saying something.

"S-sorry, what was that?" I stammer. "How can you help? Well, the thing is, we've just recently moved to this charming little town and we're keen to get our youngest boy enrolled in your charming school. Heard...charming things?" Morgan's eyes widen even further. "Minimal bullying, adequate teaching," I rattle on. "No...um... asbestos in the ceilings."

"Not that I'm aware of," the secretary says doubtfully. "But perhaps we can start at the beginning? If I could take your name?"

"My name? You want my name? As in...*my* name?"

"Yes, your name."

I look at Morgan. I look at Róisín. They look back. Every name in the history of the world has suddenly decided to spill out of my brain. Morgan covers her face with her hands. After an excruciating eternity, I bellow into the phone, "Craven! That's me. Mr Craven. Craven's my name. Craven."

"Well, Mr Craven," Miss Hendricks says in a tone that

indicates she may have met her match in the eccentricity stakes. "I'm afraid you've called on the very last day of term. The head has gone home and there aren't any teachers still on the premises. Only me and the caretaker. Perhaps I can schedule a meeting for the start of next term?"

"No!" I bellow again.

"No?" Miss Hendricks twitters.

"No," I say, pulling it back a notch. "It has to be today. In the next half hour, in fact. I…well, I want to get a feel for the place. You know, before I entrust my boy to the care of Ferrivale High. You might think this is a bit silly of me, Miss Hendricks, but I wonder, do you believe in destiny? Fate, karma, um, feng shui?"

Morgan is kicking me in the shin, but I can tell by the ripple of enthusiasm at the other end of the line that I'm on the right track. I can almost hear the eager tinkling of those sacred pendants.

"Do you know, Mr Craven, I do," she says. "I think it is very important that every soul find its proper allotted space in the universe. That is what you are driving at, isn't it?"

"*Possibly?*" I wince.

"Then you must be sure that your child is a correct fit for Ferrivale High. And we can't have the anxiety of that question hanging over your family all summer. So of course, do drop by as soon as you like, and we will see what the fates have in store for us."

"Oh. Okay, thank you. See you in a bit then." Ending the call, I rest my head against the mirror and let out a long sigh. Without turning to her, I seek Morgan's professional opinion on my performance. "Go on then, any notes?"

"Only that you're a better director than you are an actor," she says. "And that you're now stuck with that stupid voice."

I close my eyes. "Róisín? I think my moustache is drooping."

I ease myself as carefully as I can into Dean Loomis's portable deathtrap. Or, as Cas's brother insists on calling this rusted-to-hell Nissan Micra, his "honey wagon". I'm not sure which honey last had the pleasure of catching a lift with him, but she appears to have left her verruca sock wedged between the back seats.

Chocolate drop eyes, almost an exact match for Cas's, though perhaps less kind, crinkle at me in the rear-view mirror.

"You've got up to some stupid crap in your time, Jesse boy." Dean twists around in the driver's seat, planting a thick forearm on the passenger headrest. "But you nerds are out of your tiny minds if you think anyone is going to fall for this. What are you supposed to be anyway, the world's least convincing accountant?"

"Nice to see you too, Dean," I mutter.

He bounces back into his seat, slapping his hands against the steering wheel and howling. "What the hell's with the accent? Are you a method actor now or something?"

"I am trying to stay in character," I tell him tartly.

A hand reaches out from the passenger side and gives Dean's shoulder a slap. Then my best friend turns to face me. "Take no notice," Cas says. "I think Morgan's friend has done an amazing job. Anyway, we're moviemakers, right? In the business of illusions? I really think we can pull this off."

"Thanks, mate." I use a forefinger to smooth down my old-man 'tache. I actually find it quite soothing, like petting a docile hamster that has lost its sense of direction and crawled onto my upper lip. "Anyway, I reckon Miss Hendricks has bought the story, so far. I only wish Morgan could've taken over this part, but she said improv isn't her thing."

"Hendricks?" Dean cackles. "Is that crazy old bint still on reception? Oh well then, maybe your chances of pulling this off have increased a little. And if she sees through it, you could always say it was an end of term prank. You little freaks wouldn't believe the crazy stunts me and my mates used to get away with back in the day."

I try very hard not to roll my eyes. I *would* believe Dean's stories, basically because I've heard them a million times before. How he and the bunch of no-hopers he still hangs around with a decade later used to rule Ferrivale High. How they egged teachers' cars, pranked the nerds, pulled the girls they liked. Every banal joke and strutting victory tinged with a cruelty that makes me wonder yet again how these Loomis boys can possibly be brothers.

Cas gives me an uncertain smile and slides back into his seat.

"So, Jesse boy, how's that hot mum of yours?" Dean asks.

He turns the ignition and at the third attempt the rust-bucket shudders into life.

"Dean," Cas says quietly.

"Still hot, apparently," I say. "Whatever you said to her in the supermarket last week went down well anyway. And by that, I mean it's a miracle she didn't throw you through the nearest window."

This is pretty much all Dean ever says to me these days – smartarse quips about my mum, little digs about my sexuality. It's been this way ever since I came out. Before then he was more or less indifferent to me, but afterwards there's been an edge to his attitude. I never say anything to Cas about it, though I know he notices, and squirms.

Cas doesn't exactly hero worship his older brother – he's too smart not to see Dean's flaws for himself – but he feels this huge sense of obligation towards him. Like me, their dad died when they were both quite young; then Cas's mum vanished pretty much overnight with some guy she met at the local pub. After that, Nanna Laura moved into the flat and she and Dean have raised Cas between them. It was either that or my best friend would have had to go into care. Of course, what with Nanna's increasing dementia, it is now almost entirely down to Dean to provide for the family, which to his credit he always has. And he does love Cas a lot, so we at least have that in common.

I take a quick glance back at the Adeyemi-Perera house. At an upstairs window Morgan and Róisín wave and give me a thumbs up. I stroke my moustache meditatively in response.

"So have you got something to say to Jess?" Cas asks his brother, drawing my attention back to the car.

"What? Oh yeah. Sorry to hear about the surgery stuff." Dean hurtles us out the drive and down the hill leading through town. "Have they given you good odds?"

"On?" I say, gripping my seat belt.

"Making it? Surviving the op?"

"Probably better than me surviving this car journey," I mumble.

"Huh?" Dean shouts over the screech of the engine. "Speak up, Jesse boy."

I shake my head. Faces beyond the window pass in panicky snatches. A car horn blares at us as Dean jumps a red light. I start to ask if we could possibly have some air-con back here before realizing that four functioning wheels is probably the most luxurious feature this chariot of Hades has to offer. Sitting forward, I peer through the flyspecked windscreen. It seems like only seconds since we left Morgan's and yet there's the sign for Ferrivale High up ahead. Dean swings us into the empty car park and slams on the handbrake. Not a teacher's car in sight and only Miss Hendricks's bicycle still propped in the stands.

"All right, nerds." Dean grins at me in the rear-view. "Let's *Ocean's Eleven* this mother."

We're striding nonchalantly across the car park (correction: the Loomises are striding nonchalantly; I'm slouching a step behind while slowly baking alive inside Mr Adeyemi-Perera's business suit) when Dean calls over his shoulder, "Did you hear our cousin Louis's coming to stay for a few weeks?"

I'm not worried about blushing because I'm fairly certain my entire face is already beetroot-red. "Uh-huh," I pant. "I did."

"And?" Dean asks.

"And what?"

"Well, you'll get on, won't you? Him being a queer too."

It seems that even Cas can't let that one pass. "Dean, what the hell?"

"What? That's their word now, isn't it? They've reclaimed it." He spins around, shooting me gun-fingers and winking. "Good for you guys. And why wouldn't Jesse boy and Lou-Lou get on? They must have loads in common – musicals, that Drag Race show, that Olympic diver guy, not to mention both loving the—"

"Stop," Cas snaps. "Just stop, okay?"

I think all three of us are a little stunned. It's the most Cas has ever talked back to Dean, certainly in my hearing. At his words, I feel my lousy heart fill up until all I want to do is rush forward and throw my arms around my best friend. But already I can see Cas retreating again. One glare from Dean and he's back in his place – the grateful little brother.

"Don't throw a hissy fit, Casper," Dean snaps back. "Jesse knows I'm only joking. Not everyone can be alpha males like us Loomis boys, am I right?"

Cas keeps his mouth shut.

As we near the main reception block, I trot to catch up with Cas. Dean is checking his phone and not paying us any attention.

"About Louis," I say. "Do you think he's definitely up for a part in the film?"

Cas gives me the side-eye. "I told you, yes. Why are you asking again?"

"Well, the thing is…" My hand grips the mobile in my pocket. "I had a look at his Insta page last night and I—"

"Yeah, I noticed you liked his comment on my post."

There's no particular tone to Cas's voice, but still I feel my toes curl. "He's very…" I grope for the right word.

"Striking, don't you think? Like, the camera loves him? I think we could definitely find him a part in *ZomHon*."

"Didn't you say he'd have to audition like everyone else?" Cas says drily.

"Oh yeah, he'd still have to do that. But I thought, even if I wrote him a bit part, then we might—"

"Just don't start relying on him, is all I'm saying," Cas interrupts. "Like I told you, his side of the family have always been a bunch of selfish pricks, only out for themselves. They've never given a toss about us or Nanna. If Louis gets a better offer, you won't see him for dust."

"All right, game faces on," Dean says. We've now reached the entrance. With a nod from Dean, the Loomis brothers plant their backs against the wall either side of the main door. "So you keep that crazy old bint busy in the office for ten minutes and we'll do the rest. Understand, Jesse boy?"

I give my moustache a final delicate stroke. In the reflection of the glazed entrance, it seems that Róisín's miracle transformation is holding up – crow's feet and grey hair present and correct, jowls still slightly sagging. If I fail to convince Miss Hendricks it won't be because I don't *look* like a forty-year-old Antipodean businessman. I smooth down my tie and push through into the entrance hall, mentally batting away any disappointment I feel at Cas's assessment of his cousin.

"Mr Craven, yoo-hoo!"

Bouffant hair impaled with a pencil pokes out from the reception's sliding window. The secretary waves at me and a dozen sacred icons tinkle at her wrist.

"Come round to the door, I'll let you through," she chirrups. "I'm sure you're already getting a feeling about the place but let's see, shall we?"

Perhaps I'm overdoing it, throwing curious glances around the entrance hall, moving slowly as if I'm soaking up the karmic atmosphere of a corridor that reeks of sweaty teenagers and cheap floor polish. The door next to the sliding window is opened and I'm ushered through. Miss Hendricks's inner sanctum is visited only by shitheads like Ethan Murray who need their behaviour reports stamping or else kids who feel sick and require a parent to be called. I've never been in serious trouble and I've never been ill at school. Well, not until this week anyway. Now, following a cardiac event behind the gym, I'm about to temporarily relieve Ferrivale High of thousands of pounds worth of equipment. Funny how quickly things can change.

Miss Hendricks's back is turned as she leads me into the office. Out of the corner of my eye, I see two figures scurry past and head off down the hall.

"Did you hear something?" Miss Hendricks asks. She has reached her desk, a neatly ordered workplace overlooked by timetable printouts and a big laminated poster of Elvis Presley. I kick the door shut with the heel of my shoe.

"Not a thing."

"Really?" She frowns. "I could have sworn—"

"Could've been a breeze." I scramble around in the rat's nest of my brain for something that sounds even vaguely plausible. "Or the plumbing. Or maybe you've got mice behind the walls."

"I truly don't think we—"

"Are you lonesome tonight?" I say a bit desperately.

Miss Hendricks blinks at me. "I'm sorry?"

"Elvis. Gotta love the King." I gesture at the poster behind her – a sweaty middle-aged man in a sparkly jumpsuit, top lip curled, his hair almost as bouffanty as Miss Hendricks's.

"Oh yes." She beams, turning an adoring gaze on the poster. "A great spirit. So soulful, so eternal. I've always been an immense fan."

"Me too." I nod solemnly. "Pity about the whole dying on the toilet thing."

"Oh, but that's just nonsense," Miss Hendricks objects, her face flushing. "A made-up story put about by the CIA after he returned *home*."

She casts a significant look upwards, her dreamy gaze seeming to move beyond the water-stained ceiling tiles and into realms unknown. I don't think she means that Elvis is currently nursing a cup of tea in the staffroom upstairs, although I suppose anything's possible. Cas once claimed to have seen Taylor Swift in the pet food aisle at Lidl.

She's still staring into the celestial beyond when I catch a shadow on the wall. My head flips around in time to see the Loomis brothers hefting a huge box past the sliding window. If at this moment Miss Hendricks happens to glance over my shoulder, then the game's up.

"So," I say, "what do you need from me?"

The secretary jumps. I've moved around the desk to stand beside her, drawing her focus away from the entrance hall.

"Oh, you startled me." She giggles. And then her eyes narrow. "You know, Mr Craven, you do look a little familiar. Did you say you're new to Ferrivale?"

Is my make-up running? Is my moustache sliding off my face? All I know is that we're too close for comfort.

"Miss Hendricks, would you do me an enormous favour? Could you go and stand on the other side of the desk? Yes, just where I was a second ago. I would love to get the vibe of this place from your perspective. That's perfect, thank you." She's in position just as Cas and Dean dash back past the glass. "Yes, wonderful. I'm feeling a very, um, nurturing atmosphere here."

Miss Hendricks's smile becomes almost ecstatic. "I always say there is a colour to the aura of this office. I wonder, can you see it, Mr Craven?"

"I can!" I say, loudly enough to cover the sound of Cas

dropping something heavy just outside the window. "Oh yes, it's very…"

"Purple," Miss Hendricks volunteers, clapping her hands together.

"Purple." I nod dubiously. "Maybe. I would have said puce, myself, but I can definitely see how some people might interpret it as purple."

I've made a mistake. I can tell straight away from how she flares her nostrils and draws her lips into a thin line. Perhaps it's rude to second guess the exact shade of a school office's psychic aura? Anyway, in the next moment, she's snatched the pencil out of her hair and grabbed a scrap of paper from the desk.

"Well, I've only worked here for fifteen years," she says huffily. "But I'm sure you know best. Right, so what's his name?"

It's my turn to blink at her. "What's whose name?"

She's holding the paper in her hand, pencil poised. "Your son's? I'll need his full name to register him for the new term."

"My son's name is…" Not again. Why are names so hard?! "Wesley!"

"Wesley." She looks at me. "Wesley Craven. As in, Wes Craven. Like the horror film director?"

I'm staggered she's heard of him. "I'm staggered you've heard of him," I say. "But yes. What with the coincidence of our surname and me and the wife being big *A Nightmare on Elm Street* fans, we thought why not?"

"Your wife?" A secretarial eyebrow is raised. "Strange, you don't have the aura of a married man."

"Oh, no, I'm not," I say hurriedly. "My wife's dead. Very dead. For about twenty years."

"But surely your son's only a teenager?"

"Twenty years, give or take." I squint. "You lose track, don't you?"

Miss Hendricks shakes her head, her expression softening. "I'm so sorry for your loss. She must have been very young. How did she—?"

"Crabs," I blurt out. "I mean, land crabs. Not the other kind that people sometimes get in, you know, *intimate areas*. Because I don't think those can actually kill you, they're just quite irritating, am I right?" My voice is cracking and I can hear my "Aussie" accent beginning to wander across continents. We need to wrap this up, and quickly. "Anyway, the wife. Tragic story. She was sunbathing on the beach near where we lived and, well, all they found was a shredded towel and lots of little claw marks in the sand."

Miss Hendricks's hand flies to her mouth. "Your wife was *eaten* by crabs? How is that even possible?"

"Australia has very big crabs."

Over her shoulder I see Cas and Dean holding up what

looks like a drone and beaming from ear to ear. Then Dean jerks his thumb towards the door and they both disappear.

"So there you go," I say brightly. "It was all very horrific, but I'd better be making tracks."

I have to stop myself sprinting for the exit.

"But I still require some further details on Wesley, Mr Craven," Miss Hendricks says, following me out into the hallway. "His date of birth, his previous school, any allergies."

"Allergies." I swing around, clicking my fingers. "That's the problem. You see he has a very bad allergy to…" My gaze skates around the familiar hallway. I can feel a pulse beating in my neck. I've got nothing. "Hallways?" I say, then realize it sounds like a question. "I mean, *hallways*. More of a phobia than an allergy really. It's a shame because you seem to have a lot of them here, connecting rooms to rooms the way they do. But that just won't work for Wesley."

"Surely his old school had hallways?" Miss Hendricks calls after me.

"You would have thought so, wouldn't you? Thank you for your time, though. And I think you're right about the aura of your office, by the way. Purple." I give her an apologetic wave before plunging through the door and into the car park. "Purple, all day long."

I don't believe in God. Haven't since I was nine years old, right around the time I found out how young my dad had been when he'd died. I don't know. It sort of put me off the idea that there was this benign creator out there, looking down on us, taking care of the universe. I mean, what divine plan could possibly involve robbing a baby of their father before they even got the chance to know each other? So while I don't exactly thank God that we survived the trip back to the Loomises' flat, I do pat the bonnet of Dean's death machine with something like gratitude.

The lifts are out of order in Cas's block. Not an unusual occurrence, but it makes carrying the film equipment up six flights of stairs a bit of a chore. With typical Casper dexterity, he perches a Steadicam on his hip while unlocking the door to their flat and then gliding inside. With typical Jesse doofusity, I follow, tripping over my own feet and spilling a couple of tripods into the hall.

"Not built for manual labour, are you, Jesse boy?" Dean

grunts. He elbows past me with a huge box, abs and biceps bulging under his tight black tee. It's funny, in the long-ago days of my sexual awakening, Dean had been an object of many a fantasy. Back then his indifference to me hadn't been an issue. If anything, I'd found it a bit of a turn-on – the typical bad boy seduction scenario. But then he'd found out that I was gay, and the snide little jokes and comments started up, and any interest I'd had in him evaporated entirely. Dean is still objectively attractive, there's no denying that, but he strikes me now as being like the statue of some unpleasant Greek god – a figure you can only admire with a shiver.

"Don't worry," he goes on, putting down his box and collecting up the tripods. "Us Loomis boys have got you."

"Thanks," I mutter under my breath. "Maybe you could also email someone about getting the lift fixed? If your biceps can handle that."

"What's going on?" Cas sidesteps down the hall and squares Dean's box neatly against the wall.

"Nothing. Just our Jesse getting a bit hot and bothered." Straightening up, Dean plants one hand in the small of his back and stretches. "Why don't you go and say hello to Nanna," he suggests. "Let the men finish up here."

A blush crimsons Cas's cheeks and his gaze snaps to the floor.

"Sure thing." I smile sweetly. "I'll pop the kettle on while

I'm at it. Tea with two sugars for you, Dean? I'll try my best not to mix it up with the rat poison under the sink, but no promises." I pat his shoulder as I pass; I actually feel him flinch. "You *know* what us klutzy gays can be like."

I can imagine the look I get but I'm down the hall and into the open-plan kitchen-sitting room before Dean can come up with a snarky response. As ever, the Loomis home is immaculate, everything polished to a gleam that almost hurts your eyes. There are more boxes here, this time containing the jeans and T-shirts and sunglasses Dean sells at Ferrivale market, all stacked as neatly as possible against the walls, like the world's tidiest giant Jenga. Honied sunlight plays through a gap in the curtains, trying in vain to find any spiralling dust motes to illuminate. It falls on the sleeping face of an old lady, tucked up in her chair.

As usual whenever I see Nanna Laura these days, I feel this deep pang in my chest. It doesn't seem all that long ago that she was buzzing around the Loomis flat, scolding Dean for leaving the milk out, ironing Cas's school shirts into crisp, perfect piles, laughing along to some cartoon we'd been watching on her laptop. Now she sleeps and dreams, a puzzled frown haunting her brow. I pass quietly to the side of her chair, my gaze moving across the items on her table. Pills, an empty teacup, a note from her carer. In the early stages of her illness there had been stacks of the paperback romances she loved to read. When her attention started to drift, these had been swapped for fashion magazines with glossy photos. To remind her, so Cas told me, of her days as a young fashion model. Now even these lie untouched, gathering what little dust there is in the Loomis home.

You can still see traces of that beautiful girl. A hint here and there of the carefree spirit who strutted the catwalks of London and Milan, but like with everything else in her life now, a sort of emptiness clings to Nanna Laura. Dementia is a peckish thing. It started off only nibbling at the edges of her mind, but its appetite has become insatiable. Bit by bit, it's eating Cas's grandmother alive.

I shiver a little. I've seen every kind of monster horror cinema has to offer, but this hunger? *This* truly scares me. Perhaps even more than my surgery and the idea that, once it's done, I might always be alone.

Dean's voice sails in from the hallway. "Lucky I knew old Ted from playing pool at The Feathers. Didn't realize he was the school caretaker. Thought we'd had it when he appeared around the corner like that. Remind me, I owe his grandson a pair of Nikes for looking the other way."

"He's not a bad lad, really," a voice, dry as sandpaper, rustles beside me. I look down at Nanna Laura, who smiles a vague sort of smile. "Well, even if he is, he'd do anything for his little brother, and that has to count for something, doesn't it?"

I'm not sure why, but I suddenly feel this lump in my throat. "It does." I squat down beside her and take her hand in mine. "It counts for a lot. Even if he is a bit of a bellend."

She laughs, then frowns, then laughs again. It doesn't exactly sound like the Nanna laugh of old but there are shades of it still there, tinkling at the edges. I try to laugh with her and find I can't. She looks so tiny in her chair, like a child dressed up in her parents' clothes. Her expression smooths away and I can see her struggling to place me. It takes a moment or two before a victorious grin breaks out.

"Jesse! Little Jesse Spark!" She clutches at my name like a prize, hard-won. "My little Jesse angel."

I wipe the corner of my eye with my free hand. "Yes, Nanna, it's me."

She shakes her head. "But there's something... something different about you."

"There is?" I turn to glance at myself in the reflection of the TV, and wince. After the exertions of lugging the film equipment up six flights, Róisín's make-up is running down my face while my fake moustache has somehow drifted onto my cheek. I peel it and the latex jowls away and fling them into the wastepaper basket next to Nanna's chair. "Sorry about that. Just a silly game Cas and I were playing."

She grips my hand. Her skin feels so dry, veins running under it like blue rivers. "You two boys. I remember when you'd sit up at that table, you telling your stories and our

Cas drawing the pictures. Scared me half to death, some of those tales! You were lovely then. My boys. My boys who grew up and now..." She hesitates and blushes, as if ashamed. "I don't... It's not there, you see? Not every bit of it. Only the feeling. That he won't say. That he won't. And it's so silly, and I'd make him if I could, but not now. Now I can't. Because it all slips and pulls away from me before I can be sure. Memory. It's not..." She reaches over and cups my hand in both of hers, gently, like she's sheltering something fragile and precious. "It doesn't work like those films you boys make together. You can't rewind it and play it again. It blips and flips around, do you know what I mean?"

I nod. I think I do. Memory is a funny thing, even for people who aren't being nibbled away at by dementia. It skips and cheats and edits. For example, I can barely remember Cas's mum, even though I knew her for a couple of years before she walked out on her sons. I wonder sometimes if I have deliberately cut her from the movie of our lives because keeping her would feel like a betrayal, both of Cas and Nanna.

And all at once I'm picturing a photo on a kitchen windowsill, and wondering how much my mum remembers of my dad. She was so young.

"Don't get old, Jesse love," Nanna says, drawing me back. "Don't change at all. Stay as you are, right here and now.

Young and perfect and whole. Promise me?"

Her gaze flits over my shoulder and I turn to see us both in the dark reflection of the TV. A tiny figure in a chair and a boy kneeling beside her.

Both a little scared. Both a little lost.

"I promise," I tell her, knowing it's a lie.

Because I will be changing. And soon.

17

"Would you like me to put the TV on, Nanna?"

"If you like, Je…" She blinks at me, her face crumpling. A small moment of bewilderment that causes her pain. "If you like…love."

I kiss the back of her hand and lay it gently on the arm of the chair. "Let's see if there's anything good on, shall we? Maybe one of those old romcoms you love so much? Remember how me and Cas used to moan when you made us watch them with you on Sunday afternoons? Saying how soft and sappy they were. Well, here's a little secret, between you and me, I love them too. Maybe I'm not just a horror hound, you know? Maybe I'm a bit of a romantic as well?"

I've been hunting around for the remote control. Finally discovering it buried under sofa cushions, I flourish it in triumph, only to find that Nanna has drifted back off to sleep. I place it on her table as Dean's voice bellows from the hall.

"Where's that friggin' tea, Jesse boy? Is the kettle too heavy for you or something?"

I flip my middle finger at the closed door and move over to the open-plan kitchen. It's a small but perfectly ordered space, the cooker with its spotless hobs, the shining stainless-steel sink, folded tea towels squarely stacked. I flick the switch on the kettle just as Cas steps into the room. He shoots me a smile and we stand side by side, resting our backs against the countertop, listening to Nanna's gentle snoring.

"She seems to be having a good day," I say.

"Does she?" Cas shakes his head. "She's getting worse. Little bits of her keep falling away. Some of it comes back but never completely. It's partly why I didn't want Louis coming to stay. She could do without the disruption, you know? The confusion of having a strange face around the place? Anyway, it's not like his side of the family have even seen her for years."

"Then why didn't you tell him no?"

"Because she overheard me and Dean talking about it, and all of a sudden her face lit up. '*Louis,*' she said. '*I remember Louis. Is he coming to see me?*' She was so excited."

"Ah, Cas." I give his shoulder a squeeze and feel him stiffen, just a little. "Everything okay?"

"Yeah. Course. I should probably just…"

I think about telling Cas of my encounter with Brianna's

brother this afternoon and of Ethan's threats. But one look at my best friend and I know he doesn't need any extra stress right now.

Something's wrong with him. I tell myself yet again that I have my own stuff going on, but even my surgery and the scar and *ZomHon* and the seemingly impossible prospect of trying to find a boyfriend drift into the background as I watch my best friend obsessively wiping down surfaces that already sparkle.

"Dean got a lead on a possible filming location from some old mate of his," Cas says, turning back to the kettle and pouring hot water into cups. "Maybe we could recce it tomorrow before the auditions? With the forest and the Lester house, this could be our third main location all sorted."

"Sounds great." I take my cup and stare into the swirling liquid. I feel I have to say something or I'll burst. "So here's a funny thing – I found out this afternoon that Morgan knows all about us trying to boost her confidence. Isn't that weird? We thought we were being so stealthy. I guess we should've known that she'd see right through it. So I suppose it didn't matter in the end, you not backing me up about her getting the main part in *ZomHon*."

I look up. Cas seems equally riveted by his tea. And all at once I feel a prickle of irritation. "Unless you already knew that *she* knew. But then you'd have told me, wouldn't you?"

He tries a sip of his tea. "Urgh. This is awful. Sorry, the milk must have turned. Do you want a juice or something instead?"

He takes the cup from me and starts pouring perfectly good tea down the drain. I watch his back, taut, hunched.

"She also said Brianna was a good actress. A good *performer*." I correct myself. Something about the distinction snags, as if it might be significant. "Can you believe that? In fact, she went into full-on Brianna Murray defence mode, as if she hadn't witnessed for herself just how awful Brianna was in *Little Shop of Horrors*. A lot changed that night, didn't it, Cas?"

"What do you mean?" he asks in a tight voice.

I shrug. "You got together with Brianna and our entire friendship dynamic shifted. It wasn't just the three of us any more. And it hasn't been the same since. Not even now that you and Brianna have broken up. You know, I can't stop thinking about the row I saw you guys having that night in Argento's."

"I didn't row with Brianna that night."

"No, I mean you and Morgan. Right before Brianna made her dramatic entrance and you decided to inexplicably start snogging her." I click my fingers. "A bit like how you recently, and equally inexplicably, decided to start snogging her best friend behind the bins. Is this some new character trait of yours I never knew about? A tendency to kiss random girls at the most bizarre moments? Because I have to tell you, it's very *not* on-brand for Casper Loomis."

He sighs. "Jesse, drop it."

"Drop what? Cas, I don't under—"

"All these questions. You think there's some big mystery here – about why I kissed Matilda and broke up with Brianna. Why Morgan and I haven't been getting on all that well lately. I want you to believe me when I tell you, there isn't. There just *isn't*. It's all in your head." I see him tense, gripping the countertop, his knuckles standing out sharp and white. "It's like you don't trust me or something."

"Cas, of course I trust you. But—"

"No buts," he says. "Look, I want to help you make this movie. I want it to be your ticket into the best film school in the world. I want to be with you when you go into your surgery and I want to give you the biggest, gentlest hug when you wake up. And I will. I'll do all of that because you're my best friend and I love you. But this second-guessing of me? It honestly makes me feel awful. So please, Jesse, *please* just stop."

Silence except for dripping water from the tap, the wail of a passing ambulance, Nanna shifting in her sleep.

"All right then," I tell him. "I won't say another word about it. Only—"

"Jess." He sighs.

"*Only*," I insist, "if you promise to remember that I'm here if you need to talk, about anything?"

"I know."

My heart is lead in my chest. I've given Cas my word and I'll honour it. I'll draw a line here, finally and definitely. I'll try my best to not even think of these things again. And yet this all feels like part of the drifting between me and my best friends. And it's awful.

My mobile bleeps. A video call from Morgan. I flash Cas a weak smile and hit answer. Morgan cuts straight to the chase.

"How did it go? I see you haven't been arrested for theft and maligning the honour of the Australian nation, so that's something."

She's sitting at her desk at home. Thankfully there's no sign of Róisín so I don't have to explain the binning of her magnificent moustache.

"We got a drone!" Cas whoops.

Morgan sighs indulgently. "It must be like toddlers on Christmas morning over there."

And suddenly it feels like the old days again – Cas and Morgan's teasing, the familiar banter. Except not quite. Not quite...

"So I've already got a few drama guys lined up as extras," Morgan says, her attitude businesslike. "People I've worked with before and who I know will show up on time and take direction. But I've been wracking my brains and there's no one I can think of who'd be right for the husband part. That role needs charm, charisma, vulnerability; qualities which aren't in abundant supply among the circles of Ferrivale am-dram."

"Forget the husband," I groan. "What about our wife? Because the best actor I know won't take that part." I hold up my hand when Morgan starts to protest. "Yes, yes, I'm not going to ask you again, but we're not exactly off to the best start, are we?"

"Let's see what happens with the auditions tomorrow," Cas says hopefully. "Faint heart never made fair zombie movie, Sparky."

"But it isn't just the actors," I grumble. "What about the finances? Róisín wants paying, there'll be expenses for the practical SFX, stuff we haven't even thought about yet. I don't see how we can make it work."

Suddenly everything feels a bit overwhelming and I need five minutes alone.

"Jess," Morgan says softly. "We'll figure it out, I promise."

"I know," I tell them. "I know. Just give me a sec."

I pass my phone to Cas, who tries to catch hold of my sleeve as I leave the kitchen. I move quickly down the hall, grateful that there's no sign of Dean as I head to the bathroom. I'm not sure I could cope with his bullshit right now. But I've barely had chance to lock the door before there's a gentle tap on the other side.

"Sparky? Are you…?"

I rake fingers through my messy curls and close my eyes. "I'll be okay, Cas. Really."

"It's not that," he says apologetically. "I'm really sorry, Jess, but I need you to leave."

"What?" I stare at the door. "Why?"

Silence from the hallway. Then, "Louis just called. His train got in early and he's going to be here soon and I'd rather… Look, I need to get his room ready, okay? There are a hundred things that have to be sorted. I'm not chucking you out, but—"

I pull open the door and take my phone from Cas. "It's fine," I say, heading off down the corridor. "I should probably be getting home anyway."

"Jess, I'm sorry."

I stop, sigh. I'm about to tell him it's okay. This is Cas, after all – of course he's going to want everything perfect before his cousin arrives. That's when my gaze is snagged by the open door to my right. The tiny spare room where we used to make forts when we were little kids, defending our stronghold of sheets and blankets from imaginary vampire hordes. The room is all ready for its guest – a camp bed made up, pillows plumped, a fresh towel and flannel, even a glass and a bottle of water on the bedside table. Nothing left to prepare.

For some reason my best friend wants rid of me.

"I'll see you tomorrow," I mutter, and close the front door behind me.

18

Stop imagining things.

Stop imagining things.

Stop imagining things.

The words beat in my brain like a mantra. Have beaten there ever since I left the Loomis flat last night. I tell myself that my best friends are not keeping secrets from me, that things aren't really fracturing between us, that I'm only imagining that Cas didn't want me around when his cousin arrived yesterday. I want very desperately to believe this because, as my hand steals to my chest, to the thrum of my heart, I need my friends now more than ever.

After being thrown out by Cas (yes, all right, he didn't *literally* throw me out, but allow me a moment of melodrama, please!), I'd hung around for a while outside the Loomis block. In the time it took to gallop down those six flights of stairs, I'd made up my mind that I would focus on my mission and forget everything else: make the movie and find a summer boyfriend – or at least someone who might deem me worthy of a quick snog – before I go under Dr Myers's scalpel. And so, like the world's least convincing secret agent, I had planted myself in the window of the greasy spoon cafe opposite the flats to await Louis's arrival.

I'm not exactly sure what my plan was once he showed up. Perhaps to coolly sidle across the streets with a casual, *Oh, hey, you must be Cas's incredibly gorgeous cousin, what a coincidence, bumping into you like this.* In the end, I managed three sips of the most disgusting coffee imaginable before giving up and heading home. As unlikely as it was that Louis would even look twice at someone like me, behaving like a total stalker was probably not the best first impression.

Back home, Jacques had greeted me on the front step with his usual show of affection (I immediately disinfected the wound) and I then spent a lonely evening eating heated-up lasagne and going through our *ZomHon* shooting schedule. Mum called around eight, with lots of uncharacteristic apologizing for being kept late at work, followed by a full interrogation about how I'd been feeling during the day. I'd reassured her that I was fine, then proceeded to spend a pretty sleepless night going over and over the same old questions in my head – what is going on with my friends?

Now, trudging down a dusty country lane, I grip the straps of my backpack and cast a sideways glance at Cas. I do have one bit of exciting news from that conversation with Mum, something I would usually have shared straight away. But from the moment we rendezvoused at the end of my street, there's been this odd tension between us.

The mantra beats again: *Stop imagining things.*

It's taken a short bus ride and a bit of a walk, but we've finally left the outskirts of Ferrivale behind. Glancing over my shoulder, I can see the town hunkered down in the dip of the valley, the dark blue glint of Hunter's Lake sparking between the trees, a single church spire piercing the canopy of the forest. I'm suddenly struck by how pretty my hometown looks. I guess when you see something every day you stop noticing its beauty.

I turn back, fixing my eyes on the empty lane.

"Where exactly are we going again?" I ask. "Because you should know, if we lose ourselves in this wilderness, I *will* turn feral within a couple of hours. Don't smile, I'm serious. I'll also be useless with all the day-to-day survival stuff, so it'll be down to you to build us a treehouse and hunt for food. Actually, a cute treehouse might be quite nice, as long as we have some kind of Netflix hook-up."

"We are literally three miles outside town," Cas says. "I reckon you're going to survive this arduous expedition, Sparky. Anyway, it's not much further."

My gaze skims the hedgerows and the fields of corn swaying on either side. "I didn't even know this road existed. What can possibly be out here that we can use as a location?"

171

"Patience, my child." He laughs.

I laugh too, and feel the tension ease between us.

Cas's phone chirrups. He digs out the handset and grimaces. "Video call from Stan."

Stan Shan the Cans Man – our sound guy. I groan.

"I know." Cas sighs. "But we might as well get it over and done with."

He hits answer. The face of a kid only a year older than us fills the screen, yet this kid is dressed like a character from the nineties *Matrix* movies. I'm not even joking – slicked back hair, long leather trench coat with the collar pulled up, armless sunglasses perched on the end of his nose. It really is amazing how one uber-fan can put you off an entire franchise.

"Fellow filmmakers, well met." Stan nods, as if we're mythical warriors encountering each other on a sacred quest. "I am hearing that you are in need of my technical wizardry?"

Cas grips my wrist, as if for moral support. "Hey, Stan, good to see you. Hope you're keeping well?"

"I'm keeping busy, is what I am," Stan informs us. "Busy, busy, busy. Lots of my own projects heating up, so we should probably make this brief. Is Jesse with you? Ah, there you are, Jessmeister. Thought you were hiding from me for a second there."

"No," I say. "Why would I hide from you, Stan?"

The wizard shrugs. "No reason on my side. Although I do remember both of you got a little tetchy the last time we worked together. On that HP Lovecraft rip-off of yours? No, no, we don't need to start that debate again. I think we all agreed in the end that your monster *was* a total second-rate Cthulhu." Cas's grip on my wrist tightens as I start to object. "Anyway, I've read the script you sent over. *Zombie Honeymoon*, eh? You know, it's not all that terrible. In fact, it *could* be fairly decent. But there is one crucial lesson you guys must learn if we're going to work together again."

"Oh yes," I say through clenched teeth. "And what's that?"

"Sound is thy god," Stan says serenely. "Accept that truth of filmmaking and we're golden. No offence, but you can have the most garbage script, the lousiest direction, your shot compositions can suck balls." Now it's my turn to grip Cas's wrist. "But if your sound is good then your audience will forgive pretty much anything. Agreed?"

We both take a breath and simultaneously concede. "Agreed."

"Well said!" A grin of victory from the Cans Man. "So text me over the shooting schedule and I'll see you both on-set. Byesies."

The screen goes blank.

"Don't worry," Cas mutters. "We can kill him after the wrap party."

"Slowly, please. With his own boom mic staked through his heart."

We look at each other and both burst out laughing.

"Oh, by the way," I say. "I had a chat with Mum last night. She's volunteered to sort out the catering for the whole cast and crew. Snacks, sandwiches, drinks, everything."

Cas's face lights up. "Really? Bless Momma Spark."

"Yeah," I say, my mood sinking again. "Only, that still leaves us with a huge financial black hole. I sat down and worked out a rough estimate of expenses this morning. Cas, we're looking at thousands of pounds. And I know Mum would help more if she could, but criminal solicitors don't make as much as everyone thinks. Especially not legal aid ones. She's stretching our budget just to provide the catering. I don't know. Maybe we should just—"

I'm given a stern glance. "You're not giving up, Sparky. I won't let you. There'll be an answer. Anyway..." He trots up the lane and, reaching a side road, throws out his arms in a *tah-dah* gesture. "We *have* to film this location, don't we?"

I run to catch up with him, and my jaw very nearly hits the ground. At the end of a muddy, rutted track, behind a high chain-link fence, there lies a sight of cinematic splendour – towers of metal spearing towards the cloudless sky, great heaps of steel and iron woven together into industrial works of art, the corpses of cars, waiting to be remade into something new. Breathless, we race down the track towards the junkyard and, reaching the fence, thread our fingers through the chain-link.

"So," Cas says. "What do you think?"

"It's perfect!" I gasp. "Can you imagine? We could set the pre-title sequence here, when the hitchhiker is first attacked? Then we cut to her running through the woods before the married couple pick her up on the forest road. Think of some of the shots we could achieve!"

I can see Cas is as excited as I am, his cinematographer brain racing down the avenues of this gorgeous junkyard, capturing the perfect angles as our hitchhiker flees for her life.

"We could get some of the zombies to lie in wait inside the boots of the cars," I say. "Or have them hanging off the scrapheaps, moaning and clawing. If we shot at the golden hour, imagine the light! The shado—oooooh shit!"

We've been so transfixed by the possibilities of the junkyard that neither of us have noticed the two ferocious creatures bounding in our direction. I leap backwards a second before the first dog launches itself at the fence, landing hard on my tailbone. Even Cas's natural grace seems to abandon him as he yelps and dances away from the gate. Meanwhile, I quickly check my fingers, making sure I haven't left any dangling from the chain-link.

"Shut up yer noise!" a voice bellows from beyond the fence. "They won't hurt yer, them's only babies."

A gigantic, broad-shouldered man appears out of a shack just inside the gate. He comes ambling over, smoking a roll-up, scratching his backside and reading an old newspaper. Even amid the terror coursing through me, I can't help but admire his multi-tasking. He chucks the paper aside and places two grimy hands on the heads of the Dobermanns that continue to snarl and rage at us.

"I said quiet yer noise," he growls.

"They don't seem to be taking much notice of you," Cas shouts over the barking.

"I don't mean them." A beady eye is fixed on me. "I mean him."

It's at that moment that I realize I'm screaming. My mouth clamps shut and immediately the two monstrous dogs stop barking.

"You Dean Loomis's little brother?" the man asks.

"No," I squeak.

"Obviously not." He nods. "I'm talking to the other one."

"Oh, yes, I'm Casper." Cas steps up to the gate and actually lets one of the monsters lick his fingers. Complete madness. "Dean said you'd be up for letting us use this place for a little filming?"

"I might be," the man admits. "But I'd have certain conditions."

"Which are?"

His watery dark eyes roll from Cas to me and back again. "Come inside and we can discuss them."

He pulls a ring of keys from the belt loop of his faded overalls and, selecting one, wrestles with a stubborn padlock until it snaps open. The effort makes me wonder if he ever leaves this place at all. He then whistles at the beasts, who lollop away into the shadows of the junkyard, before turning and heading back towards his shack. Meanwhile I scuttle to my feet, catching up with Cas as he steps through the open gate.

"You do realize this has all the vibe of *The Texas Chain Saw Massacre*?" I point at the rusty wrecks of cars, perhaps left behind by their vanished/cannibalized owners. Cas shrugs and I sigh, following him into the yard. "Fine. But just know, if we die here, I am *so* coming back to haunt your brother."

19

The gigantic junkyard owner waves us over to a pair of rusty oil drums. I'm not entirely sure what he means us to do with them until I see an obviously reluctant Cas take a seat. I look at my jeans, then at the greasy raised rim of the second drum, before mouthing, "*He can't be serious?*" Cas grabs my sleeve, pulling me down next to him. I manage to squirm into a fairly pain-free position while suppressing a disgusted "*Ewwww*".

"Comfy?" the man asks.

Is he joking? More beard than human, it's difficult to see his mouth at all, let alone a smile. He strikes me as a cross between the survivor of an apocalyptic disaster and a Scooby-Doo villain. If he is one of those doomsday survivalists, I'm not convinced his shack would hold up to a nuclear blast. It appears to be mainly held together with old masonry nails and optimism. Still, it does contain a vast quantity of canned food, toilet roll and tea bags, all piled up in a corner, so Armageddon might not be too arduous for him.

"Fancy a brew?" he says, catching my gaze.

"Um, nah, you're all right." For some inexplicable reason, I rub my tummy. "Had a big cup before we left home. Bi-iiiiggg old cup. Pint mug, easy. And I've got this weak bladder, so, you know, long bus ride back to town. Usually I'd bite your hand off if you offered me a brew." My eyes snap to the oily slabs of meat poking out of his sleeves, every finger raw with burns and open cuts. "But not today, ta."

Cas elbows me in the ribs and I dutifully shut up.

"Character, ain't he?" the man says, jutting his chin in my direction. "I'm Tiny, by the way."

My gaze now snaps to a different part of those grease-stained overalls. "You're what?"

"Tiny." He says it with a bewildering note of pride. "Always been Tiny, ever since I was a lad."

"Oh," I say. "I'm...sorry?"

He stares daggers at me. "What you sorry about?"

"You. Being. Well, you know what they say – it's not what you've got, it's what you..." I look at Cas for help. He boggles back at me, like I'm the one who initiated this discussion about a junkyard owner's private junk. "It's personality that's important, anyway," I reassure him. "And you have such a large, um, personality. Very loving too, I'm sure."

"Is he all right?" the man grunts at Cas.

"He's fine. He's…Jesse," Cas says, then turns to me. "This is an old friend of Dean's, Malc Liveridge. Known as Tiny because he's quite a big lad. Like it's an ironic nickname? You get it, don't you?"

"Ooooh," I say. "But I thought he meant—"

"Yes, I know what you thought he meant," Cas says out the corner of his mouth. "Now, for fuck's sake, be quiet."

I think this is probably wise advice – it usually is in my case – so I decide to let Cas do the talking.

"You said something about conditions? The problem is, Tiny, we haven't got any budget for this thing, so if you're thinking about money—"

This suggestion is waved away. "I got no need to raid yer wee piggybanks, boys. Scrap metal is gold and I'm rolling in it." He eyes us both for a moment before casting a glance around his shack. "Hold hard, do you two think I actually live here or something?" And now there's no mistaking that's he's laughing – at least, the beard is bouncing up and down. "I got a bloody mansion on the new development, brand-new Merc in the drive, and a holiday apartment on the Costa del Sol. So no, I'm not interested in pennies from a couple of schoolkids."

"Then what do you want?" Cas asks.

Tiny straightens up to his full height, his bushy head brushing the ceiling, his colossal chest threatening to pop the buttons on his overalls.

"I want a part."

I look at Cas. Cas looks at me. We both look at Tiny. "You want a—?"

"Part." He waves his hand impatiently. "In this vampire film you're making."

"Zombie."

"Zombie, vampire, same difference."

"Well, in fact there's quite a lot of difference," I say in a teacherly tone. "You see, although both are *technically* members of the undead community, zombies are—"

"Forget the distinctions between vees and zees," Cas interrupts, and ignores my outraged scowl. This is horror hound blasphemy. "The thing is, Tiny, we haven't actually got any main parts that you'd be suitable for. The only male lead is a guy in his twenties and you're...well...a little more mature than that."

"I don't care about the size of my part," says Tiny (which given my recent misunderstanding is not the most fortunate of phrasing). "I just want to be in it. Like a walk-on or a bit part or—"

"An extra?" I suggest.

He points at me. "Finally, the kid's said something I can understand. Yeah, an extra would do. One of these zombies or whatever. Do you realize how many great actors were spotted in the background of films and then made into stars? Brad Pitt, Clint Eastwood, Renée Zellweger."

"You want to be the next Renée Zellweger?"

"I think I've got a certain look," he says, ignoring me and admiring himself in the reflection of an old hubcap hanging from the wall. "Like a young Harrison Ford maybe."

"Before or after he was dropped into that trash compacter in *Star Wars*?" I wonder under my breath. This receives another elbow in the ribs from Cas.

"I can definitely see that." Cas nods approvingly. "Something about the eyes. And speaking for Jesse and myself, it would be an absolute honour to have you as a junkyard zombie in our movie. So can we call that a deal?"

I think Tiny's face lights up, again it's difficult to tell. Anyway, he spits in his palm and shakes on it with a slightly grimacing Cas.

Out in the sunshine again, I frame my hands into a camera eye view and sweep a vista of the junkyard. It really will look incredible, reanimated corpses swinging from jagged towers of metal as our hitchhiker hurtles for her life through this winding labyrinth of scrap. It almost makes me forget about all the other crap going on in my life.

We say goodbye to Tiny and his beasts, now panting like overgrown puppies at his side, and hit the road.

"Happy?" Cas asks.

"It'll make an incredible location," I say non-committally. "And all we have to do is put up with a walking beard who thinks he's the new Han Solo. How exactly does Dean know him again?"

"Probably best not to ask," Cas says, then glances at his watch. "Ah crap. How's it that time already? Jess, we better get a move on or we'll be late for the auditions. And honestly, I'd rather face both of Tiny's hellhounds any day of the week than a single pissed-off Morgan."

It turns out that Morgan's optimism for the auditions wasn't misplaced after all. In fact, it was scarily accurate. Signora Argento has had to clear all the pavement tables outside the diner because there's a line snaking right round the block. A heaving, bustling, chattering crowd, some clutching play scripts, quite a few even in costume. We have Victorian chimney sweeps, leather-jacketed greasers with spit curls, French revolutionaries ready to burst into song, and one kid in doublet and hose, staring intently at the skull in his outstretched hand. I'm not sure what kind of movie they think we're making here.

As Cas and I push our way to the door, a couple of the drama geeks recognize us and swarm forward.

"Oh hey, Joey, can I just say how excited I am to be reading for the wife in this film of yours?" a girl in a pointed hat with green face make-up chirrups at me. "So I bet you're already aware, but I played Elphaba in a recent production of *Wicked*? You probably saw my notices in the Ferrivale Gazette? '*A peculiar interpretation*'? Peculiar meaning individual, you know? Unique? Anyway, I only wanted to say—"

"Back off, witch." Morgan comes bowling out of the diner, her version of my mother's Stare working overtime. Immediately the crowd lulls into hushed murmurs. She then grabs Cas and me by our collars and drags us inside, turning only to announce to the street, "Oh and FYI, he's called *Jesse*. Rule one of successful auditions, remember the name of the bloody director."

The door bangs to behind us. I barely have time to glance around the empty diner before Signora Argento is waving a kitchen knife in front of my nose. Today she is dressed as Norman Bates's mummified mother from *Psycho*.

"I say you can hold your stupid auditions here, Jesse Sparks," she screeches. "I did not think for one moment it would lead to the total collapse of my business. There are about a million people outside that door but *she*," the murder weapon is now jabbed in the direction of an ice-cool Morgan, "says they must wait and be called through one at a time. I could be making a fortune! Enough to send Dario to catering college." She glances over her shoulder and shrieks towards the kitchen, "Where he can learn to cook a freaking burger without incinerating it!"

"I told you," Morgan says calmly. "We will let *ten* in at a time, and while they wait, they have been told they must order food. Good enough?"

Signora Argento seesaws the knife in her hand. "You did not tell me that bit…" A rarely seen smile then breaks out. "All right, open the doors, you darling girl! Let's begin. Dario! Fire up the grill!"

While Morgan turns to marshal the crowd, Cas leads the way over to our favourite booth.

"Okay." He grins. "You ready?"

I nod, shrugging off my backpack and taking out the *ZomHon* script. "As I'll ever be."

But one question has been nagging at me ever since we turned the corner and saw that huge snaking line. *Where is Louis?* I'd scanned every face and he was nowhere to be seen. Despite the numbers, I was certain I couldn't have missed him. I pull out my phone under the table and bring up his Insta page. A new photo has been posted only ten minutes ago, Louis leaning back on the rail of the Loomises' balcony, Ferrivale rolling out behind him. Sunshine dazzles in his sandy hair and his eyes are closed in a dreamy, rapt expression. The caption: *Loving this sweet little town!*

I guess he must have changed his mind about auditioning.

I touch my chest, let my hand drop again, swallow down my disappointment. Maybe I'll still get to see Louis at some point during his visit. Meanwhile, Cas nods over to Morgan, stationed at the entrance. She returns his nod, pulls open the door, and the madness begins.

"It is the Earth, *crying* out in pain! The planet saying to the human race, no *more!* That is what has *birthed* these creatures. These walking *corpses* that feed upon living flesh! We have polluted her rivers, torn up her forests, and now Mother *Nature* herself has reanimated the dead to use against us. To end the *plague* of humanity. *For ever!*"

The woman throws out her arms and Cas is forced to duck to avoid a slap in the kisser.

I nod and blow out my cheeks. "An interesting take on the wife role, Mrs Foster. Some very…bold choices."

Mrs Foster waves away what she interprets as a compliment. "It's my method, you know? I try to bring a little of myself to each part I play."

"Maybe a bit too much of yourself?" Morgan mutters under her breath.

"And with Mary O'Bannon," Mrs Foster continues, oblivious.

"Mary who?" I frown.

A wrinkled hand reaches out and pats the script on the table. "Well, there aren't any character names in this thing, only 'Wife', 'Husband', 'Hitchhiker', so I thought I'd come up with my own little backstory for her."

"That's a deliberate artistic choice," I say. "If the characters are unnamed then they're kind of anonymous. They can then act as a stand-in for any audience member to identify with. It makes the whole experience more personal, and therefore more scary."

"Mmm-hmm, mmm-hmm." Mrs Foster looks unconvinced. "Very modern of you, I'm sure. But to me, my character *is* a Mary. She feels like one, don't you think? Mary O'Bannon from North Yorkshire. Before this awful zombie apocalypse what-have-you, Mary worked at a bakery in Ripon and helped out at the church jumble sale every weekend. Also, she was a member of her library's knit-and-natter group."

Morgan leans across the table. "You see, this is the problem. The wife—"

"Mary," Mrs Foster insists.

"The *wife* is supposed to be twenty-two years old," Morgan continues. "She doesn't do jumble sales and she definitely doesn't knit. And no offence, but how old are you exactly?"

Mrs Foster draws herself up, the half-moon spectacles on the string around her neck swaying with her bosom.

"I didn't come here to be asked personal questions. My granddaughter just happened to mention that a classmate of hers had seen this casting call and I thought—"

"You're a *grandmother*?" I say, not entirely surprised.

Mrs Foster has clearly had enough. She collects her walking stick from under the table and swans dramatically, if a bit arthritically, out of the diner. It takes a while.

"Best acting she did in the whole audition," Morgan says drily. "Next!"

Argento's is buzzing with people. Despite Morgan's best efforts, it was impossible to keep the crowd outside and so now they are all packed onto tables and into booths, chowing down on Mystic Pizzas and Big Kahuna Burgers. Signora Argento is so happy she's comped us a giant portion of cheesy nachos, which Cas and I pick at without much enthusiasm. Two hours in and things aren't going well. We've had "I Dreamed a Dream" from *Les Mis* shrieked at us so many times that finally Morgan stood up on her chair and publicly reminded everyone that *Zombie Honeymoon* wasn't a musical, and that she would personally disembowel the next Fantine who dared to emote a note. Apart from West End blockbusters, we've also had a smattering of Shakespeare. The skull kid rocked up but barely got beyond "To be or not to be" before Morgan informed him it was "Not to be" and he promptly exited, hugging the skull to his chest. As for me, I've given up hope, both of finding our lead actors and of Louis making an appearance.

I plant my head on the table and groan. "Just tell me when it's over."

"Lots of theatre nerds still to get through," Morgan says, in what for her is an upbeat tone. "Don't give up yet."

When I finally lift my face (Cas peeling a stray nacho from my forehead), it's to find the queen of Ferrivale High marching through the open door of Argento's and straight towards our booth. She doesn't have her entourage in tow today, but people like Brianna Murray don't require regular sycophants. Perfect strangers are more than capable of providing admiring gazes and whispers of approval. These she receives as her due as she cuts her way through the crowd towards us. I cast a sideways glance at Cas, who suddenly appears to be fascinated by the state of his fingernails.

"Look, I hope I'm not pushing in." Brianna sighs, sliding into the booth next to Morgan. "But my evening is utterly hectic, so I wondered if you'd be complete sweethearts and see me now? Is that even the teensiest bit possible?"

I open my mouth to say Brianna will have to wait her turn when Morgan cuts in. "Fine by me. What do you think, Cas?"

Cas remains fixated on his cuticles. "I've not got a problem with it."

"Great," Morgan says, passing Brianna some script

pages. "We have a few scenes marked up. Take a look and begin when you're ready."

I shrug and we all fall into a comfortless silence while Brianna skim-reads the scenes. Occasionally, she licks a forefinger to turn the page, glancing up and smiling warmly at me and Morgan. She seems pretty much indifferent to Cas – in contrast to the brutal reception he received outside the drama studio the other day. I wonder if I'm right about her forgiving him, thinking that he'd then shoot her more sympathetically in the movie. Arrogant enough to believe she's a shoo-in for a part, it's just the kind of game she might play.

Finally, she closes her eyes and hands the script back to Morgan. "Would you read with me?" she asks. Morgan nods. "Then I think I'm ready."

I stare at Brianna. "You might want to keep hold of those pages."

"No need," she assures me, eyes still shut. "I'm not a total airhead, you know."

"Oh, no, I mean, no one thought you were. Right, guys?"

Morgan touches Brianna's elbow. "If you're sure?"

I sometimes forget this side of Morgan, maybe because I see it very rarely. But the odd times I have witnessed her in rehearsals, it's always struck me what a nurturing teacher she can be, especially to those performers less naturally talented than herself. It's like the harder edges of her personality take a back seat and she opens up, providing advice and guidance. I see a touch of that now in how she handles Brianna.

"I'm good to go when you are," she says.

Cas keeps his head down, but I'm fascinated. A transformation is happening right in front of me. It starts with standard Brianna, finally opening her eyes and plucking up a spoon from the table to check her reflection in the bowl. Then, as she lays it down again, a twist of the lips, a shade of uncertainty. I'm thinking again of the girl at the *Little Shop* after-show party, crying, inconsolable; the same girl I met on the hill yesterday on my way to Morgan's. And then all at once that girl is gone too, and I'm looking at a young woman caught between the deepest grief and the most bone-chilling terror.

"I can't do this any more," she says, tears starting in her eyes. "It's too much."

"You have to." Morgan, reading her part as the hitchhiker. "There's no other choice. Not now."

Then Brianna lets out this sound and I rock back in my seat. It's somewhere between a sigh and a groan, like the acceptance of a pain that must be borne. I didn't write that in the script; it comes entirely from her. And now even Cas looks up, mesmerized.

"You don't understand," Brianna says, choking on the

words. "You're a stranger. But he is my life. *My life*. And you want me to—?"

"You must," Morgan insists quietly. "To save us, you must."

I can picture the scene in my head – three figures in the gloomy parlour of the Lester house, the undead clawing and scratching at the boarded-up windows, alerted by the moans of the newly reanimated husband. Infected by a zombie bite, he lies chained at the feet of the hitchhiker, who has just passed a shotgun to the wife. While it plays out in my imagination, I watch the tears slide down Brianna's cheeks.

"Fine," she says with a snarl of rage. "I'll do it, if that's what you want. I'll kill the man I love and I'll bury him with my bare hands. And afterwards, well, then you can answer a question for me. Just one question. The only question worth asking now. Here, in this place."

"Yes?" Morgan says.

Brianna stares at her and suddenly I feel my own tears start to prickle. "Who exactly are the monsters?"

It takes a moment for us to realize that the entire diner has gone quiet. Even Signora Argento has stopped berating the waiting staff and is looking over at us. Then she puts her hands together. It starts like that – a ripple, one or two tables applauding, but soon the enthusiasm builds into a full standing ovation. Brianna blinks and glances around.

And in that instant the old Brianna returns, accepting the adulation as no more than she deserves.

"Well," I breathe once the clapping has died down. "That was…"

I look at Cas and Morgan for help.

"Can you give us a second?" Morgan asks.

Brianna rises regally from her chair. "Sure. Oh, and one last thing I should mention, though I don't want it to sway your decision in any way. It's just, my dad has said, if I *am* lucky enough to be cast, he'd love to donate a little something to the budget. Can't have his girl appear in anything cheap and shoddy, you see? Would five grand be okay?"

She doesn't wait for an answer, simply folds herself into the adoring crowd.

After a stunned silence, I blow out my cheeks. "What just happened?"

Cas stirs. "She was pretty good, I thought."

"Pretty good," I muse. "Cas, she was the best performer we've seen all afternoon! With the exception of Morgan, she's probably the best we've ever seen. How has this happened?"

Morgan shrugs. "I told, you she's a better actress than any of us thought."

"But *how*? Only three months ago she was the worst thing I'd seen onstage since Cas's third shepherd. Remember that Year One nativity when you simultaneously peed yourself and vomited all over the wise men?"

"Yes, thank you, Sparky. I've not forgotten."

"The fact is, Brianna just blew our minds," Morgan says curtly. "And she is offering you more than enough money to finance this thing."

"And," Cas chips in, "with Brianna onboard we aren't likely to run into any problems with her sociopath brother over the summer. Feels like a win on all fronts to me."

"Except one." They both stare at me like they have no idea what I'm talking about. "Well." I bristle. "I hate to bring it up, because apparently I'm not allowed to *pry* into things that don't concern me, but Brianna is your ex, Cas, or had you forgotten? This is going to be a difficult enough shoot without any personal dramas in the mix."

"Then we'll let bygones be bygones, shall we?"

I almost jump out of my seat. I hadn't noticed that Brianna had returned to our table. Now she lays a red-taloned hand on my shoulder, and I watch Cas wilt before my eyes.

"I can promise to be professional on-set if Casper can do the same? Is that a nod, Cas? Good. Then what do you say, Jesse?"

I'm completely sick of this. If my best friend insists on keeping secrets from me then he can't complain if there are consequences. I stand up and shake Brianna's hand.

"You've got the part, congrats."

She squeals and pulls me into a hug. "Oh, you fabulous human! I won't let you down, I promise."

Then, raising her arms in triumph, she is cheered out of the diner.

"Well." I sigh, sitting back down. "That was unexpected. Any notes?"

Cas is picking at the cold nachos while Morgan examines the menu.

"All right then," I say. "In that case, let's find me a husband."

My mood keeps flipping between stunned surprise (have we really just cast Brianna as our lead?) and mounting despair (there doesn't appear to be a single male actor in Ferrivale that can match her). I linger on that first thought for a moment, asking myself yet again – how has Brianna improved so much? The answer is obvious, I guess – the Murrays are loaded. Swimming pools, personal assistants, they've got it all, and as Brianna indicated, they're also very much about appearances. That's why Mr Murray is willing to donate five thousand pounds from his pig farming empire to our student film – so that his little girl looks good onscreen. I remember the effect her parents' scathing review of her performance in *Little Shop of Horrors* had on Brianna, reducing the demon queen to tears. Knowing she wouldn't give up on her dream, they must have paid for acting lessons. And bloody good ones at that.

The only thing the Murray money can't buy us is a decent male lead. I cast a gloomy look around the almost deserted diner. We've now seen everyone and the closest we've come to our *ZomHon* hubby is a Year Nine student who read well but who, even if we popped him on a box, would only come up to Brianna's shoulder.

"Maybe we could do something with that kid after all." Morgan sighs, as if reading my mind. "I mean, Tom Cruise has got away with it for years."

"There's only so much magic I can work with camera angles. Unless we put him in high heels?" Cas pushes out a contemplative bottom lip. "Could work."

I don't say anything. Just pick a stray nacho from the bowl and watch the last of the Ferrivale thespians leave. At least we've cast all the smaller roles and the extras, although at the moment that feels like cold comfort.

Signora Argento comes striding over, wiping her *Psycho* knife on a tea towel. I'm thinking those red stains are probably tomato sauce from a freshly carved pizza, but with our friendly neighbourhood diner owner, all bets are off.

"That's that then," she announces. "Now can you please get the hell out of my restaurant?"

"Why?" I blink. "Is there a fire?"

"Does he think he's cute?" she asks Morgan and Cas. "He's not cute. No, we must clean up and prepare for our evening customers. You know, adults who buy proper meals and don't spend two hours sharing a single bowl of complimentary nachos."

"I think you've done a pretty roaring trade," Morgan says, nodding at tables heaving under the weight of empty glasses and dirty dishes.

"It was…acceptable," the signora agrees begrudgingly. "But please, now go away."

"Charming," Morgan mutters, though even she seems too dispirited to get into a row, and so we all start collecting up our gear.

"That girl, she was something, no?" Signora Argento smiles, clearly pleased that she'll soon be rid of us. "The pretty one with the red hair and the Medusa attitude? I always thought she was a bit, well, like my poor Dario?" At the sound of her son's name, a deafening crash echoes out from the kitchen. "Who is an idiot that I ought to have strangled at birth!"

With that, she stalks away, knife raised.

Morgan and Cas are making vague reassurances that everything will be all right while I slide my script into my backpack. How can it be "all right" when the crucial third member of our cast is nowhere to be found? Honestly, at this point I'm all out of ideas. If only Louis hadn't changed his mind about auditioning. He certainly has the look I imagined for our *ZomHon* husband and, from his Insta photos, he seems to have a tonne of acting experience. Maybe I could get Cas to have a wor—

I hear the diner door click open.

"Oh, hey, guys, am I too late to try out?"

I haven't heard his voice before. Well, not since he was about eleven years old anyway. But I know it's him. It has to be. A smooth, rich, chocolatey sort of voice. Absolute perfection… For the part, I mean.

I have my back to the door. To him. I'll get one chance to make a good impression. I'm suddenly acutely aware of several hours spent sweating over terrible auditions and munching my way through a bowl of cheesy nachos. I breathe into my hand and wrinkle my nose. Not great. Then, borrowing a little trick of Brianna's, I snatch up the nearest piece of cutlery and try to catch my reflection. Unfortunately my random selection turns out to be a fork rather than a spoon. In the tines, I can just make out a hint of untamed poodle curls and a pair of eyebrows that only a werewolf would be proud to call his own.

Meanwhile Morgan's mind-reading skills seem to be on fire tonight as she slips a breath mint into my hand. I pop it into my mouth (almost choking, naturally), do my best to pat down my curls, and finally turn to face Louis Loomis.

There's a light just above the doorway, designed to fall on the hostess station. Now it falls squarely on the most stunning boy I have ever seen, illuminating him like a spotlight on a stage. He looked incredible in his Instagram posts, but in real life? All I can say is that Morgan has discreetly leaned in and placed a finger under my jaw, snapping it shut. He has something of the Loomis brothers about him, the full lips, the wavy hair, but Louis is leaner, more angular, and those cheekbones do indeed go on for days. He steps out of the light and comes towards us. He walks with a lazy sort of ease, like he's known us our entire lives. He's dressed in faded dark jeans with black leather boots and the kind of billowy open-neck shirt you imagine Jane Austen heroes flouncing around in. Only Louis doesn't flounce. He *glides*.

Stepping up to the booth, he directs those denim-blue eyes at Morgan. "Oh my gosh, Morgan Adeyemi-Perera? So there's no reason you should know this, but I saw you last summer in the UK Youth Play festival. Your Mrs Lovett in *Sweeney Todd* was just…chef's kiss!" He laughs, a full, deep laugh. "Which is sort of appropriate, I guess? Given the part? Anyway, you were completely spellbinding; your interpretation of the role and your incredible singing voice. I wanted to say hi afterwards, but I felt a bit…well."

"A bit what?" Morgan asks.

It's funny, whenever Cas and I have given compliments on her performance, Morgs has always dismissed them as ridiculous. But with Louis, she seems genuinely touched.

"Intimidated?" He hooks his thumbs into his belt, rocking back onto his heels. It's sort of adorable. "I wanted to ask you a tonne of questions about how I could improve my technique. You are honestly *so* good, Morgan."

I beam at my friend. Mainly because she is beaming.

And then suddenly both my hands are taken and it's like the rest of the diner has fallen away. I am the sole focus of Louis's attention, the only person in the room. I feel the touch of the beads and bracelets around his wrists, cool against my skin. Standing back, still holding my hands, he gives me an up-and-down look. But not *the* up-and-down look. Not the one I've been receiving most of my life. This is different.

"Look at you, Jesse Spark, all grown up. You know, I am a bit in awe of you."

It takes a massive effort for me to return his gaze. "Um, you are?"

"Very much so," he says, cocking his head to one side. "I know we've only met once or twice, and I haven't seen you for years, but I've been keeping tabs on you. Getting Cas to send me your movies and stuff. You've grown so much as a filmmaker. That noir thriller you guys made last summer, with the murdered fiancé in the bath tub? Just a sublime nod to Clouzot's *Les Diaboliques*." A little blush colours his cheeks. "Unless I misunderstood the reference?"

I realize I haven't answered him. I've just been staring. Morgan coughs and I shake my head. "Oh, absolutely, it was a homage to *Diaboliques*."

"And to the bathroom scene in *The Shining*," Cas says drily.

Louis smiles at his cousin. "Then it's even cleverer than I thought. And your shot compositions were completely incredible, cuz. What a talented trio you are." He looks at each of us in turn. "And I bet this new film will be your best yet. So…?"

Louis finally lets go of my hands, which makes my heart sink a little. "Is it okay if I audition?"

Our heads all spin around as impassioned screaming and threats of infanticide echo out from the kitchen. Poor Dario.

"We really need to leave," Morgan says.

Turning back to us, Louis frowns. "Am I late or something? Because I thought Cas said auditions started at seven?"

"I said five," Cas mutters. "And you've missed them."

I shoot Cas a look. His attitude is grumpy, even a little hostile. I know he was a bit miffed about his cousin coming to stay, but it isn't as if Louis has pushed himself on the Loomises. And honestly, I'm not picking up any of the nasty vibes Cas seems to associate with Louis's side of the family.

Louis looks genuinely upset. "Oh God. My mistake then. I'm so sorry, guys. Have I missed my chance?"

My hand steals to the inside pocket of my jacket. The letter from Dr Myers confirming my surgery date is still there, laid against my breast like a constant reminder. I take a breath. If I'm going to do this, I better do it. No more excuses, no more delays, no more making plans and never following through. It's now or never, Jesse Spark…

I mean, he'll probably say no anyway. Won't he? And even if he says yes, it won't go anywhere. I mean, look at him. Why would a guy like that be interested in a gangly, crazy-haired, epic-eyebrowed nerd like me? It's completely ridic—

"My mum's at boxercise," I blurt out.

Three pairs of eyes blink at me.

"Okay," Louis says. "That's really…good? Exercise and self-defence and endorphins and all that."

"No," I cut in. "I mean, we'd have the house to ourselves. If you wanted to audition there?"

Louis presses his hands together and bounces onto his toes. "Really? Are you sure? That would mean the world to me. I happened to take a look at the script Cas left on the kitchen table this afternoon. Read some of it while making Nanna her tea, and I'm not just saying this, I think it's a really special project. Even if I don't end up getting a part, I want you guys to know that."

"Well then," I say, collecting up my bag. "Shall we?"

Morgan stirs. "Do you want us to come too?"

"No!" I almost bellow at her, then laugh nervously. "No, it's cool. You and Cas can do something else."

Cas stares at me. "Like what?"

"Something…" I shrug. "Else?"

I can sense them watching us as we leave, as Louis opens the door and I manage to step into the street without tripping over a passing cat or faceplanting the nearest lamp post. They're probably as amazed as I am. Not only by the uncharacteristic non-klutziness but by the spectacle of me inviting an actual boy home. I cast a quick final glance through the diner window to find my best friends having words. I can't hear what they're saying but their whole vibe catapults me right back to that night three months ago and their angry, heated row after the Easter show. And you know what? I really *don't care*. Let them keep their stupid secrets.

It's time I concentrated on me.

"Hey, you." Louis smiles, nudging my shoulder. "Everything okay?"

"Everything's fine," I smile back. "Just brilliantly...fine."

22

"I love the fact that you don't name the characters in the script," Louis says brightly. "Such a clever idea. I'm only guessing, but is it so that they become mirrors for the audience? Like, if we don't personalize them in that way, we can imagine ourselves in their shoes? Making their choices, facing their fears?"

I almost hug him. "Exactly! Thank you. At last, someone gets it."

We beam at each other. It's only been ten minutes since we left the diner but already we've discovered so much in common – a shared love of horror and thriller movies, as well as manga comics and ancient cartoons from the 1980s. In fact, we've just finished a debate about who is the hottest ThunderCat, Lion-O or Tygra (a victory for Tygra based on the outcome of rock, paper, scissors), when a familiar car bumps up onto the pavement beside us.

"Ah, crap," I groan.

Louis shoots me a concerned glance as the driver's

window of the vintage VW Beetle whirs down to reveal a grinning Ethan Murray. He has a sidekick sitting beside him in the passenger seat, a kid I don't recognize with a crew cut and a tongue stud that looks a microbe away from bubonic plague.

"Nice to see you again, Jessica. Out on a date?" Ethan shouts while pumping the accelerator so that the engine roars. I'm not quite sure what point this is supposed to prove. Maybe that he has the basic primate skills of gripping a wheel while using his foot at the same time. "We didn't get to talk properly the other day about what happened at prom. No hard feelings, eh?"

"Never where you're concerned," I mutter under my breath.

"And who's this pretty boy then?" Ethan coos.

"Oh yes, please do introduce me to your friends, Jesse," Louis says, bending down and peering into the car. "They look so fun. The one showing off that little tongue stud, what a Petri dish of oozy cuteness. No, darling, please don't say anything and ruin your brooding allure. And then we have the alpha male." He plants an elbow on the open window and treats Ethan to a wink. "Aren't you the charmer? And you think I'm pretty? Too pretty for you to handle, that's for sure."

Ethan jerks away. "Bloody queers everywhere these days."

Louis laughs, spinning round to face me. "He's discovered our secret, Jesse. And I thought I was being so discreet."

"Laugh it up, you little bumboy," Ethan grunts. "And you, Jessica, don't think that I'm done with you and your mate Loomis either. He humiliated my sister and no one gets away with shaming a Murray. No one."

He tries to spit on the pavement where we stand but, misfiring, sends a runner of phlegm skating down the side of his driver's door.

"Might want to clean that up." Louis sighs. "It's such a sweet little car."

Ethan throws a few more homophobic slurs our way before roaring off into the night.

"Bless. Are there many like that in Ferrivale?" Louis says, looking after him.

"A few. That particular one also happens to be our leading lady's twin brother. Don't ask, it's a long story."

We continue on our way through town. It's a sultry summer's evening, the bars and restaurants buzzing, friends and couples squeezed onto outdoor tables or sprawled across tartan blankets in the park. Laughing, holding hands, sharing private jokes. Louis snares the gaze of virtually every person we pass, yet he seems oblivious to their attention. Even the odd wolf whistle doesn't faze him. I can only imagine the whispered comments:

What a hottie.

Yeah, but look at the other one.

They can't be together, can they?

Pluh-ease. Not unless the hot guy's had some kind of aneurism.

"Hey! So I just had this random memory from when we were kids!" Louis says, his face lighting up. "Nanna Laura's seventieth birthday party. We played murder in the dark in Dean's bedroom and I ran straight into the closet door and almost knocked myself out. Jesus, I was such a snotty little thing back then."

"Yeah." I grin. "I mean, no. You weren't all that snotty. Just the standard amount of mucus for an eight-year-old."

He laughs and bumps his shoulder against mine. "You say the sweetest things, Sparky."

I stop dead. We're halfway through the park, almost home. I can see my road up ahead, the streetlight on the corner blinking into life. Insects swoon around the sudden glow, billowing, fascinated. Louis has walked on several paces before he realizes I'm no longer at his side.

"Everything okay?" he asks, trotting back. "Did I say something wrong?"

"No, it's just…you called me Sparky. Only Cas ever—"

He looks pained. "I'm sorry. I didn't realize it was a special thing between the two of you. I've heard him refer to you as Sparky so many times, I thought…I really am sorry, Jesse. I know I can be a bit much sometimes. A bit full on? Everyone says so. It's not my place to come barging into your life and presume I can pick up things that you guys have shared together. You and Cas have such a special friendship."

Do we? We used to. These past few days, though? The sense that he is keeping things from me, putting barriers up between us. I just don't know any more.

"You can call me whatever you like," I tell Louis, tugging at his sleeve until my forefinger accidentally brushes the inside of his palm. "Now, come on, you've got an audition to get through."

Thankfully there's no sign of Mum or the Thing of Evil as we step inside the house. I take off my jacket and tell Louis to grab a seat in the lounge while I bring my GoPro camera down from upstairs. My plan is to tape his audition and then send it off to Cas and Morgan for their approval. If they've finished their oh-so-mysterious argument by then, of course.

Louis lingers at the bottom of the stairs. "Do you have your camera all set up in your room?"

I pause on the landing. "Yeah. But it's honestly no hassle."

"Don't be silly," he says, bounding up the stairs three at a time. "Makes no sense to dismantle everything on my account. As long as you don't mind me invading your bedroom, that is?"

I pray he doesn't notice my Adam's apple yo-yoing in my throat. It is quite an epic gulp after all. Apart from Cas, I've never had a boy in my bedroom before, and certainly not a boy of my persuasion. *Of my persuasion?* I mentally shudder. Why does my inner voice sometimes sound like a Victorian schoolmistress?

"Absolutely no problem at all," I say, guiding him across the landing.

My hand pauses before gripping the door handle. Have I put my boxers in the laundry basket? Are there any mugs lying around like questionable chemistry experiments? Why hasn't my mum nagged me more about the state of my room? This looming disaster is entirely her fault. Closing my eyes, I push open the door.

"Oh, this is so adorable," Louis says, sidestepping past me.

I open one eye, then the other, and let go of a huge breath. For the first time since I was about eleven, my mum has cleaned my room. I guess she either got tired of asking or maybe decided to take pity on me because of the whole heart situation. I'm not sure how that makes me feel, though right now I am grateful that we're not walking into a toxic wasteland.

"Did you and Cas make these?" Louis is standing at a big table I have set up by the window. Arranged across it is a collection of dioramas from famous horror movies, all built out of modelling clay, cardboard, and gallons of glue. There's the staircase scene from Tod Browning's classic *Dracula*, the eerie Count greeting his guest; Jason Vorhees chasing a hapless teenager through the woods at Camp Crystal Lake; monochrome zombies surrounding the farmhouse in *Night of the Living Dead*. I go and stand beside him, smiling a little.

"Yeah, we did. Took us hours. Years." My smile drops. "Kids' stuff."

"No," Louis says. "These were important, to both of you."

"They were." I nod. "Anyway, let's get started, shall we?"

I slip off my backpack and flip through the script until I find a couple of scenes we can work on. I then hand them to Louis while I sort out the GoPro.

"This is great," he says, leafing through the pages. "You really are a talented writer, you know?"

"I'm a hack," I say, attaching the camera to a tripod and setting it up to face my desk chair. "But I'm an okay director, and Cas is a wonderful cinematographer. Somehow we make the material look decent."

"Respectfully, I disagree. Some of these lines really sing, and believe me, I've read a *lot* of crappy scripts, so I know good stuff when I see it. I want to be a writer too, you know? Possibly even more than being an actor. I just love storytelling; making up these fictional worlds and having my characters move through them. In fact, I'm working on a project at the moment. Nothing as ambitious as this, just a sort of one-man play. Dreams of the Edinburgh Fringe." He laughs self-deprecatingly.

"What's it about?" I ask. "I'd love to take a look."

"Truly? That would be so kind, once it's ready. I'm still researching stuff at the moment." He goes and sits on my bed, plucking up a throw cushion and hugging it to his chest. "Isn't it funny, I've done about a million auditions – everything from proper films to deodorant commercials – and I still get nervous every time."

"No need to be nervous," I say, trying my best *not* to imagine Louis deodorizing his fabulous firm torso. "It's only the two of us."

"Perfect." He draws up his legs and tucks them under him. "Is it all right if I sit here for the reading? I don't know why, but it feels sort of comforting."

"Sure." I reposition the GoPro to face my bed (where a beautiful boy is now perched; I certainly didn't expect that when I woke up this morning) and take the desk chair myself.

"Can I ask you something, Jesse?" he says. "You can say no if you'd rather not talk about it."

I glance at the camera monitor to find him staring back intently. "Of course."

He runs his forefinger around his knee, dropping his

gaze. "What do you think of my cousins? I mean, I know you and Cas are tight, obviously. It's just…I don't know. I probably shouldn't say anything."

"No." I nod. "Go on."

"Well, they've agreed to me staying, but it's like they don't really want me around, you know? I mean, I get that Dean has this thing about me being gay. He makes it pretty obvious. But Cas seems off with me too for some reason. All I wanted to do was drop in and see them for a couple of weeks, because it has been ages and we are family after all. But now I'm here…"

I feel a flush of anger. I know Cas has this grudge against Louis's family, thinking they're snobbish and self-serving, but he shouldn't project that prejudice onto a cousin he hasn't seen in years.

"I don't know what to tell you," I say. "I'm only sorry you're being made to feel that way. If you want me to have a word with Cas…?"

"No, no." He waves the suggestion away. "I'm probably being silly."

"I promise you, you're not the one being silly."

"Anyway." Louis pats the script pages spread out beside him. "I've chosen the bit from scene seventeen? After the honeymoon couple see their first zombie attack. If that's okay, I think I'm ready."

I know the part he means, and try my best not to blush.

Instead, I hit record, settle back in my chair, and start to read the stage directions. "Fade in. Exterior: day. Late afternoon. Twilight shadows are already falling across the farmyard. The wife and husband are sitting together, huddled in the darkness thrown by a large hay bale. They are terrified, breathless, their clothes bloodied. They speak in urgent whispers."

I glance up to find Louis with his head in his hands. Slowly he drags his fingers down his face, revealing the stark horror in his eyes. "What is happening? What is happening? What is hap—"

"Shhh," I read. "Please, love, you have to be quiet. They'll hear you."

"They?" He shakes his head, like a determined toddler. "But they're not real. Can't be real. It's just a nightmare, has to be."

"But we heard it on the car radio. It's happening all over. The dead returning."

"No. No, no, no. The world can't change like this," he insists. "Not overnight. Not just like that. Not for us."

And suddenly he's slipped from the bed and is kneeling in front of me, his gaze hooking mine. "Tell me it isn't real. Please."

"Shhh," I implore him again.

In the movie in my mind, the dead are stirring in the fields all around us, waking up, reanimating, hungry.

Sheltered behind the bale, the newly-wed husband lays his head in his wife's lap. In my bedroom, Louis does the same.

"The world was just starting for us, now it's ending?" he says softly. "It's not fair."

"I know," I whisper. "I know."

"We had for ever and now… Whatever happens, I want you to remember. Always remember. I love—"

At that moment, the door swings open and my mum barges into the room, her arms piled high with laundry. "Jesse, listen, I'm glad you're home. There's been another letter from the hospital and I need to talk to you for a seco— Oh my God." Catching sight of us, she drops the pants, socks and T-shirts all over the floor. "Oh my God. Oh my…" Her hand flies to her mouth as Louis's head springs out of my lap. "I'm so— I'm sorry, boys, I didn't realize you were in the middle of—"

"Mum? It isn't what it looks like." I jump out of the chair, almost kneeing Louis in the forehead in the process. "We were practising, that's all."

My mum stares at us both as we scramble to our feet and stand together, side by side. "*Practising?*"

"I meant rehearsing." I wince.

"Rehearsing for what?"

Louis gives me a sly side-eye. "The end of the world?"

Saying that we can talk when I'm less *occupied*, Mum leaves the bedroom door open a crack as she beats a hasty retreat. A crack more than wide enough for the Thing of Evil to squeeze through. I watch as Jacques sidles over to the bed, but before I can warn Louis of any imminent danger, he has leaned down and gathered the softly purring monster into his lap. I watch in horror as the creature that I am convinced has been plotting my death since its kittenhood lies back to have its tummy scritched.

"Aw, and who are you then, handsome boy?" Louis coos, bringing his face to within striking distance.

I'm amazed. Jacques never lets anyone pet him, let alone a stranger. The demon is almost certainly lulling Louis into a false sense of security. Any moment now a vicious claw will be produced. More than willing to sacrifice my poor looks on the altar of Louis's perfect features, I jump up and grab a suddenly snarling Jacques from between his legs.

"Sorry," I shout over the yowling, "as you can see, he has significant anger management issues. Let me just shut him in the bathroom for a bit. He seems to have a personal vendetta against my rubber duck, so he'll be happy enough in there."

I finally manage to wrangle Jacques into the bathroom before resting my head against the closed door. *Did you just tell the most gorgeous boy you've ever met that you have a rubber duckie? And now you're seriously thinking of asking him out?* Well, I was… Cringing, I turn back towards my bedroom only to have my malfunctioning heart almost leap out my mouth.

"Jesus Christ, Mother! What is it with you and this new stealth mode? Have you had some kind of parental upgrade or something?"

She jabs a finger down the corridor and whispers, "Who is that?"

"That is Louis. Cas's cousin?" I whisper back.

She places her hand at about the height of her hip. "That Louis? But last time I saw him, he was—"

I widen my eyes in mock startlement. "I know! Weird, isn't it? How kids grow between the age of eight and seventeen? Almost like it's some natural process that has happened to every human being since the dawn of the species."

This receives a brief flicker of the Stare. "So you were

rehearsing, were you? Maybe I should have a read of this script of yours."

I roll my eyes and slip past her. My hand is on the door handle when I pause and turn back. "You didn't really think we were…you know? Come on, Mum, seriously? Me and a boy like that?"

She looks back at me, the Stare gone, replaced by a very different sort of expression. "Jesse, why do you always…?" She shakes her head. "Look, is this something you've had on your mind? Maybe something that's being exacerbated by the operation? You know we can talk about anything."

I give a casual shrug. "Don't be silly. I only meant that he's generally way out of my league. What did you need to tell me anyway?" I ask before she can interrogate me any further. "When you very rudely burst in, you said something about another letter from the hospital."

Mum blinks. "Oh yes, I've got it here." She goes to the banister where she's laid her work jacket. Digging into the pocket, she brings out an envelope, which she passes to me. "Sorry I opened it, but I saw the hospital stamp and thought it might be important. They need you to come in for a pre-op procedure next week. It's called an angiogram. They inject a dye into your veins and then view the blood flow on a monitor. It's to check you haven't got any potential blockages before the surgery. You're awake the whole time but they give you a local anaesthetic, so you don't feel a thing. The procedure itself only takes about half an hour and you can come home afterwards. No overnight stay." She sees my face fall. "I know. One bloody thing after another, isn't it?"

"Yeah." I snatch my eyes away from the diagram of a patient on a surgery table, a long thin pipe trailing out their wrist. "Still, it doesn't sound like anything too major. Not compared to massive open-heart surgery anyway."

I give a hollow laugh and Mum flinches. "Jesse…"

"It's fine," I say, folding up the letter and slipping it into my back pocket. "And by the way, you don't have to worry about the movie. No blow-job scenes, I swear."

I push open the door, some old joke about Jacques ready to go, when I collide straight into Louis. We both gasp in surprise and freeze for a moment. We're chest to chest, eye to eye. I feel his hand come up automatically and rest on my hip, as if to steady himself. I watch his lips part and spread slowly into a smile.

"You startled me," he breathes.

"You too." I shake my head. "I mean, I'm sorry."

We make a bit of a mess of stepping away from each other, me banging the back of my head against the closed door, Louis almost tripping over his own feet. Perhaps simply by being in my presence he has become infected with terminal klutziness.

"Are you leaving?" I ask.

"Yeah, sorry. I promised I'd see Nanna before she goes to bed. Is that okay? I mean, do you have enough footage for the audition and everything?"

"Oh. Of course. Sure." I nod. "And give Nanna my love, won't you?"

He touches my shoulder. "I will. You know we talked about you today? She seems to have forgotten almost everyone but she remembers Jesse Spark. Stories about you and Cas, what you were like together as little kids, how you've been there for him. I think you're very special to her. In fact, she said something that worried me, and I was going to ask you about it, but maybe it's none of my business?" His grip tightens a little. "Or maybe she got her wires crossed."

"What is it?" I ask.

"She said she overheard Cas telling Dean that you were going to have an operation? She said he sounded really upset."

I take a breath. He was always going to find out about it sooner or later. Film sets are hives of gossip. "It's true. I've got this medical procedure coming up. I need to have…" The image of Doc Myers's third sketch rises in my mind – the incision diagram, illustrating that devastating, life-changing scar. "It's no biggie." I shrug. "Just a simple op to correct a useless bit of my heart."

"Oh, thank goodness." His hand comes down to gently

pat my chest. "Can't have our maestro being poorly, can we?"

"No. I, um, guess not."

"Well, I better be off. Thank you so much for tonight."

I follow him downstairs to the front door. There's no sign of my mum, and so he asks me to wish her goodnight and to apologize for his part in the misunderstanding earlier. He's almost at the end of the drive when he looks back.

"Oh, I meant to say, will you let me know when the others have had chance to look at my audition?" He grins. "You might have to cut right at the bit before your mum came in. But yeah, I'd love to know what they thought—"

"You got the part," I tell him. Screw it, I'm not sending the video to the others. For some reason, I feel like I've been steered and manipulated all the way through this pre-shoot process. I can't explain it exactly, but it's a sense I've started to get – that I'm playing a role in some kind of drama and that someone has forgotten to give me the script. Well, that stops here. This is my movie and I'm making an executive decision. "You were great, Louis," I say. "And if you want it, the husband role is yours."

"Really?" He rushes back down the drive and throws his arms around me. "That is amazing! You don't know how much it means to me. Honestly, this role is so brilliant, plus I'll get to see you guys work together and everything else that goes on – it'll be so valuable." Louis stops to catch his breath. "You've made my summer, Jesse Spark."

Leaning in, he kisses my cheek. Only a feather light touch, there and then gone, but still it sets my stupid heart racing. I very nearly call after him as he trots away down the road, waving a triumphant fist in the air. The words are there, dancing behind my lips. Simple, unoriginal words, spoken in various ways by billions of people across thousands of years, right from when this whole ridiculous romantic rigmarole began: *Would you like to go out with me sometime?*

But *not* spoken by people like me to people like Louis. At least, not with any glimmer of hope that they might say yes. The idea is preposterous, and in a few short weeks will be even more so.

I go back into the house and close the door behind me.

24

Zombies are waiting in the woods, sipping iced coffees, choreographing dance routines with their friends, making goofy videos for their TikTok followers. One panicky member of the undead is being chased around by a wasp while another watches on, mildly entertained, as they chow down on one of my mum's home-made breakfast burritos.

It is the first day of filming, and three days since we cast our lead actors. The past seventy-two hours have been organized chaos, a lot of it taking place under our roof. Morgan has been rehearsing with Louis and Brianna, who continues, rather bafflingly, to shine. Not only this, but with some positive reinforcement from Bree of all people (*"Darling, please come and have a teensy peek, you look utterly fabulous!"*), Morgan has even managed to watch herself on playback of rehearsals without squirming. In fact, Bree has been sprinkling Morgan with what I can only describe as a lot of little micro-motivations, all apparently sincere, praising her acting and appearance, and it seems to be having an effect. I've never seen Morgs as comfortable in her own skin. It makes me wonder what Cas and I got so wrong in our efforts to boost her confidence.

In other news, Mr Murray has come through with the promised five thou, so we've been able to pay Róisín, who's been darting around experimenting on any extras that happen to cross her path. The results look incredible, although our postman is not a fan. After years of suffering at the paws of Jacques, the final straw came when a screaming creature with a peeling face burst out the front door one morning and chased him down the drive. Mum wrote an apologetic email, explaining it was only a teenager having an allergic reaction to zombie make-up, but the Post Office said the poor man's nerves could no longer take the strain of delivering mail to our house.

Meanwhile, the SFX guys Cas has managed to rustle up have put together a sort of lab in our basement. I've seen some of the practical effects they've developed and, just like with Róisín, I'm impressed. The umbrella-through-the-zombie's-chest idea Cas first imagined in his sketchbook? I really think these guys are going to make it work. The only downside is the hammering, drilling and occasional small explosion, but Mum has been a trooper. Her attitude seems to be *out of sight, out of mind* as she ignores the smoke seeping from under the basement door and runs around making sure the cast and crew are all fed and watered.

Until today my role has been mainly supervisory, checking in on rehearsals, giving a couple of performance notes, approving effects and make-up designs. I've also run out to the Lester house and the junkyard a couple of times with Cas to plan shots. He remains quiet and a little tetchy, especially around Louis, which bugs the shit out of me. Several times I've been on the verge of asking him what exactly his problem is with his cousin, but to be honest, I've given up trying to understand his nonsense.

The one good thing is the operation has barely crossed my mind. It really is amazing how movies – both watching them and making them – can help to shut out the worries of the real world. That's part of their magic, I guess.

Suddenly Róisín comes striding out of the forest, a purple-haired tornado in make-up-spattered overalls, heading straight for us. "JS, little update. You need to kick this thing off. Pronto. My zombies are melting in the heat."

We're standing on one side of the road that cuts through the wood. It's 6 a.m. on a Tuesday morning so there isn't much traffic, although the sun is already pretty ferocious. Just behind us, Stan Shan the Cans Man is assembling his boom mic, headphones and laptop. There's no attitude today, no sly quips. Say what you like about Stan, on-set he's a complete pro. Meanwhile, dressed in her gore-stained hitchhiker costume, Morgan is helping Cas to strap the Steadicam to his shoulders.

"Ouch!" he snaps as she clips something into place. "Watch what you're doing."

Morgan steps back, hands raised. "Soh-ree. Next time you can dress yourself."

Yeah, so things haven't improved there either. In fact if anything the drifting between the three of us seems to have worsened. Still, they're here with me, committed to the project, so I guess our friendship is holding. For now anyway.

"Thanks, Róisín," I say. "If you could gather them all together, I'll be calling action in the next few minutes." She nods and whirls back across the road. Pulling out today's shooting pages from my bag, I fix my attention on the script. "Was Dean okay lending us the car?"

Cas nods. "He parked it up earlier and got one of his trader mates to give him a lift back to the market. He wasn't too happy about it; said if 'his baby' came back with a single scratch he'd murder us both in our beds. But he did give Louis a couple of lessons in how to handle it."

I look up to find Cas swaying from foot to foot, acclimatizing to the weight of the camera. "But Louis told me he had a licence. He knows how to drive, doesn't he?"

"Sure, but he's never driven anything like Dean's *Christine*-mobile," Cas says, referencing the classic Stephen

King movie about a demon car that goes on a deadly rampage. "Maybe we should dig into the budget and pay him some danger money?"

The three of us look at each other and smile. It's a tiny moment, almost insignificant in the past few weeks of building tension, but I think we all feel it – the echo of old times reaching out, the happy memories of a hundred films that have all led up to this one big project. However, the good vibes don't last long.

"Where is Louis?" I ask. "We really do need to make a start."

"He wanted to jog here," Cas says shortly. "Build up some sweat so that he could be in character for the scene. It's his 'method'."

"Oh, how terrible of him," Morgan shoots back. "To take his part seriously."

"Talking about taking things seriously, why the hell are you wearing your glasses?" Cas demands.

"I couldn't find my contacts this morning, is that all right with you?"

"But you can't wear your glasses in this scene and not in the rest of the movie. What are we going to say? That your character popped off to get corrective eye surgery in the middle of a zombie apocalypse? And if you are wearing glasses the whole time, then I'll need to keep checking for reflections and lens flare."

"It's fine," Morgan insists. "I can take them off for this scene and wing it."

"You can't 'wing it'," Cas objects. "You're blind as a bat without them."

Morgan stares daggers at him. "It. Will. Be. Fine."

Cas throws out his arms. "It'll be fine. Do you hear that, Sparky? All fine because Morgan says so and Morgan is never wrong about anything."

"No." Morgan nods. "I'm not. Because unlike some people, I know where I stand and I'm not afraid to—"

"Stop!" I shout at them. Stan, who has been testing sound levels nearby, almost jumps out of his skin. I think he might be about to say something before he sees the expression on my face. "I mean it," I seethe. "Just stop, both of you."

"Jess," Morgan begins, but I hold up my hand.

"No, you need to listen. I am so beyond caring about what is going on with the two of you."

"There's nothing going—"

"Didn't you hear me, Cas? I do *not* care. But this stupid bickering ends, right here, right now. While we're on-set, while we're shooting, you two are going to behave like the bloody professionals I know you are. Because all this bullshit?" I wave at the space between them. "It's disrespectful. Not only to me but Stan and Róisín and Brianna and Louis and everyone who's trying to make this thing work. And I know you want it to work too, so please, let's get through this one last project together and then you can go back to being as awful as you like to one another."

I can see the shimmer of tears in both of their eyes.

"I promise," Morgan says quietly.

"Me too." Cas nods. "But, Sparky, this one last project? What do you mean?"

"I don't know," I say truthfully. "Only, I'm not sure I want to go through this again, not the way things have been with you two anyway."

Before either of them can respond, Louis comes jogging up. He's grinning from ear to ear, bursting with energy despite his six-mile run from the Loomis flat. He's wearing his husband costume, a wing-tip collar shirt with cummerbund and a frayed wedding suit that Morgan found in a local charity shop. He must have raised some eyebrows as he raced through town. Now he shrugs off his backpack and swaps his trainers for a pair of shiny dress shoes.

"Not late, am I? My character's supposed to be under extreme stress, so I thought I'd—"

"You won't even be in close-up," Cas says drily. "So what's the point?"

Louis smiles. "Oh well, it might help my performance."

"It's a great idea," I say.

Completely unfazed by his cousin's rudeness, Louis beams, throws his arms around me and plants a kiss on the side of my cheek. I can feel a supernova blush engulfing my entire body.

"Bless you, lovely one," he says. "So, are we good to go? If we are, I can help get everyone together."

I watch him dash off across the road, zipping between clusters of zombie extras, sharing a word and a joke with each. They all laugh and smile, and I'm suddenly reminded of how Cas used to be in the time before prom. The social butterfly accepted by every group within the school. I glance over at my friend, now broodily examining his Steadicam monitor.

Louis comes jogging back. "Good to go, maestro."

I don't know how he does it. Six a.m. in the blistering heat, dressed in a twenty-year-old tuxedo, and he remains stunning. No wonder I can't summon the courage to ask him out. And I've tried, believe me. Over the past three days it has sometimes felt like we've been getting closer. Little looks and smiles exchanged, the odd private joke, intense chats over the coffee machine in our kitchen at home, laughing and debating, discussing acting and directing and our favourite movies, words of praise and reassurance after rehearsals, the brush of his hand on mine, the occasional lingering look and touch. In those moments, I've felt scared and excited, hopeful and intimidated... And then I have a quiet word with myself. He is kind and tactile with everyone. It means nothing.

Although one tiny sliver of hope comes back to me, time and again – the comment he posted under my picture on Cas's Instagram: *Looking cute, Emerald Eyes.*

He thinks I'm cute.

But come on. Everyone says everything's cute these days – tricycles, grandmothers, sunsets, Henry Hoovers. I mean, my mum thinks my Chewbacca eyebrows are cute, so clearly the word has lost all meaning. And that peck on the cheek just now? It's just his way. Isn't it?

"All right, zombies, enough TikToking," Morgan says, bringing the dozen or so undead to order. "We've got about an hour to get this scene in the can before the road starts getting busy. So listen up."

She turns to me, a small smile on her lips. I'm already regretting the harsh words I used with her and Cas, but I can't take them back now.

"Okay," I say, clapping my hands together. "Here's our scene – the hitchhiker has just escaped a zombie attack at the junkyard. That's the opening to the movie. We then cut to our honeymoon couple, who have recently had their own encounter at a local farm. The wife is asleep in the back seat, so we didn't need Brianna today." I catch one or two relieved looks. She has been great in rehearsals but out of character, she's still Brianna, and that can be a lot. "They're travelling through the forest as the hitchhiker staggers into the road and flags them down," I continue.

"Pursued by you guys. So I want plenty of energy. This will be a long establishing shot and we'll pick up with close-ups later. All good?" I turn to Morgan. "Get yourself set up by the tree we marked, you can leave your glasses behind the trunk or something. When you see Dean's car you sprint out, got it?"

Morgan nods. "See red car, run towards it. I think I can handle that acting challenge."

"Right then. Places, everyone!"

Louis gives my hand a squeeze before heading off towards Dean's car, parked up a little way down the road. "Well done, maestro."

I grin and pull out the clapperboard from my bag, snapping it in front of Cas's lens. "Zombie Honeymoon, scene twenty, take one. And...ACTION!"

Morgan starts fleeing through the trees, stumbling, staggering, clumsy with exhaustion. Her eyes are wild, her face drawn long with terror. Her head keeps snapping back to view the ravenous corpses that chase her. Sunlight pours through the branches, caging the action in bars of black and gold. It looks great.

"Help! Jesus, please, someone help me!" she shrieks. "HELP!"

"This is good," I murmur to Cas. I see him nod. "And here comes Louis."

A red car screeches to a halt as Morgan emerges onto

the road. We watch her hurtle round the bonnet, battering her hands on the passenger window, screaming to be let in. The door pops open and she throws herself inside just as the zombies burst from the treeline, claw-like hands scraping at the driver's door. A moment later, the car has screeched off into the distance.

"And cut!" I shout. "Brilliant! Well done, everyone. Let's get Louis and Morgan back and then reset for close-ups."

"Um, Jess?"

I turn to Cas. He doesn't appear quite as thrilled as I am. Instead he's grimacing and pointing over my shoulder. I spin around to see Dean's car crawling slowly up the road towards us.

Louis winds down the passenger window and shouts out, "Sorry, couldn't get it to start first time. Do you want me to try again?"

There is no sign of a passenger sitting next to him.

I close my eyes. "Cas, please tell me that Morgan didn't just mistake a different red car for Dean's and throw herself inside, screaming that she was being chased by zombies?"

"Not quite," Cas says, handing me a page from the script. "It's actually a bit worse than that."

I don't need to read the lines. I know them by heart.

Safely inside the car, the panicked hitchhiker grabs the husband, shrieking in his face.

HITCHHIKER: *They're dead! All dead! My friends – murdered! Ripped to pieces! Eaten alive! We need to get to the police! Now!*

25

"For the last time, Jesse, once I realized I was in the wrong bloody car, of course I told the driver that we were making a movie, and that my friends hadn't really been murdered and cannibalized in the woods by a gang of what, by that point, he started insisting 'must be illegal immigrants'." She pauses to roll her eyes. "Racist Ferrivale strikes again. Anyway, by the time I managed to calm him down we'd almost reached the police station. He was pretty furious at being made a fool of – which I guess I can understand, even if he is a dumbass bigot – so he insisted on coming in to make a formal complaint against us. And here we are."

Here we are indeed – Morgan, Cas, Louis and I, all sitting in a line, awaiting our fate. There's a guy with bruised knuckles the size of Maltesers sitting opposite, plucking at a split lip and frowning at us. I guess we must make a strange sight, even for Ferrivale police station – Louis in his frayed wedding outfit, Morgan hunched over in her blood-stained hiker gear, Cas with a camera still strapped to his chest.

After we realized what had happened, Louis drove us here in Dean's car. Always an experience, but we survived, and now at least Morgan has her glasses back.

"One positive," Cas says. "I reviewed the footage on the way over here and the scene looks incredible. The way that guy tore off down the road? It was like he was genuinely terrified. He even left skid marks on the tarmac."

"Probably on his underwear too," Louis says.

We turn to him and, I don't think any of us can help it, we burst out laughing.

"I can use some editing software to make his car match up with Dean's in future shots," Cas continues. "So all in all, I'd say it's been a pretty successful first day."

I nod. "The zombies really sold it too. The mindless confusion as they milled about in the road afterwards was super convincing."

Morgan stares at both of us. "Well, I'm delighted that my imminent prosecution has all been worthwhile."

We lapse back into silence while I glance up at the clock above the reception desk. It's been two hours since our interviews and with each passing minute the dread curdles in my stomach. Not so much of the police – the constable who took our statements seemed more amused than anything else, especially when I started outlining the history of zombie representation in film. (Don't ask, it seemed important at the time.) No, it's the other authority figure that is currently negotiating our fate who terrifies me.

As if sensing my mounting unease, Louis wraps an arm around my shoulder. "You okay, maestro?"

"I fancy a coffee," Morgan announces, standing up. "I think I saw a machine in the hall. Cas, come and help me select the least revolting option."

Cas snaps his head in her direction. "What? No thanks, I don't want one."

"Not about you," she says, dragging him out of his seat and marching him away.

Meanwhile, Louis slides closer until his thigh is pressed against mine. "How are you feeling?"

I resist the urge to lay my head on his shoulder. "Nervous? Petrified? I don't know. It feels like everything about these missions of mine has been doomed from the start. The hassle getting hold of the film equipment, and now this? It honestly might be easier if it was all brought to an end today rather than prolonging the agony."

"Yeah." Louis nods. "Maybe you're right. Quit while you're ahead, eh?"

I stiffen. "What?"

He pokes me gently in the ribs, which soon turns into a bout of tickling. "See? You don't really believe that," he says when I reluctantly tell him to quit it. "So let's have no more defeatist talk. Whatever happens, you're going to finish this movie and it's going to be brilliant. After all," he waggles his head, as if shaking out a long luxurious mane, "it is your duty to showcase the incredible talents of the greatest actress the world has ever seen."

I can't help laughing. It's like Brianna is in the room. When I compliment him, Louis shrugs. "I have been rehearsing with her for three days. It's like she's in my head now."

"She definitely has that effect," I agree. "But seriously, can I ask, what do you think of her as an actor?"

He seems to consider before answering. "I'm not sure. She feels fresh, you know? What I mean is, most of us are a bit worn and jaded, even by seventeen. We've been round the am-dram block a few times and got the war stories to prove it. Like, you can tell after only a few minutes chatting to her that Morgan has lived and breathed the scene for years. But Bree? I know she's been in a few shows, and she is good in her way, but it all feels sort of artificial. As if the rehearsal itself has been carefully rehearsed. Does that make sense?"

I nod slowly. What he's saying chimes with my own thoughts.

"Anyway, if I can be selfish for a moment," he continues. "You can't give up on *ZomHon* because I need this movie on my audition reel for drama school. So there."

"Well, that's reason enough for me to carry on." I smile.

"And how's the research going for your one-man play? Will that be part of your applications too?"

He nods enthusiastically. "I hope so. Just being here is really helping with the writing. Getting some space away from my parents, I mean."

"I'm glad. You know if I can help in any way…?"

"Bless you." He gives me a long look. "You're a good soul, aren't you, Jesse Spark? Not many like you in the film world. Everyone out for themselves, mostly. But not you… Anyway, there is one thing that puzzles me. You just said it felt like everything about your missions was doomed. *Missions*. So *ZomHon* aside, what exactly are you up to, maestro?"

He arches a pantomime eyebrow and I lower my gaze.

"C'mon," he pats my knee, "you can tell me. No judgement here." When I hesitate again, he sighs. "Well, if you won't tell me then I might have to skip to another inappropriate subject that is none of my business – I don't think you were telling me the whole truth the other night."

I look up. "About what?"

"Your heart?"

"Oh."

"You said it was 'no biggie'." He opens wide those huge denim-blue eyes. "I heard Morgan talking to Cas about it. Open-heart surgery definitely counts as a biggie, Jess. I've researched it a bit online and—"

"Ow!" I yelp as he swats my arm. "Is this how you treat all your poorly friends?"

"The ones who lie to me, yes."

I sigh. "I'm sorry. Really. But we'd only just properly met, and I didn't want to make a huge deal out of it, that's all. Forgive me?"

Finally he turns to face me again. "Yes, I forgive you. Idiot."

"And I forgive you for the slap."

"Do not test me, Jesse," he says, breaking into a smile. "And I still want to know about this second mysterious mission of yours. But only when you're ready."

It's then that the realization hits – if he's researched the op he must know about the scar. And if he knows, then what have I got to lose in asking him out? Other than having to endure the mortifying moment during which his face crinkles with pity and he sighs, *Oh no. I'm really sorry, Jess, but I just couldn't ever think of you in that way.*

"Are you worried about it?" he asks, drawing me out of my thoughts.

I blink. "About?"

"The surgery." He shakes his head. "Silly question. Who wouldn't be worried?"

"I'm worried about the *idea* of it," I say truthfully. "You know, in an abstract sort of way. I know it's coming and that I've got to go through with it; that I don't have a choice.

So I guess I've made peace with that. I suppose what worries me is the pain afterwards and the recovery time. But it feels so immense that I can't really imagine it, so I've been focusing on other things. Not just the movie but…"

"Yes?" he asks gently.

"Louis." I swallow hard, my nerves tingling. Just do it. Just ask him. "Would you like to—"

His phone bleeps. "Sorry, I'll just…" He looks at the caller ID. "It's my darling on-screen wife. I'd better answer or she'll only keep calling."

I nod. "Of course."

He taps the screen and a steaming Brianna appears. I don't mean she's drunk, she's literally steaming. Clouds of it billow around her as she steps out of a marble-tiled bathroom, a towel wrapped around her head.

"What the actual hell is going on?" she demands. "The WhatsApp group is going crazy. Stories about Morgan being abducted by some sleaze and the police shutting down production. Is it true? Because Daddy will want his money back if the film isn't going ahead."

"There's a WhatsApp group?" I whisper to Louis.

"Yeah. Aren't you a member?"

I shake my head. Of course I wouldn't get invited to a group dedicated to my own bloody movie.

"Well?" Brianna glares down the lens.

"It's going to be fine, Bree," Louis assures her. "No one

is shutting down production and Morgan hasn't been abducted."

"She better not have been. I've put a lot of work into building my girl up recently, making her see how fabulous she is. No one messes with Morgan. Urgh!" She shakes her head. "I knew I should have been on-set today. None of this would have happened if I'd been around."

"Your character is supposed to be lying down in the back of the car," I remind her. "She's sleeping when they pick up the hitchhiker. You wouldn't have been onscreen even if you had been there."

Although I'm certain Brianna would have engineered an appearance somehow, perhaps sitting up, yawning and stretching like a Disney princess just as the zombies attacked. Louis reassures her again that everything will be okay and, ending the call, turns to me.

"Sorry. You were saying would I like to…?"

"Oh." I blush. "Yes. So I only wondered if you'd like to—?"

"Jesse!"

"What?" I spin around to confront the latest interruption. "What, what, wha—? Oh, hi, Mum."

My mother looks positively homicidal. Standing beside her is PC Bradstreet, the constable who took our statements. Just then Cas and Morgan reappear, though I notice neither of them are holding cups of coffee. Mum sweeps us all with the Stare.

"After much persuasion by myself and PC Bradstreet, we have managed to convince Mr Winthrope not to press charges. He has accepted that his name appearing in the press as someone who believed a cannibal apocalypse was in progress might not be great for his professional reputation."

"What does he do?" Morgan asks.

"Wait!" Cas cuts in. "I recognize that name. Winthrope. Isn't he the head of that posh private school outside town? Oh, I bet his students would just *love* to hear this little story."

"They won't be hearing it," PC Bradstreet says. "Not from anyone. Understand?"

We all nod solemnly.

"I think you should thank your lucky stars you had someone as formidable as Miss Spark in your corner today. It was she who talked Mr Winthrope around." He gives my mum a respectful nod. "Her being a defence lawyer, we're not always on the same side, but I think this was the right outcome. However, this film of yours?"

I can feel official eyes boring into me. "Yes?"

"Sounds fun!" He grins. "Love a good horror movie myself. Gorier the better. So you can carry on with the project, only please try not to frighten any more members of the general public out of their wits. At least, not until the premiere." He nods to my mum and starts to turn away before hitting the brakes. "Oh, one last thing, kids. Where did you get all that film equipment?"

"Mr Prentice from school loaned it to us," Cas and I blurt out, almost in unison.

This receives a long, cool look. "Toby Prentice? Drama teacher at Ferrivale High? Very unique dress sense?" We nod. *Oh crap.* "We play poker together every Thursday night. I thought he was out of the country? So I guess he must have given you guys permission to use it before he left." We nod again. "Expensive gear by the look of that camera. He must really trust you." Can you nod too much? Is an excess of nodding suspicious? We do it anyway. "All right then. I look forward to buying my ticket for opening night."

"I am *not* happy," Mum says, once PC Bradstreet has departed. "Poor Mr Winthrope was still shaking in his boots when I arrived at the station." The Stare softens. "Which was admittedly hilarious. Anyway, the four of you, please try to stay out of trouble and…vamoose!"

We don't need telling twice. We're up and out of the building in ten seconds flat.

Cas and Morgan are a little way ahead of us, discussing whether the light is still good enough for more establishing shots of the road, when I impulsively grab Louis's sleeve.

"Hey, so that thing I was going to ask you?"

He stops and smiles. "Oh yes, we were talking about your heart. Was it about that?"

"It was…" *Not about that. Go on. Tell him it was about asking him out on a date. For God's sake, Jesse, just say the words!* "Yes," I say. "About my heart. I was going to ask if you'd maybe consider…" *You idiot. You massive fucking idiot!* "Coming with me to this little pre-op procedure I have to have done. It's the day after tomorrow. Cas is shooting second unit stuff that day and Morgan is busy with something else she has planned. I mean, it's no problem if you can't."

"Of course I'll come," he says, throwing his arm around me. "It's what friends are for, right?"

I force a smile. "Yeah. Thanks. Absolutely. Friends."

I bite my thumbnail, glance at my phone. Should I call him? Maybe I didn't tell him the right time? Or the right day? Or even the right hospital? I mean, this is me we're talking about. I can very easily picture Louis standing outside a different cardiac surgery department, wondering where the hell I've got to. Although if that was the case, surely he would have called by now?

I pull out Dr Myers's letter, confirming to myself that at least *I* am where I should be. Then my finger goes back to hovering over Louis's contact. What if he's been in an accident? Run over or mugged or face-planted the side of a stationary bus while crossing the road (it happens, okay?). If he has injured himself while coming to support me then I'll never forgive myself.

Ten minutes to go. *Come on, Louis.* I was only allowed one person to accompany me today, and so when Mum asked if I'd like to do something special after the procedure as a treat, I told her it was okay and that a friend had said he'd come with me. She'd smiled, saying that it was kind of Cas to volunteer. When I told her it wasn't Cas I'd asked, but Louis, the smile had become a bit fixed and unnatural.

"That's very considerate of him," she said.

Something in her tone had made me look up from my cereal. "What's that supposed to mean?"

"Nothing. I'm just a little surprised, that's all."

"What's surprising about it? Louis has been a good friend."

"Yes. For about a week."

I'd put down my spoon and glared at her. "And?"

"Well, you've been best friends with Morgan—"

"Morgan isn't around," I muttered. "Even though our shooting schedule is right up to the wire, she's asked for the whole day off. Going to see some West End play or something. It's so selfish. She could at least have helped Cas out with some of the second unit shooting, even if it was only for a couple of hours before she left."

I'd immediately felt bad after saying it. Morgan has put tons of work into *ZomHon* and she'd seemed really excited about the show. I guess I was just in a stressed-out mood this morning. Although it's only a small pre-op procedure, the angiogram feels like step one on the path to the big surgery, looming so close now on the horizon.

"Well," Mum had continued, "what about Cas? Couldn't he have come along with you for an hour?"

I'd got up at that point and chucked my bowl into the sink. "I didn't want him to come, all right? He's been really prickly and grumpy on-set and I'm getting sick of it. So I asked Louis, who has been nothing but kind and considerate. But by that look on your face, I can see you have some kind of problem with him. So come on, out with it, I know you're dying to tell me."

Mum surprised me then. We didn't get into a massive row or anything. She just came over and wrapped her arms around me.

"Good luck today, Jesse bear," she said. "Please call as soon as you're done. You know where I am if you need me."

I stood at the sink for a while after she left, staring into space. I'd picked up the vibe that she wasn't the biggest Louis fan after that first night when she walked in on us filming his audition. Something about her attitude around him has been off ever since. Mum is usually a good judge of character – in her line of work, she has to be – but whatever her instinct is with Louis, this time she's wrong. Even now, waiting for him in the doorway of the hospital, I know she's wrong.

"Jesse Spark, please report to waiting area 5B."

My name being called over a tannoy.

I swipe away from Louis on my mobile and bring up my mum and then Cas. Even if I called, there wouldn't be enough time for them to arrive before the procedure. And if I did, they'd both immediately jump to the conclusion that Louis has let me down, when I know he'll have a good reason for not being here.

Then why don't you message him? a mean little voice asks in my head. *Because you're afraid to hear the truth, aren't you? That either he's forgotten or can't be bothered or found someone much better to spend his time with. You really think he'd waste such a beautiful summer's day on you? Bury himself in a dingy hospital waiting room for an already nondescript boy that he knows must soon become a hideous, scarred freak? All right then, call him. Go on. I dare you,* maestro.

Phone clenched in my fist, I turn and walk into the hospital, the voice still cackling at me.

He doesn't want you now and he sure as hell won't want you later.

No one will.

Not ever.

Get used to it.

"Jesse, is it?" A nurse at cardiac reception greets me. I can hardly remember the walk through the corridors to waiting area 5B. "Are you all right, dear?"

I quickly wipe my eyes with the back of my hand. "Yeah. Sorry. It's coming out of the daylight and the air-con in here and…everything."

She looks sympathetic. "I understand. It's a lot to be coping with, isn't it? Is anyone with you today?"

"No." I shake my head. "Just me."

"Well just you is just perfect. My name's Stella, by the way. Now, I'll get you all checked in and then we can gown you up for the big performance. It'll be over before you know it, I promise."

We sit in a corner of the empty waiting room and go through a brief medical questionnaire. The whole thing reminds me of Big Si with his alluring lumberjack beard and his clipboard. It seems centuries ago that I laid on that bed, the probe skating around my chest, slowly revealing the truth about my stupid heart. I wonder if Si is on duty today. It would be nice to see a friendly face. Not that Stella isn't friendly; in fact, she even manages to make me laugh once or twice.

"All done," she says, ticking the final box. "Now, off you pop into the far end cubicle and change into the gown provided. You can leave your clothes in there. Someone will come and collect you and take you to Dr Myers and his team when they're ready. Is that all right?"

I nod dumbly and head into the cubicle. Changing into the gown, I sit on this little wooden bench and take one last look at my phone. No missed calls, no texts. I scroll through a few news feeds, just to distract myself. A dog has rescued a kid from a burning building; a politician has been caught fiddling his taxes; they're casting for some new fantasy film in London based on a bestselling YA novel; a football team

I've never heard of has beaten another football team I've never heard of.

I switch off my phone and let my mind drift across the miles to the old Lester house. Yesterday's filming there went pretty well, Brianna and Louis knocking a really intense scene right out of the park. The extras were great too, throwing themselves into a particularly gruesome moment where they all had to eat a mass of gungy tofu designed to resemble various bits of human anatomy. In fact, only Morgan seemed off her game. Which is unusual as Brianna's boosting of her acting ability and screen presence seems to be doing wonders for her confidence. She and Cas have also honoured their promise and there hasn't been as much bickering between them, but still she was tense and brittle all day, snapping at everyone.

A knock at the cubicle door. They're ready for me.

I follow a nurse down the corridor and into a chilly room that looks like the kind of operating theatre you see in movies, only smaller. There's a team of about five people standing beside a narrow bed, all gowned up and wearing masks. They seem friendly, waving gloved hands and saying hello. I recognize Dr Myers from his glasses and the sniffly voice coming from behind the mask.

"Hello again, young man. How have you been keeping?"

"Good, thank you," I say, taking in the narrow surgery bed and the huge X-ray machine standing over it.

"Excellent." Dr Myers's gaze flickers to my hands, my fingers twisting and untwisting themselves. "Do you know," he says in a kindly tone, addressing his colleagues, "this young man is a very gifted filmmaker."

They all make interested noises.

"Now, Jesse, will you pop up onto the bed for me? That's great, thank you. I'm just going to sterilize this area around your wrist and give you a little local anaesthetic before we begin." I stare up at the brilliant white machinery while Dr Myers injects the anaesthetic into my wrist. It stings a little. "Theeere we go. Yes indeed, ladies and gents," he says, handing something to the nurse beside him. "We may well be in the presence of the next Stanley Kubrick or Akira Kurosawa. His mum even sent me a couple of his films to take a look at."

I stare at Doc Myers. "She did?"

"At my request. Very proud of you, as she should be." He takes a scalpel from one of the others, but I barely notice it. He keeps my attention fixed on him. "And I watched them all. Fascinating use of shadows and perspective in that black and white vampire movie of yours. Influenced by the German Expressionist movement?"

I almost smile. "You like old movies?"

He gives a dry little laugh. "To me, some of them are not so old. Now, I'm making this small incision into your radial artery, okay, Jesse? You tell me if you feel any pain and we'll take care of that right away. There…we…go. Good. So, listen up, team, we need to take special care of this one because he will go on to do great things one day, I'm sure."

The rest of the procedure goes by pretty quickly. Dr Myers keeps me informed and distracted throughout the whole thing, which is an impressive trick. At one point he tells me that the catheter tube he has threaded through my wrist has now reached my heart – I don't feel a thing! – and they are injecting a dye into my bloodstream which will show up on the X-ray, highlighting if there are any blockages they need to know about. The dye whooshing around my body is a bit of a weird sensation, almost making me feel like I've wet myself. Dr Myers assures me I haven't and that the scan shows no blockages.

"So we are all clear for the main event," he says happily.

"Oh," I murmur. "Good."

He tells me he is fitting a compression band to my wrist. Because they have opened an artery to insert the catheter tube, the band needs to be slowly loosened over an hour or two so that I don't start bleeding from the puncture site. I'm to stay in a treatment room until then.

"The next time I see you will be in just over a fortnight, okay, Jesse? Now, is there anything else you're worried about regarding the surgery?" I shake my head. "You're sure?" Dr Myers looks at me for a moment from behind those thick glasses, as if he doesn't quite buy my denial.

"We're going to get you through this, young man," he says. "Have no fear."

Stella the nurse meets me outside the theatre and takes me to the treatment room. My clothes are there, neatly folded on a bed, my phone sitting on top. The plastic compression band is really tight around my wrist, and as I sink onto the bed, I can feel a dull ache pulsing along my arm. I guess the local anaesthetic must be wearing off. Stella tells me this is normal and that I should avoid lifting anything too heavy for the next forty-eight hours.

"That won't be a problem," I say. "I'm not exactly a gym bunny. In fact, I never lift anything heavier than the kettle."

"Good. I'll be back in about an hour to loosen the band. In the meantime, try to relax. Oh, and I almost forgot." She's at the door when she spins around. "There's a very handsome young man here to see you."

My freshly-X-rayed heart leaps. I suppose Stella must see something in my face because she smiles. "Your boyfriend?"

I blush and blow out my cheeks. "No. I don't have a boyfriend."

"Well, he seemed very keen to visit you," she says with a wink. "Would you like me to bring him in?"

I nod, trying not to wag my head too enthusiastically.

Smiling, Stella heads off while I desperately try to make myself more presentable. Not an easy task in a hospital gown. Even if my arm wasn't aching like it had just been run over by a steamroller, there would be no time to get dressed. The best I can do is smooth down my gown and rake a hand through my dishevelled poodle mop. I'm guessing he must have got caught up in traffic or maybe the bus was late or…

"Here he is then," Stella announces, ushering my visitor in with another wink. "Now I'll leave you two alone."

Cas stands in the doorway, annoyance and concern battling across his features. Finally, he sighs.

"Sparky, what the hell?"

"How did you know I was here?"

We're both sitting on the bed, cradling cups of hot chocolate brought in by Stella. Before leaving us, she shoots me a wink and a warm, cheeky smile.

"Your mum," Cas says, frowning after the nurse and taking a sip of his drink. "She brought over some sandwiches and snacks while we were out shooting. Just happened to mention what was going on. Why didn't you tell me?"

He sounds really angry.

"I said I was going to the doctor's," I mumble.

"This," he gestures at my wrist, "is not 'going to the doctor's', Sparky."

"It's nothing," I say. "Only a little procedure they had to do before the main operation. Come on, Cas, you know what film sets can be like. One rumour that I'm in hospital and everyone would have started panicking that the production was being shut down. It wasn't worth worrying them."

"So I'm only part of the crew now, am I? Can't be trusted not to spread gossip?"

I sigh and try to reach out to him, forgetting for a moment about my wrist. The movement sends a sharp ache throbbing along my arm and I wince. "It's okay," I tell Cas through gritted teeth, "I'm fine. But look, you were supposed to be out shooting second unit stuff today. Important shots that'll set up the third act of the movie. You were more valuable to me there than here."

"Was I?" he asks in a flat tone.

I nod dumbly. What else can I say? That I could only bring one person along with me today and that I didn't choose my best friend since childhood because... I look at him, clutching his cup, his eyes downcast. Because I wanted to get close to someone else before it was too late? Because I would have liked to share this moment of vulnerability with Louis and not with him? *Because, honestly, Cas, we seem to be drifting further and further apart lately.*

Whatever my justifications, I still feel a deep twist of guilt about my choice.

"I should phone my mum," I say. "Let her know I survived."

Cas says he'll get us some snacks from the vending machine while I make the call. I watch him go, rummaging in his pockets for change.

"Is Louis looking after you?" Mum asks once I've finished telling her about the procedure. "Do you two need a lift home? I can arrange a taxi if I'm not finished at work."

"No," I say, avoiding the first question. "It's fine. I have some money."

"Well, all right then, if you're sure? And Jesse?" It's not often you hear an apologetic note in my mother's voice. "Will you thank Louis on my behalf? For looking after you? It was very good of him."

"Sure. Bye, Mum."

I'm still looking down at the blank screen of my phone when Cas returns, arms overflowing with crisps, chocolate bars and fizzy drinks. "Wasn't sure what you'd fancy so I've brought a selection. Got a few weird looks from the nurses; I suppose they don't encourage this much junk food in the cardiac unit."

I opt for a Mars bar, which due to the compression band Cas has to help me unwrap.

"Shall I cut it into nibble size chunks for you?" He smiles.

"Do not mock the afflicted," I say between bites. "Or I'll lay a gay hex on your head. We have the power, you know."

He cracks open a can of lemonade and places it on the table beside me. "How are you doing anyway? We haven't really talked for a while. About the heart stuff."

I shrug. "Suppose I'll just be glad when it's all over and finished with."

He looks up. "You're talking about the operation?"

"Of course. What else?"

"Nothing, I guess." He gets up and goes to the window that looks out onto the hospital car park. "Anyway, I might have some good news. You know how we were thinking we'd have to use some rubbish royalty-free music off the internet for our soundtrack? Well, Stan has hooked me up with this local musician. He's in a band called Dancing for the Super Worm. I know," he says. "Weird name. But the lead singer, Caleb, he writes his own stuff and from what I've heard, it's pretty good. Very synthy, like John Carpenter wrote for *Halloween*? I thought we could get him to score *ZomHon*; maybe even put some of his more upbeat songs over a few of the action sequences. You know, like juxtaposition?" He turns and grins at me, and I remember that walk into school when we discussed his storyboard ideas. It feels like years ago now.

"Two unexpected things colliding." I smile back.

"Here, see what you think."

He passes me an earbud and hits play on his phone. We listen to a couple of really great tracks – a sweet, mysterious, Celtic-infused instrumental called "The Last Firefox"; a superbly camp pop song called "Boy Queen"; a clever, trippy tune with hilarious lyrics titled "Noah Can't Even";

and "The Shadow Glass", an eighties-style power ballad, all punchy snare drum and wailing guitars. It's an eclectic mix but you can tell it's all from the same musical mind and, honestly, it's freaking brilliant.

"That last tune would work so well over the end credits," I say as Cas hits pause. "And if Caleb could put together some thoughts for a complete score?"

"I've already asked him." Cas nods. "Sorry if that was overstepping, I know this is your baby, but I also knew you'd dig the hell out of those songs."

"What did he say?"

"I gave him a look at some of the early rushes," Cas says, meaning the raw, unedited footage we've shot so far. "He was impressed. I think he'd like to get into composing for film, so this could be a great experience for him. He has his own recording studio set up in his parents' basement, so he's able to lay down the tracks there, no problem. But."

"Oh, God, don't tell me. He wants paying."

Cas laughs. "Not quite. He wants us to go to a Super Worm gig. Next Friday at Hinchcliffes."

"AKA the sleaziest nightclub in town? Urgh. How will we even get in? Neither of us is eighteen yet."

"It's a teen band night, so they're not serving alcohol. He'd like us to bring the whole *ZomHon* crew if possible. His band's pretty new and I think he's worried that no one will show up."

"Sounds fun." I grin. "One last big night out before I get sliced and diced. Although, thinking about it, the next day will be our last scheduled shooting day with Brianna and Morgan's big finale scene. We'll all need to be on our game to get that one in the can."

"We'll stay for an hour at Hinchcliffes," Cas assures me. "And all home by midnight, I promise."

"Sounds like a plan." I nod. "So if Caleb can get his score written and recorded while I'm in hospital recovering, we can then work on the edit together once I get home."

"One last project, eh?" Cas says quietly.

I shake my head. "Cas, I didn't me—"

"Well, aren't you the popular patient?" Our heads snap towards the door and to nurse Stella. "Not one but two handsome young men come to visit. If this continues I'll have to set up a VIP guest list at reception. But seriously, Jesse, rules are rules and it's only one visitor per patient, so?"

Louis hovers at the nurse's side, his fingers twisting around the hem of his T-shirt. He mouths a sheepish *sorry* and gives me a little wave.

"It's okay," Cas mutters, abruptly rising from the bed. "I can go."

"Oh, cuz, no," Louis says. "I didn't realize you'd be here. Of course you should stay. I can wait outside or maybe see Jesse later when he gets home. How are you anyway, Jess? Did it all go okay?"

"Um. Yeah, it went really…well." I cast a glance at Cas. "Actually, Louis, could you give us a sec?"

Louis looks between us and nods. He and Stella then retreat to the corridor while Cas comes to stand in front of me, his palm out. It takes a moment for me to understand that he wants his earbud back.

"So it seems you told at least one person what was really happening today?" He takes the bud and pockets it. "Nice." He turns and heads for the door.

"Cas, wait," I call after him. "You don't understand. I didn't choose Louis because he's a better friend than you or anything like that. It's just, I've had the surgery on my mind a lot lately and there's… Well, there's something I've wanted to… Needed to—"

"To what?" Cas asks, throwing out his arms. "Jesse, you're not making any bloody sense."

I should tell him. Explain my plan to make a connection, one intimate connection before I go under Doc Myers's scalpel and all that becomes impossible for me. Once I might have told him. But now, looking up at my oldest friend, seeing the anger and hurt in his eyes— All at once my sense of guilt is overridden by a surge of anger. I'm not the one who's caused all this drifting between us. That's entirely the fault of Cas and Morgan; Cas has no right to feel angry about anything.

"Actually, it's none of your business," I say coldly.

"So thank you for coming, and on your way out, please tell Louis I'm free to see him now."

Cas stares at me for a moment. And then he's through the door and past a bemused-looking Stella before I can even think of saying another word. Stella clearly picks up on the vibe of the situation because she makes quick work of loosening the band on my wrist before asking if everything's all right.

"Sure." I nod. "Thank you."

"Well, you press that buzzer if you need anything. I'll be back in another hour to loosen the band again and then you can probably go home." She treats Louis to a no-nonsense look. "And I don't want any dramas in here, all right? Jesse is my priority and he's recovering from a significant procedure. I don't want him upset. You're a big lad," she says, squaring up to him. "But I've thrown bigger and much uglier than you out of this place before. *Comprendé?*"

Louis looks somewhere between intimidated and crestfallen, until Stella pats his arm and says she'll bring him a hot chocolate. Once she has bustled away, he takes a step or two into the room, still tugging at his T-shirt like a guilty toddler.

"I'm so sorry," he says. "I feel really awful about not being here for you."

"Don't worry about it," I tell him. "I've been fine."

"It's just, Dean got me out of bed at the crack of dawn, saying it was about time I earned my keep. He said it in this jokey way, only I'm never really sure if he's joking or not. Does that make sense?" I nod. It does. Dean has that typical bully's trick of claiming that all his "playful" threats and insults are said in fun, while at the same time keeping up an undercurrent of menace. He gets off on it, I guess. "Anyway, he dragged me along to the market to help out on his stall. I didn't mind, it was interesting, seeing him work. He's kind of an actor in his own right, you know? Like one minute he's the charming grandson to all the little old ladies, next he's this streetwise hardman selling flashy trainers and sports gear to kids." Louis pauses for a second, as if taking some kind of mental note, then shakes his head. "So I thought I'd work the stall for a few hours and still have plenty of time to make it to the hospital. Only once we got set up, I realized I'd left my phone back at the flat. Then Dean disappears for ages with some mate of his and by the time he comes back, I know I'm going to be late. Honestly, Jess, I got here as soon as I could."

"Wouldn't Dean lend you his phone when he came back?" I ask. I don't want to make him feel bad, and of course I believe him, but still, the story feels a little weak.

"I didn't think to ask." Louis slides into the place on the bed recently occupied by Cas. "I was so angry when he got back. I'd told him I needed to get away by ten; he knew I was coming to support you. I threw my money belt at him and ran all the way here."

Close up, I can see the sheen of sweat still cooling on his brow, the golden hair plastered to the nape of his neck. He taps my bare knee with his forefinger.

"Forgive me?"

"Psshaw." I smile. "Of course."

"I hope Cas does, too," he says forlornly. "I really didn't mean to butt in just now."

"Cas will be fine," I say, while at the same time wondering, will he? That look on his face when he stormed out. I mentally shake myself. Screw Cas. He can't expect me to rely on him when he's been so absent lately. He and Morgan started all this unspoken weirdness between us, so if he feels abandoned and pushed aside? Join the bloody club! "Or he won't." I shrug. "Either way, it isn't your fault."

Louis takes my good hand in his and gives it a gentle squeeze. "Is everything all right with you two?"

"I don't know." I sigh. "I wish I did."

We sit in silence for a while, the random squeaks and groans and bleeps of the hospital filling the void.

"Well," Louis says at last. "Tell me about what's been going on with you. I want to hear all the gory details." He looks at my banded wrist and winces. "That looks like it might leave a nasty scar."

28

I look across darkening fields of corn. Soon the sun will begin to throw an angry cloak across the horizon, splashing the landscape in shades of red. For now, it glints in every warped and fractured surface of the junkyard, a thousand suns shimmering in fragments of shattered windscreen. It's the golden hour. Almost time to shoot our scene. I need to get my brain in gear.

And then my gaze strays to Louis, huddled together with Morgan and Brianna beside the junkyard owner's shed, rehearsing the scene. He looks up from his script, smiles at me, and my thoughts fly back to those words he spoke at the hospital.

A nasty scar.

Simple words that have haunted me for the past week. Louis didn't mean anything by them, I know that. Just a casual comment anyone might make under the circumstances. But in the seven days since the angiogram, I've become obsessed with that tiny mark left on my wrist.

Every time I wash my hands, every time I hold my phone, every time I lift a drink to my lips, I see it – a neat, pale little dot, not much bigger than a pimple really, and if it does leave a permanent scar, it won't be much of one. But still it blazes there, a minuscule ugliness, like the promise of more hideous things to come.

And they will be coming very soon.

Only eight days to go.

Eight days and I still haven't summoned the courage to ask Louis out. Because if he thinks that insignificant blemish is "nasty", what must he imagine an open-heart surgery scar will look like?

Anyway, I have my excuses all ready whenever I miss my opportunity. Although we've been together every day, sunup to sundown, a movie in production is like an army and I am the general. I've barely had time to eat. Someone is always around, asking me questions about scene blocking, SFX, make-up design. And of course, Cas is always at my side. Not the ideal situation in which to propose a date, especially as he seems even more resentful of Louis after the whole hospital saga. I've got no idea what the atmosphere must be like in the Loomis flat but on-set it is pretty negative between them, at least on Cas's side. Louis, meanwhile, seems oblivious to it all, continuing to treat his cousin with the same kindness and respect he does everyone else.

I need to make a decision, one way or another. Tomorrow is our last day of shooting. The big finale at the Lester house when Brianna's grieving wife and Morgan's messed-up hitchhiker must make their stand against the zombie hordes. After that, the cast will have done their job and Louis's part in *ZomHon* will be over. His time in Ferrivale is almost up.

I'll think about it later. Let's get back to what I'm good at.

"Okay, everyone, gather round," I say, clapping my hands together.

They all crowd in – the zombie extras, Brianna, Louis and Morgan, Stan Shannon ready with his boom mic, Cas checking the settings on the high-def camera, and finally Róisín and Tiny. The gigantic junkyard owner is beaming from ear to ear. I can tell because he put up no resistance at all when Róisín demanded he shave off his beard so that she could apply his make-up properly. I'm not sure he looks any more like Harrison Ford without the face fungus, but he does look a hell of a lot better, even with rotting false teeth and hollowed-out cheeks.

"So exciting," he bellows, and several of his fellow zombies jump out of their skin. "Aren't you excited? You do know that Brad Pitt, Clint Eastwood and Renée Zellweger all started their careers as background artists? So let's listen up to our director."

Tiny's newfound respect for me is refreshing. He's even agreed to chain up his beloved dogs – Dolly and Daphne – at the back of the yard for the duration of filming. We can still hear their distant howling, but Stan says that will only add to the eeriness of the soundtrack.

"Right," I say. "Thank you, Tiny. So this scene comes just before the fateful moment back at the house where the wife –" I nod to Brianna – "has to make the ultimate sacrifice and put an end to her husband, who has been infected by a zombie. The bite happens here, at the junkyard. The couple and the hitchhiker have realized they need weapons, so they come to scavenge for supplies. But when they arrive, they find a nest of the undead waiting for them, and poor Louis here gets a little gnawed." Louis grins, holding up his right arm, which already sports Róisín's incredible oozing make-up effect. "Very good." I laugh along with cast and crew. "And yes, I agree, it is amazing how he can make even a zombie bite look sexy."

The words are out before I can stop them.

Luckily, or unluckily, at that exact moment a car roars up to the gate, distracting everyone. I see Brianna's eyes narrow and scars of colour whip into her cheeks. She turns and marches over to the chain-link fence, swiftly followed by Morgan and Louis.

"What the hell do you think you're doing here?" she demands.

Ethan slides out of the VW Beetle and comes strolling over to his twin sister. Reaching the gate, he spits on the ground before speaking.

"It's a nice evening so I thought I'd have a little burn out into the countryside." He stretches, lifting his face to the still-simmering sun. "Also, I overheard you talking to one of these losers on the phone before you left, and it got me curious about what you've been up to recently. You know, sis, hanging out with a bunch of weirdos, playing at being their friend? It's doing nothing for your rep. And anyway, we all know you're not the best at this acting thing, right? So why don't you stop embarrassing yourself."

I've now reached the gate and I'm close enough to see Brianna's bravado begin to falter. She's suddenly back to being that girl I glimpsed at the after-show party, consumed with doubt.

"We don't have time for this bullshit," Cas mutters.

Ethan's gaze flicks in his direction. "Hey, Cassandra. Oh, and Jessica's here too. And the pretty new boy." He flashes Louis a grin. "The whole queer little fag gang. And look, you've even got yourself some new members. What the fuck are you all supposed to be anyway?" His smile turns into a sneer as he strides over, smashing his palms against the chain-link so that the whole fence shakes. One or two of the zombies step back, but most hold their ground, which only infuriates Ethan further. "Don't go thinking I've forgotten about prom," he spits at me and Cas. "No one humiliates a member of my family and gets away with it."

"I don't care about any of that," Bree shouts back. "Not any more."

"I don't care whether you care or not." Ethan shrugs. "It's not about you. Don't you get it, Bree? It reflects badly on *me* to have my sister hanging with freaks and making a proper tit of herself. And anyway, these two need to be taught a lesson."

"Is that right? And who exactly are you, you pasty-faced little gobshite?"

If it were possible, Ethan's complexion suddenly turns even paler. We all stand aside as the giant of the junkyard ambles up to the gate, snapping open the padlock and throwing it aside.

"I asked you a question." Tiny rattles the security chains free and pulls open the gate. "What. Is. Your. Name?"

Ethan stumbles backwards, his eyes like saucers as he fumbles in his pocket for his car keys.

"I don't want any trouble," he says, a hand raised as if to ward off the junkyard owner.

"Course you don't." We all know that this roar is normal volume for Tiny, but Ethan's legs seem to give way at the sound and he lands hard on his tailbone. "Nasty wee vermin like you never do want trouble with big old bruisers like me." Towering over the cowering bully, Tiny grabs Ethan by the collar and lifts him to his feet. "But that's your mistake."

"Please don't hurt him," Brianna calls out.

"Don't you worry," Tiny shouts over his shoulder. "I won't harm a shivering hair on his head. Just going to see him off the premises is all." Ethan's trainers shuffle across the dirt track as he is hauled back to his car. "Keys?"

Still in a virtual sitting position, Ethan drags them out of his pocket and hands them to Tiny.

"Much obliged." Tiny thumbs the fob, the Volkswagen bleeps, the driver's door is yanked open, and Ethan deposited inside. "Now then, all comfy? Good. My suggestion is that you head straight home and get yourself an early night. You've had a tiring time here, trying to play the big man, but we've got a movie to make. So off you pop."

He throws Ethan the keys and, turning to us with a wink, saunters back to the gate.

"This isn't over," Ethan half-shouts, half-sobs, jabbing a finger at me and Cas. "I prom—"

Tiny has had enough. "I said, GET OUT!"

Ethan doesn't need telling twice. He slams the key into the ignition and a moment later is tearing off down the track, rooster-tails of dust kicked up in his wake. Watching him flee, the dead let out a raucous cheer and they all crowd around Tiny. He shoos them away and calls out to me and Cas.

"Better get started, eh? The light's wasting."

He's right. The sun is creeping further towards the horizon; the shadows are lengthening. I glance at Cas and see him watching the dust resettle on the road. I wonder if he's thinking what I'm thinking – that it would make a lot more sense if Ethan Murray was Dean Loomis's brother rather than him. Even with everything that's happened in recent weeks – the moodiness, the secrets, the drifting – Cas is still ten times the person Ethan and Dean will ever be.

"Right then," I say, clapping my hands again. "Excitement over. Everyone, take your positions and we'll go for a first take. Just the short scene with the wife, husband and hitchhiker before they realize the junkyard is infested with zeds. Then we'll move on quickly to the big chase sequence."

We set up the shot, the action focused at the mouth of one of those avenues of towering trash. While the extras move out of frame, Cas tests the light, Stan angles the boom mic, and I give our leads their motivation. The characters have finished scavenging for supplies when the wife hears a noise coming from somewhere among the junk piles.

"So lots of tension," I conclude. "String it out as long as you can, Bree. And…action."

They are hunched together over their packs when Bree's head snaps up.

"Listen," she says, breathless. "Did you hear that? Sounded like something moving. Something big… Stop. I know that look." She glares at Louis/the husband. "Don't tell me it's only the rats. You didn't believe me back at the… Back at the… Shit."

She shakes her head, eyes downcast, and I call, "Cut."

"Bree," I say gently, "the line is 'You didn't believe me back at the power station, and remember what happened there?' Okay, good to go again, Cas? And…action!"

The scene restarts and we reach the same line.

"You didn't believe me back at the petrol station—"

"Cut," I call, and tears start in Bree's eyes. "It's okay," I say, and remind her of the line. "Let's go again."

We hit the same spot.

"You didn't believe me back at the railway sta—"

"Cut!" I try my best to keep the irritation out of my voice.

I hear a sigh from Stan and catch a couple of the extras rolling their eyes. We go again, hit the same line.

"You didn't believe me… You didn't… Fuck!" Bree cries. "Power station! Power station! Why can't I…?" She stands up, brushing away Louis's comforting hand. "I can't. I can't. I'm sorry, guys, I just… I'm done."

She walks off towards the gate and Cas lowers the

camera while Morgan comes to stand beside us. Bree finds a perch on an old tractor tyre and puts her head in her hands. Meanwhile Louis has crossed the yard and is shuffling up next to her. Beside me, Morgan sniffs at the sleeve of her now fairly funky hitchhiker's outfit. After a fortnight running around in the same costumes, all the actors are starting to whiff a bit.

"You'll need to have a word," she says.

"Me?" I blink. "Um, okay. But what do you think's wrong?"

"Here's an idea," she snaps back. "Why don't you go and ask?"

I sigh. This routine is getting really old – grumpy Cas and snappy Morgan. It's like they're a double act, except for the fact that they're barely talking to one another. Morgan in particular has been ratty all week, jumping down everyone's throat at the slightest thing. She didn't even seem to enjoy her trip to London to see the show. Anyway, I plaster on the best smile I can and head over to see what's wrong with my leading lady.

"Hey, Bree, everything all right?"

Louis looks up at me and shakes his head.

"I can't," Brianna says, her voice shaking. "What's the point? You've all been really nice to me, especially Morgs, but everyone knows what's going on here. You only cast me in this thing because my dad offered some money towards the budget. If it wasn't for that…" She breaks down in tears. "Ethan's a nasty piece of shit. Has been ever since we were little kids. He gets off on making people's lives a misery. I'm sorry about what he said to you, Jesse. He's always looking for what he thinks are people's weaknesses, and in his twisted mind he thinks being gay is a weakness. But one thing he's right about is me. I need to stop this. Stop embarrassing myself."

"Brianna? Hey, look at me." I crouch down so that I'm eye-level with her. "Do you want to hear the honest truth?"

She looks a little scared, but still she nods.

"All right then, here it is." I take a breath. "If someone had told me three weeks ago that I'd have cast Brianna Murray in *any* role in this movie, I would have laughed in their face. Of course, that might depend on whose face it was. If it had been *yours*, I probably would have backed quickly away and hidden in the nearest closet for the next couple of hours."

She laughs, wiping away a few stray tears. "I suppose I can be a bit much sometimes."

"Hmmm." I frown. "Lady Gaga can be a bit much sometimes. You're on another level." This receives a playful slap on the wrist. "That was deserved," I admit. "But what I'm trying to say is, you blew me away in your audition."

"Blew us all away." Morgan has come up behind me and lays a hand on my shoulder.

"And yes, the money from your dad is helpful," I admit. "But there was no chance after seeing you audition that we weren't going to cast you. So do me a favour?" She sits up a little straighter. "Ignore your dumbass brother. Ignore your parents. Ignore anyone who tries to pull you down. Put on your game face, Brianna Murray, and come and act the hell out of this scene."

"Listen to him, Bree," Cas says. He is now standing at my right shoulder, Morgan at my left. In this moment, we're a team again, pulling together. "You've done some amazing work these past few weeks. Everyone thinks so. Right, Morgan?"

Morgs nods, and for a second something passes between my two best friends. A gentle glance, a look of understanding.

Brianna studies her ex. "You mean that? You're not just saying it?"

"I'm saying it because it's true," Cas grunts. "Now let's get to work. We're wasting daylight."

29

"Great pep talk, maestro. You really got through to Brianna."

"Thanks, Louis," I say. "I appreciate that."

He snaps me a playful salute and heads off. Confidence restored, Bree has aced the scene and we've now set up for the big chase sequence. Leads and extras are all starting to take their positions across the junkyard, hitting their marks. Only a fortnight ago our *ZomHon* sets were chaos, extras not paying attention to where they ought to be, wandering around with phones in their hands, chewing gum, chattering. Now Cas, Morgan and I have whipped them into a focused, efficient unit. I can't help being a little proud.

Cas is with Morgan, Louis and Bree at the far end of a narrow avenue that cuts through mountains of scrap metal. He has the Steadicam strapped to his body so that he can capture all the action as they flee for their lives. Our married couple and hitchhiker are already in character, their faces drawn into expressions of panic and desperation, each hunched forward, ready to run when I call action. One of our older extras has experience of stunt work and so has managed to rig up some safety harnesses to which half a dozen hungry zombies are tethered. They reach down from high platforms of wood and steel that Tiny has bolted into place and made safe, their clutching hands casting spectacular shadows. Meanwhile, swarming behind our heroes, a terrifying mob of the undead is ready for the chase.

I stand with Stan Shannon beside the stationary high-def camera, mounted on a tripod at the mouth of the avenue. Through the monitor I can already see what an incredible scene this is going to make. But we need to capture it now, while we have the light.

"Ready?" I ask Stan.

He nods, pulling one headphone aside. "Those mutts are really making a racket, but I think I can work with it in the edit."

He's right. Echoing through the twisting maze of the junkyard, the furious howls of the guard dogs are enough to make even the most brain-dead zombie quake in their rags. I guess Dolly and Daphne aren't used to so many strangers invading their territory.

"Right then, let's do this thing." I pick up the clapperboard and snap it in front of the camera. "*Zombie Honeymoon*, scene one hundred and six, take one. And... Action!"

The chase begins.

It's only a thirty second segment. A quick flash of action in the sweep of our eighty-minute movie. But I think it will stick in the mind of the audience for a very long time. As I watch it play out before me, I know that in one take we have captured something special. Maybe even iconic. The brutal shafts and spires of scrap, rising like ruined skyscrapers; the avenue between them, an inky canyon full of dense, velvety shadow through which our heroes must scramble, the screeching horde at their backs. And the light! The light is stunning, throwing shards of sunset across the faces of the living and the dead.

"Cut!"

They come to a breathless halt just past the stationary camera. Cas, who has performed a miracle by racing alongside while keeping out of the main shot, looks up from the Steadicam viewer and beams. We don't need words. We've worked on so many films together that a look alone will do it. He's caught his own version of the scene and, spliced together with mine in the edit, it's going to take *ZomHon* to a whole new level.

"That was very special," Stan says, hooking his headphones around his neck and lightly punching my shoulder. "You've really got something here, you know?"

I smile back at him. "Thanks, Can Man." I then try to quieten down the excited chatter. Everyone is beaming at each other, even Morgan. They seem to know that we've caught a slice of cinematic magic, but the light is still good and no director worth his salt banks on one take. "Right, guys, thank you so much, but we need to get a couple more in the can, so please head back to your marks."

No one complains. They're all buzzing.

We manage another three takes before the sun deserts us. They're pretty good but nothing compared to the drama and urgency of that first. I call everyone over to view it on Stan's laptop and there is much whooping and high-fiving.

"Did you see me at the back?" Tiny bellows excitedly. "I was in frame for at least ten seconds. You couldn't miss me, right?"

"You're eighteen feet taller than any other zombie." Cas grins. "No one's gonna miss you, big fella."

"Fantastic work, JS." Róisín nods. "You've done my make-up proud."

"You've done us all proud," Brianna agrees, clutching both my hands in hers. "You know all these years we've been at school together and I never realized – you're actually a little bit of a genius, aren't you, Jesse Spark?"

When I try to tell them it was a team effort, Morgan cuts in. "If I were you, I'd take that compliment and run with it. It's not like Bree gives them out very often. In fact, I'd put it on the film poster – 'A little bit of a genius' from the lips of the one and only Brianna Murray."

Brianna laughs and throws her arm around Morgan's neck. Watching them, I can only laugh too. My best friend and the queen of Ferrivale High sharing a joke, who would have thought it?

Louis rocks his shoulder against mine. Just that little bump is enough to make my heart leap and a big smile spread across my face. "Bravo, maestro," he says. "Bravo."

And suddenly my smile slips as I see Cas's grin fall away.

"We're not done yet," I say, clapping my hands. "We need to get a couple of establishing drone shots of the junkyard, so if the zombies could start randomly milling around the place, that would be great. Remember, your motivation is yummy brains and where to get hold of them." As the extras immediately launch into a quick improv workshop about how to tackle this challenge (honestly, actors) and Cas begins setting up the drone, I go and find Tiny. He's standing outside his shed, smoking a rollie and looking up at the hazy night sky. "Hey, so I wanted to say thank you for everything. Letting us use the yard and...Tiny? Are you okay?"

His gaze remains fixed on the moonless sky, a glimmer or two now sparking against the bruised purple.

"Stars," he whispers. "They're mostly long gone, you know? Burned out millions of years ago. But we still see them, still reach for them." He turns and stubs out the cigarette against the shed door. The tip flares for a moment, like a dying star. "I'm not an idiot, Jesse. I know that some big Hollywood casting director isn't going to spot me in the background of your film and offer me a three-picture contract. I know I'm probably going to work here in this junkyard for the rest of my life. And that's fine. I get a good living out of it and that makes me luckier than most. But here's the thing – we all need a dream to cling to. Something bigger and brighter than our everyday lives. Something that still shines, even though in our heart of hearts we know it's impossible. We have to at least give it a shot, do you get me? We have to try."

I look over to where Louis stands, chatting animatedly with Brianna and Morgan.

"I think I do," I say. "Yeah."

"Hmm. Well, I best go see to my girls. Sounds like they're really spooked by all this activity, bless 'em." He stalks off into his kingdom of scrap, calling over his shoulder, "And no need to thank me, Jesse lad. It was my pleasure."

A dry night wind swirls the dust around my feet. I let my hand steal to my heart as I think of some words Brianna once said to me on the hillside leading to Morgan's house – *reach for those stars*.

"We have to give it a shot," I murmur to myself. "We have to try."

I take a deep breath and start walking towards Louis.

"Drone's all good to go," Cas says, stepping into my path. "I'll get Tiny to put on the security lights to light it up a bit. How many flyovers do you want?"

"What?" I blink at him.

"Drone?" He lifts the machine and waggles it in front of me. "Earth to Jesse. How many shots?"

"Oh, I don't know." I shake my head. "You decide."

Frowning, he turns and follows my gaze to where Louis stands, still chatting with his co-stars. "Well, I can see you're preoccupied with more important things," Cas says acidly. "So please, don't let me get in the way of your raging libido. I can get on with the less glamorous work while you trot off and have your fun. After all, I've had a lot of practice lately."

I stare at him. "What the hell is that supposed to mean?"

He turns back to face me, eyes narrowed. "Nothing much. Only that it's been the story of this whole production. Cas is given the second unit grunt jobs while you spend all your time with him."

"What time?" I fire back. "I haven't had a minute to myself. None of us have. We've been shooting and editing every second of every day. But you know what, Cas? I think I get what this is all about. The hospital, right? Okay then, do you really want me to tell you why I asked Louis instead of you?"

"Oh, I think I can guess why," he says with a bitter laugh.

I can feel the rage screaming up my spine, boiling under my skin. "Can you? Well then, you must know that—"

"Guys?" Morgan calls to us.

"Just give me a minute," I call back and refocus on Cas. "The reason I asked Louis is because this surgery is going to leave me with the biggest sc—"

"GUYS!"

"What?" we both shout in unison, heads flipping round to where Morgan is pointing towards the mouth of the avenue. And then, again in unison, "Oh shit."

One of Tiny's hellhounds has got loose and is galloping towards us. I know that dogs don't *literally* gallop, but this thing is the size of a pony. Zombies are already scattering, pulling themselves up onto piles of scrap, throwing themselves under old tin baths and into the cages of rusty shopping trolleys. Cas and I take one look at the slavering jaws bearing down on us and our argument is forgotten.

Hugging the drone to his chest with one hand, grabbing my sleeve with the other, Cas sprints off towards Tiny's shed. It's sweet that he's trying to save me, but there is one problem with his impromptu plan – I am built neither for coordination nor speed. We're halfway to the shed when I trip over some invisible obstacle and Cas's fingers slip from my shirt. By the time he realizes he's lost me, it's too late. My chin planted in the dirt, I glance up to see him reach the wooden door and spin around, a look of horror on his face.

"Go!" I shout at him. "Get inside!"

He shakes his head and looks like he's about to run back to rescue me. But that's madness. Cas is the most gifted cinematographer of his generation and I won't let him be mauled to death on my account.

I throw myself to the right, heading away from the shed and into another of the branching pathways of the junkyard. No need to check on the proximity of the hellhound, I felt the heat of its breath on my ankle as I scrabbled to my feet. I can hear Cas calling after me but his words are drowned out by a frustrated snap and snarl. I run as best I can, arms windmilling, legs doing their thing. I don't make it far. Because of course I've chosen not only the shortest avenue in the whole place but one that culminates in a dead end.

I turn, heart in my mouth.

"Nice doggy," I squeak. "Now listen, I know Tiny will be really pissed off if you eat me, so please give that some thought before you do anything rash."

The Dobermann is having none of it. A river of drool slides from its lower lip as it bows its head, ready to pounce.

And then suddenly I hear a metallic screech, and a strong hand grabs me, and I'm being dragged into the back seat of some derelict car. I land on my back as my rescuer slams the door shut, just as a pair of meaty paws hits the grimy window. We hear an outraged howl; the complaint of a pooch denied its chow. Catching my breath, I take in my surroundings – some old jalopy propped up on breeze blocks, engineless, half-gutted, left to rot. I'm only glad its doors and windows remain intact.

And then I look up into the face of the boy leaning over me.

"Oh hey, fancy meeting you here."

Louis smiles. "Close one, maestro. Are you okay?"

I nod. Take a breath.

Reach for those stars.

"Would you like to go to the club with me tonight?" I blurt out.

He frowns. "Sure. We're all going, aren't we? To see this singer who might write the music for the movie? Sounds fun."

"Absolutely. One hundred per cent. Fun." I agree. "But I was thinking…" I look up into that perfect face – the dark blue eyes, the cute, quizzical smile, the cheekbones – the *cheekbones*, for God's sake! – and shake my head. "Nothing. Just being silly."

"No, Jess, you were going to say something," he coaxes. "What?"

"Well, I—"

A meaty fist hammers the window and we both jump. "Sorry about that, lads," Tiny bellows from outside. "She got away from me for a second there. All safe now, though. You can come out."

"Did you hear that, Jesse?" Louis winks. "We can come out. Shall you tell him or shall I? Been there, Tiny, done that, got the sparkly rainbow T-shirt!"

"Yeah." I force a dry chuckle. "Hilarious."

An hour after narrowly avoiding being eaten alive by a junkyard hellhound, I'm ringing the Loomises' doorbell with the fixed determination that tonight will be the night. Finally. No ifs, no buts, no interruptions, no retreats, no misunderstandings. I'm going to ask Louis out. Just you wait and see.

Dean opens the door, right at the moment that I'm checking my armpits. I've just climbed six flights of stairs after all and it's a warm evening. I'm wearing my best jeans and a brand-new retro *Ghostbusters* tee. Which has nothing to do with Louis happening to mention the other day that the original film was his favourite eighties movie.

"Christ," Dean says, wafting a hand in front of his face and stepping into the communal hallway. "Did something die out here?"

"Very funny," I mutter.

"I'm serious," he says, following me into the flat and pretending to gag. "I should get onto the council about the drains. Or maybe one of the flats upstairs forgot to flush. Aw, no need to look at me like that, Jesse boy, I'm only joshing. You smell great. I can smell the Lynx Africa from here. But I gotta ask, are you seriously thinking of heading out to a club dressed like that? I get that you and Cas like your dorky stuff, and in his case I suppose it doesn't matter, but you must be the only gay boy I've ever met who has no fashion sense whatsoever. So come on, tell me, are you an outcast amongst your fellow homosexuals?"

I'm standing at the end of the hall, the lounge door in front of me, my fists clenched. Three years of this bullshit. Three grinding years of crap innuendos and cheap jokes. And I've put up with it, why? Because Dean Loomis is some big swaggering intimidating bully that I'm frightened to challenge? No. I've endured it on Cas's behalf. Because my best friend looks up to his brother. Because he thinks he owes Dean for keeping the family together after their mum left. Owes him undying, uncritical loyalty to the point where Cas compromises his opinions, his values, the essence of who he is, and all because he's grateful for something that any loving brother would have done.

Well, I don't owe Dean anything. And the way things are right now, I don't feel I owe Cas either. And so I turn around and ask, "What exactly is your problem with me, Dean?"

The stupid smug smile tightens. "What do you mean, Jesse b—?"

"I'm not a boy," I say, taking a step towards him. "I'm a man. An out and proud gay man. So please stop trying to belittle me."

"Well, if you can't take a joke."

He tries to saunter off down the hall, but I catch hold of his shoulder and turn him back to face me. "Sorry, I haven't finished speaking. Can you respect me enough to at least hear me out?"

He straightens up, puffs out his chest. "What have you got to say, then?"

It's funny, but my heart feels completely still for once. I'm not filled with pent-up rage; I'm not worried about what Cas will think of me talking to his brother like this; I'm not even bothered if Dean loses his rag and knocks me out. I let the words flow.

"Firstly, you don't have to answer my question. In fact, I'm not the slightest bit interested in what your problem is with me. Because it's *your* problem, not mine. So it can be rooted in your ridiculous machismo or some dumbass opinions you got off your friends or inherited from your family or society. It can be that you don't like me personally and have decided that my sexuality is a soft target. Or it could be that you are just a massive dickhead and this is how you express it. To be honest, I don't care and I never have. But what irritates the *fuck* out of me is the impact it has on your brother. You don't seem to care that, every time you insult me, Cas dies a little inside. Because you know what, Dean? He wants nothing more than to turn around and tell you to shut the hell up. He wants to stick up for his best friend. But because for some reason you're his hero, he lets it slide, even though he thinks what you say hurts me. It doesn't." I shrug. "You fail every time. It doesn't hurt *me* in the slightest."

Dean's eyes flicker. His jaw clenches. He looks away, starts to laugh, a harsh, bitter sound. Then stops abruptly.

"What I am bothered about," I continue, determined to get through this, "and you should be bothered too, if you really love him, is that it hurts Cas. It hurts him so much."

He looks back at me then, a sort of defiance in his eyes. Anger there, but something else too. Something I can't quite interpret. "Not sure why you think you have the right to talk to me like this," he mutters. "In my own home."

"I have the right, Dean," I tell him. "Believe me."

I turn to the lounge door, reaching for the handle.

"Jesse?"

Here it comes. "What?"

When he doesn't answer I glance over my shoulder. He seems somehow smaller. Diminished, deflated.

"I didn't… I mean, I don't know what to…"

The pause seems to go on for an eternity. He looks down at his hands, staring at them as if they're a stranger's. Then he grabs his jacket from the hook by the door and heads out of the flat. I look at the empty coat peg for a while, wondering if I should go after him. He seemed so…not shaken exactly. I don't know. Whatever his faults, and there are many, Dean has looked after Cas and their grandmother all these years, probably sacrificing things in the process that I have no idea about. But then even if I did manage to catch up with him, what could I say? Dean and I are such different people.

Head still full of questions, I push open the lounge door.

"Who is it? Who's there?"

"It's all right, Nanna," I say soothingly. "It's only me. It's Jesse."

The frightened frown slowly evens out and Nanna Laura gives me a shaky smile. "My little Jesse angel. Come here, let me look at you."

I kneel beside her chair and she folds my hand into hers. "How are you feeling today, Nanna?"

"Old. Old and useless." She sighs and sits back, fumbling at the buttons of her cardigan. She's wearing a little pewter pendant today; a gift Cas and I chipped in to buy her on a school trip to the Tower of London. I don't know why, but the sight of it brings a lump to my throat. "Is it breakfast time yet?" she asks, glancing over her chairback to the darkened kitchen. "Not that I'm hungry. Don't ever seem hungry these days."

"It's suppertime," I say, stroking the back of her hand. "Your carer will be here soon and she can get you a snack before bed. Or I can rustle you up something now if you like? Toast and raspberry jam? Your favourite?"

"Not hungry," she says. "Anyway, sweetheart, you'll get your nice clean clothes all mucky. I know you and jam of old. It'll be everywhere except on the toast."

She reaches out and ruffles my curls, just like Cas used to.

"Was that one of the boys I heard out in the hallway?" she asks. "Dean or Casper. Or the other one. I get their voices mixed up a bit these days."

I look up at her, the woman who has been almost as much of a grandmother to me as to my best friend. Who has known me since for ever and who knows me still, despite the darkness nibbling at her.

"It was Dean," I tell her softly. "He's gone for a walk, I think."

She nods, her voice unsteady. "He's not all bad, you know? He tries. He tries…"

I open my mouth to say something when Nanna's night carer comes bustling into the room, full of gentle questions and good humour. I say goodnight to them both and start down the corridor towards Louis's room. I'd thought I would find either him or Cas with Nanna in the lounge. We'd agreed that I'd meet them here before we all went onto the club. Maybe they're still getting ready.

I smooth down my *Ghostbusters* tee, and knock. "Louis, it's Jess. Are you ready?"

No answer. Opening the door, I find Cas hunched over the camp bed. He has something in his hands – Louis's notebook. I recognize it from on the set. The journal he sometimes brings out to jot notes in between takes; the one that contains all his ideas for the one-man play he's been working on.

"Oh, hi, Sparky. I think he's popped down to the garage to get some gum. Or something. I was just in here tidying up a bit…" The colour is high in his cheeks. He looks both guilty and defiant. He drops the notebook onto the bed and smooths down the duvet before turning back to me. "You know what? I think maybe you should see…" He presses his lips together and shakes his head. "No, forget it."

"Cas," I murmur. "What are you doing? What's going on?"

He hesitates, licks his lips. "The film. It's going really well, isn't it?"

"Yes." I nod. "But—"

"Really well. One last project together." He passes a hand over his brow. "You know something, Sparky?"

"What?"

"Once we've got this thing cut and edited and ready to screen, I don't think there'll be a film school in the world that would turn you away. *ZomHon* is your calling card. It's the beginning for you. Of everything." He takes one last look back into the room before closing the door. "Come on, let's get out of here."

The music hits us the moment we step inside the club. There's just no mistaking Dancing for the Super Worm. Their sound is woven through every drumbeat and guitar lick, an individuality captured by the stunning voice of their lead singer, Caleb Rush. He's onstage now, a commanding presence in black leather jacket, cut-off denim shorts, fishnet shirt and thigh-high zipper boots. It seems that his worries about no one showing up were unfounded; Hinchcliffes is heaving, the dancefloor rammed with bodies.

Caleb has the crowd eating out of his hand. He's belting out a tune called "Wranglestone", hitting an insane high note that makes the place erupt. Even the staff behind the bar give it some love, whistling and holding up their hands in praise.

"Wow," I call to Louis and Cas over the roar. "He really is something."

Louis nods. He's dancing on the spot, already lost in the

music. Meanwhile Cas stands to one side, arms folded, eyes fixed on the stage. After a goodnight kiss for Nanna Laura, he'd led me out of the flat, down the stairs and across the road to the all-night garage at a breakneck pace. We'd met Louis on the forecourt, who seemed his usual self, catching us both in a hug and saying how excited he was for the night ahead. I watched Cas stiffen like a board. He's barely said a word since.

What the hell was he doing with that notebook back in Louis's room?

"Hey, you guys! Over here!" Brianna waves at us from the bar area. She's in a group with Morgan, Róisín, Stan and some of our zombie extras, all sipping very sickly-looking virgin cocktails. Cas starts heading over while I gently shake Louis out of his dance reverie.

"Huh?" He blinks those enormous blue eyes at me. "Oh, sorry. I was away with the fairies for a second there."

I can almost hear the snide Dean joke in my head. Except... I don't know; I'm not sure he would have said anything at all. Not now. The image of Cas's brother in the hallway comes back to me, a figure somehow diminished.

"How very *diva* of you to turn up after everyone else has arrived," Bree scolds. She leans in to kiss me on both cheeks. Close up, I think I can smell a whiff of rum in the cocktail she's holding. She confirms my suspicion by leaning in again and whispering, "My cousin works here.

If you fancy a real drink, 's no problemo."

"Best not," I say, patting my chest. "You know, with the whole operation thing coming up."

Thrusting her glass into Morgan's hands, Brianna grapples me into the fiercest hug I've ever endured. "That's right. You poor darling…um…" She looks up from my neck, clicking her fingers at Louis. "What is that cute thing you keep calling him? Something Italian? Pinocchio? Magneto?"

"That's an *X-Men* villain," Stan mutters.

"Maestro," Louis volunteers.

"Maestro!" Brianna says triumphantly, as if it was her invention all along. "You poor little maestro. But I want you to know that we are friends now, and when your crappy heart is all fixed up, I'm going to visit and take care of you and give you the biggest makeover. Because honestly, darl? Those eyebrows really need some attention."

"Um. Thanks?" I say, suddenly very self-conscious.

"Hush," she commands, releasing me from the hug. "You are super adorable and you deserve it. But promise me one thing, yes? All of you?"

Everyone gives her their word, although most look a little nervous. With Brianna we could be promising her just about anything.

"Whatever happens after the last day of filming tomorrow, you won't ever think badly of me. Because I have really tried to earn my place here. I've gone home every night and rehearsed my lines over and over. I've taken this whole thing more seriously than anything in my entire life. Morgan can tell you. And Louis. And even Cas, I think." She gives him this almost pleading look; in response he offers her a reluctant nod. "However it started, I want you to remember that I really did give this film my all."

And with that she weaves back to the bar and places another order.

"That was…weird," I say to Cas.

He shrugs. "That was Bree."

"Do you think she'll be okay for filming tomorrow?"

"She'll be fine." His gaze strays back to his ex. "I think she's still stressed about Ethan showing up on-set today. Everybody thinks Bree has this perfect life, but I've been around her family. Believe me, toxic doesn't even begin to cover it."

Caleb has started a new number and we all turn back to the stage. The performance is as captivating as before, but I find my attention drifting now and then to Morgan. She stands gripping the handrail that leads down to the sunken dancefloor. She looks distracted, far away. And then suddenly she's back in the room, focused on the swaying bodies below. She lets go of the rail, almost snatching her hands back as if the bar is hot to the touch, and folds her arms tight across her chest.

"Jesse! I've been meaning to ask you something." Louis grabs my hand, snagging my attention with an uncharacteristically nervous smile. "I think it's time."

"Time?" I echo. My throat feels very dry. "For what?"

He frames my face between his palms, his eyes locked on mine. "Promise you'll be gentle with me?" All I can do is nod. Then suddenly he's flourishing his phone and laughing. "I'm going to ping you over the script for my play. It's finally ready and I want you to give me your honest opinion, okay?" His fingers flash across the screen and the mobile in my pocket chirrups. "There." He sighs. "You have my heart. Now, let's dance!"

"Oh no, that's really not a good idea," I say. "Anyway, I should go talk to Mor—"

"Talk to her later. I need to see your moves, maestro!"

"My what?" We're halfway down the steps, Louis already snaking his hips as we descend into this grooving, grinding alien world. "But I don't have moves. Seriously, can't I just watch?"

"No. You may not."

Louis has not only guided me onto the dancefloor, he has somehow managed to clear a space for us right in the middle. It's amazing really, how the other kids fall back and make room. They're either dying to see this gorgeous boy in action or else staggered by his choice of dance partner. Probably both. I can certainly see a few raised eyebrows and whispers being exchanged. I swallow hard as he plants his forearms on my shoulders and starts swaying to the beat.

"You can't go through your whole life watching," he says. "Sometimes you have to step into the movie and play a part."

He links his fingers behind my neck and pulls me close. "Whatever it takes, you have to claw your way up onto that screen and once you're there? Make sure you stay there. Now, come on, show me what you've got."

Lights spin and pulse from the ceiling, washing across the crowd that has loosely gathered around us. I can see the curiosity in their faces, the anticipation, the mockery, the disbelief. Or am I imagining it? Are they really watching us or is it only the paranoia in my head? That mean little voice that insists, *He will never want you. Not now. Not later. Not ever.* But another voice now answers back, *He's just given you his script. His heart. That has to mean something, right?* From the stage, the music swells, Caleb crooning along to some upbeat love song.

I reach out. Louis's eyes are closed, his head thrown back. I can feel my palms brush against his hips. I step closer and—

"Thank you, guys! That's the end of our first set, but we'll be back with more very soon. In the meantime, the DJ has some classic bangers lined up for you."

Louis opens his eyes and I immediately plant my hands at my sides. He blinks over at the stage and pouts as the band strides off into the wings.

"Oh that sucks. And I was just about to see your—"

"Moves, yes. Oh well, maybe next time."

He winks. "I will hold you to that… But, wait. Britney!"

A cheer goes up as the pop icon's "Till the World Ends" starts booming through the speakers. Louis tries to keep me on the floor but I tell him I need a breather (which is pretty laughable as I have yet to bust a single move) and head back through the throng towards the bar, cursing myself the whole way. *Why is this so hard?*

Over in a corner I spy Cas and Morgan. It's rare to see them together these days, let alone talking, but even before I get within earshot, I can tell this isn't a happy conversation.

"What you need to do is stop trying to interfere. I'm serious, Cas. You made your decision and now you have to live with it. I've done what I can to help you out, even though I still think you're a fucking idiot, but I won't sit back and watch you ruin this for him. I won't."

"I'm not trying to ruin anything, Morgan. It's not about me."

"Of course it's about you. Right from the beginning, this whole thing—"

"I want him to be happy. But not like this."

"And why not? Answer me that."

"What's going on here, guys?" They both spin around to face me.

"Sparky." Cas gasps. "I thought you were dancing."

I look from one to the other. They both appear startled and at a loss as to what to say. I've had about enough of this – the silence, the secrets. I'm ready to start tearing into them with questions that will make the Spanish Inquisition seem like a friendly pub quiz when the lead singer of Dancing for the Super Worm taps Cas on the shoulder. Morgan immediately sees her chance to escape, making a beeline for the gang at the bar.

"Caleb." Cas grins, looking like a man who has just been saved from drowning. "That was amazing. I mean it. Just incredible. Oh, this is Jesse, by the way. Our director."

Offstage, the strutting lead singer is a very different personality, replaced by a shy, softly-spoken guy who finds it difficult to maintain eye contact.

"How lovely to meet you," he says, shaking my hand. "I'm such a big fan. The footage Cas showed me the other day? There's a real raw power there. To be honest, I can't believe you'd even consider having me onboard to write the score." He blushes. "Although I suppose I'm getting ahead of myself."

I stare at him. "Are you kidding? I was about to get down on my knees and beg you to let us use your music."

His blush becomes bright crimson. "Really? I mean,

I obviously put a lot of work into my stuff, but it's not *that* good."

"It's not good," Cas says. "It's freaking spectacular."

Caleb breaks out into this adorable nervous laughter and his blush goes into hyperdrive.

"So can we say you're our composer?" I ask.

"On one condition." He nods. "You use my latest song in the movie. I wrote it last night and I'm going to play it in the next set. I hope you'll like it."

I can tell Cas wants Caleb to stick around but the singer says he's needed backstage and scoots off. But my best friend needn't have worried. There's already another little drama unfolding to keep me from questioning him about his row with Morgan.

"I love you guys so much!" Brianna squeals, throwing her arms around Morgan and Róisín and spilling her latest drink in the process. "You're my fam. My crew. We're sisters now, right?" She glances blearily at Stan. "And brothers. No. I mean, you're the brother and I'm the sister. Or whatever. Anyway. Selfies! We have to have lots of selfies tonight. Everyone squeeze in, squeeze in. You too, Casper and Jesse. Or no. Wait, I want one just with me and Morgs."

"No," Morgan says bluntly, wiping the rum and Coke from her denim jacket. "Thank you."

"But you must," Brianna insists. She drops her glass onto the bar and, by some miracle, it stays upright. "C'mon, it'll be fun. I'll show you this great new filter I just downloaded. It makes your skin sparkle."

Morgan shrugs Brianna's arm from her shoulder. "I said, no."

"But we'll look *so* cute together." Bree pouts. "You have such gorgeous eyes, Morgs. They really light up when you smile. And your figure is so now. *Fssst!* You are hot, girl. So stop being a moody-bum and get in this selfie."

"No." She again pushes Brianna's arm away. "Please, stop."

"But I want you to."

"Well, I don't."

"But why?" Once more, the attempt to drape her arm around Morgan's shoulder. Once more the rebuff. "You're being so mean to me when all I want to do is—"

"Jesus Christ, will you fucking *listen*," Morgan explodes. "I don't look *cute*, okay? I don't have gorgeous eyes and a nice figure, so stop bloody patronizing me. I know for a fact there isn't a filter in the world that can make me look acceptable."

"That's not true," Brianna says in a stunned voice. "I mean, you don't need filters at all. Morgs, you're stunning. How many times do I have to keep saying it for you to believe me?"

"Oh, but I did believe you," Morgan says. "Or at least I started to. All those compliments and kind words on-set and in rehearsals, they almost had me fooled."

"I wasn't trying to fool you," Bree insists. "You've given me so much, Morgan. I only wanted you to see what I see. What we all see."

"And I was stupid enough to believe you." Morgs nods. "Stupid enough to believe the lie. That I was in some way okay-looking. When the truth is simple – I'm ugly. Fat and lumpy and ugly." She states it as though it was a matter of unquestionable fact. "And you don't have to take my word for it. That's the view of the biggest casting directors in Hollywood. So yeah, it's fucking official, all right?"

32

"Morgs, what's going on?" I ask.

She is calmer now, though her eyes are red with tears she hasn't let fall.

We've left Hinchcliffes and ducked into the alleyway that runs between the club and the takeaway next door. It's still relatively early so there are no ravenous clubbers queueing outside for their fast-food fix just yet. In fact, aside from the heaps of garbage bags stacked against one wall, we have the alley pretty much to ourselves. I notice in passing how Cas steps carefully over a greenish spill oozing from one split bag. It seems that, despite snogging Matilda behind the bins at prom, his phobia is still a thing.

"Do you remember the script I was reading when you came by a couple of weeks ago?" Morgan asks me. "The day I introduced you to Róisín?"

Brianna and Cas glance over at me. Stan, Róisín and the others have all stayed upstairs, probably not wanting to intrude after what was clearly a difficult moment for

Morgan. Last I looked, Louis had still been on the dancefloor, oblivious to the drama that had just unfolded at the bar.

"Sure," I say. "I teased you about cheating on me with other directors."

Morgan nods. "You said you were happy for me to be seeing other creatives. Well, that's just what I've done. You guys have heard of *The Marsha Rivera Chronicles*, right?"

Brianna stirs. Morgan's outburst in the club appears to have sobered her up. "That trilogy about the British witch who's sent to a sorcery college in LA? My mum loves those books. She says she identifies with the main character on some deep level, though honestly, I think she's having a midlife crisis." Her eyes go wide. "Wait, aren't they about to make the movie version? It's been all over my socials for months. The producers said they were looking for an unknown to star as the lead."

"I downloaded a leaked script off the internet," Morgan says. "That's what I was reading when you arrived, Jess. Thought I'd try to get a head start on the other Marsha hopefuls. Rehearse, prepare, get myself in character. All the usual nonsense."

Suddenly it clicks. I knew Morgan would never have deserted *ZomHon* over anything as trivial as some show she wanted to see. It had to be more serious than that. And then I remember being in the changing cubicle at the hospital, scrolling through my news feed as I waited to be called in for the angiogram. A story about auditions taking place in London for some big fantasy movie.

"Why didn't you tell us?" I ask. "I had my procedure, but I'm sure Cas would have come down with you. Supported you on the day."

Cas nods.

"And me," Brianna says quietly, trying to catch hold of Morgan's hand. "You've helped me so much recently, of course I'd have been there to cheer you on."

Morgs shakes her head. "Don't any of you get it? Cas, Jess? This stupid mission of yours to boost my confidence, to reassure me? It's typically sweet and considerate of you, and also typically moronic. The more that you guys insist that my issues about how I look are all in my head, that I'm in fact this gorgeous leading lady, the more my brain screams, *But they're your friends, of course they're going to say that. It's their job.*"

"But you are beautiful," I say. "You should see yourself the way we see you, up onscreen. Strong and powerful and captivating."

"Listen to him," Cas agrees. "It's true."

She gives us both a sad little smile. "But you love me, don't you?"

"Of course we do," I say.

"Always have, always will," Cas confirms.

"And because you love me, I don't believe you." Morgan nods. "I'm sorry, but I'll always think of them as kind words, nothing more."

"Well, I'm not your best friend," Bree says with a sassy click of her fingers. "In fact, up until quite recently, I didn't even like you very much. So you can rely on my unbiased judgement that you, Miss Adeyemi-Perera, are a fierce, stunning woman, and it will be my pleasure to kick the arse of anyone who says different."

Morgan shakes her head. "Thank you, Bree. And you know something? You *have* been making me feel better about myself recently. I started to believe all your kind comments because you *weren't* my friend and had no reason to simply be nice to me. But there's one problem with that now – we have grown close these past few weeks and so, like with Jesse and Cas, I'm starting to think it's all just kindness. But let me say right here and now, I'm sorry for having a go at you in the club. It wasn't fair to take this all out on you."

"So you don't believe me any more when I tell you you're absolutely bloody gorgeous?" When Morgan shrugs Brianna throws out her hands. "There is just no convincing this girl."

"There isn't," Morgan agrees. "And that isn't your fault. The problem is, I can't dig seventeen years of comments and criticisms out of my head just to make you all feel better. If I could, I'd do it for myself too."

"You mean your mum?" I say.

"Yes, but not only her. It's everything. Society, culture, social media. A constant noise telling us all we're not good enough."

"And people like me, too?" Brianna says thoughtfully. "I'm part of that noise too."

"People like you *used* to be, maybe," Morgan admits. "And so I tried to pretend it didn't bother me. That it was all ridiculous, superficial nonsense. And it *is*. What I told you the other day is true, Jess. I'm not interested in those flimsy lead roles where girls are only expected to stand there and look pretty and say five lines for every dozen given to the men. I'm a character actor. I want my *work* to matter, not how I look. But still there's that voice needling in the back of my brain, insisting over and over – fat, fat, fat; ugly, ugly, ugly."

My hand steals to my chest. I know that voice. I've heard it too. I should say something, admit to the fear that's eating me up inside. Tell Morgan that she isn't alone in feeling this way.

"But admitting that I listen to that voice?" she goes on. "Never. I'm Morgan Adeyemi-Perera. I'm stoical, strong. I don't give a fuck about such things. Except when I do."

I look at my best friend. She is clearly upset, her hands shaking a little, her eyes so raw with the tears she refuses to let fall. Yet her voice is calm, controlled, her words smooth and articulate. This is and always has been Morgan. Always able to calmly analyse anything and anyone, even herself.

"Do you want to talk about what happened in London?" Cas asks gently. "You don't have to."

"There isn't much to tell." She shrugs. "In fact, when I look back on it, the whole thing is a bit banal and pathetic. I heard about the open auditions through a friend I went to drama camp with last year. I'd read the *Marsha Rivera* books and enjoyed them – a fun, inclusive take on a witchcraft story. Gay witches, Black witches, trans and non-binary witches, all proudly standing together against evil, hateful enemies. Only it seems no one told the producers that. Anyway, I didn't tell anyone what I was doing, just caught the train to the auditions by myself. I wasn't even particularly nervous waiting to go in, though I did notice that most of the kids being put through to the next round looked very similar. All skinny with great figures and flawless skin.

"Finally, I was called in. I thought I did pretty well, right up until the Q&A with the casting director and her team. They didn't ask me a single thing about my take on the character or my acting experience. It was all about how I looked. Oh, they were careful how they phrased it, of course. You can't just come out and call people a fat freak any more. It was all little hints like, *if we asked you back, we would like you to consider how Marsha is described in the books and if you can do something about that? You know, a petite girl who is good at sports and takes her health seriously. Something to think about."*

"That is *not* how Marsha is in the books," Brianna says, her face like thunder. "What did you tell them?"

"I told them to fuck off."

"No!" Bree beams.

"No. I didn't. I thanked them very politely for their notes on my performance and I left. Got straight back on the train where I…" She takes a long breath. "Where I phoned my mum and told her I needed her help. To lose some weight, to change myself."

"Oh, Morgan," I sigh.

"Don't worry. By the time I got home, I'd come to my senses. Told her what she could do with her diet and exercise regime. She went into meltdown, of course. Kept going on about me ruining my chances."

"Such bullshit," Cas mutters.

"Maybe, maybe not. But the prejudice of those producers? That isn't my problem. That's what I tell myself anyway, and most of the time I believe it. I can only do my best work and let that stand for itself. That's what I should be judged on and that's what I believe. It really is. But still that voice inside my head?" She shrugs. "It's something I need to work on, maybe even speak to someone about, I don't know."

None of us really know what to say. Morgan says she's tired but that she's okay and will see us tomorrow for the last day of shooting. We walk her to the cab rank where she promises to message Brianna once she's safely home. We all give her a hug and while Cas and Bree head back into the club, I linger as the next taxi pulls up to the kerb.

"I'm sorry you didn't feel you could talk to us about any of this," I say. "And I'm sorry about our stupid mission too. We thought we were helping."

She pauses, one foot inside the taxi, the other planted on the pavement. "It's not your fault. You were only doing your best for me. You always have." She then does a very un-Morgan thing. She takes my face in her hands and gently kisses my forehead. "Go be happy, Jesse. You deserve it more than anyone I know."

I watch until the cab vanishes around the corner, my own secret still held fast in my failing heart. *I hear the voice too, Morgs. Every day.* But it is easier to reassure a friend than reassure yourself.

I show the bouncer my wristband and wander back into the club. So many thoughts in my head – anger at how Morgan was treated at the audition; the ways in which we, her friends, have tried to help and yet ultimately failed her; how my own newfound issues about my appearance mirror so much of what she has been feeling about herself; the expectations that are placed upon us, and those we place upon ourselves, to achieve some absurd "ideal". I tell myself how hollow it all is. How ridiculous. How meaningless.

And yet.

And yet when I see Louis on that dancefloor – stunning, beautiful, perfect Louis – all these rational thoughts fly away. I have only days now. Hours before Dr Myers's life-saving scalpel transforms me into something unwanted. And so I move slowly across the club, ignoring Brianna, who calls to me from the bar. Sidestepping Cas, who tries to start up a conversation about tomorrow's shoot.

Reach for those stars.

I drift down the steps to the dancefloor.

Go be happy.

I squeeze my way through the dancers. They don't part as easily for me as they did for Louis, but bit by bit I make my way towards him.

He shines. He glows. So beautiful.

"Okay, ladies and gentlemen, here is our brand-new song – 'An Undying Heart' – played for the first time tonight. It goes out to Jesse Spark and Casper Loomis. I hope you like it, boys!"

Louis has turned to face the stage, where Caleb is swaying gently to the opening bars of a sweet, melodic tune, hands gripping the microphone.

"It's only love; Not the end of all things; Not a world torn apart..."

I press my hand against my chest. Brush my fingers against Louis's arm.

"*Only love; Just a crack in your soul; An unmade work of art…*"

At my touch, he spins around, beaming, full of joy.

I smile.

"*Only love; And what's love, after all?*"

Open my mouth to speak. To say the words.

At last.

Just say them.

"*To an undying heart?*"

"Jesse!" He throws his arms around me, hugs me tight. "Where have you been? I've got such exciting news. Guess what?"

"Louis, I wanted to ask you—"

"I've asked Caleb out on a date!" he cries. "Isn't that exciting? I wanted you to be the first to know. He's so clever and handsome, and I'd never have met him without you. It's like you're my lucky charm. Ever since I came to Ferrivale, you've been there, bringing me all these blessings." He steps back, holding me at arm's length, those denim-blue eyes sparkling in the strobing light. "My sweet maestro. Anyway, what did you want to ask me?"

I look past his shoulder, to the gorgeous lead singer. And of course they belong together.

They're perfect.

"Nothing," I say. "It doesn't matter any more."
"*Let it burn; Let it fall; Let the hungry darkness have it all;*
Make it stop before it starts;
Quiet this undying heart."

"Ten minutes earlier. Just ten minutes and…"

And what? I stare at the image on the wall opposite my bed. That stupid *Freddy vs Jason* poster. I remember lying here weeks ago, talking to myself, coming up with my hopeless mission. Find a summer boyfriend. Experience one brief moment of connection, of touch, of intimacy, of love even, before the surgery made all that impossible. Part of me knew how laughable it was, even back then. The truth is, no boy has ever expressed any interest in me. The sum total of my romantic experiences consists of kissing a cute classmate in a closet at Julia Odili's birthday party and then getting an erection that everyone laughed about afterwards. Ha ha ha. That's Jesse Spark. Not unattractive exactly (well, not yet), just a bit plain and pathetic.

And you expected me to ask Louis out and for him to say yes? Ha ha ha ha ha ha ha! *Please*. Dragging my heels was self-preservation; a way to delay the inevitable. I only thank my lucky stars for Caleb Rush. Imagine the scene if he hadn't been there tonight – the unbearable look of pity on Louis's face, the agonized contortions as he tried to come up with some excuse.

"Oh, Jess, I'm flattered you'd even consider asking me, because you're such a very special guy. But the truth is, I couldn't ever think of you in that way. Please don't say this has ruined our friendship, though, because that's the most important thing in the world to me."

Blah blah blah.

A lucky escape. For both of us.

I hear the click of the front door downstairs. It's not Mum. She was already in bed when I got home, though she shuffled out into the hall in dressing gown and slippers when she heard me come in.

"Did you have a good night, love?" she'd asked.

"Fabulous. You know me and nightclubs."

I don't think there was anything particular in my tone, but still she stopped me at my door. "Jesse bear. What's the matter?"

"Nothing at all," I told her. "The world is exactly as it should be."

She held my gaze for a long time. I didn't feel even a prickle of tears.

I'd done all my crying on the long walk home.

"I wish you'd talk to me," she said at last.

"We don't talk," I reminded her. "It works for us."

"Jesse, please—"

"Fine. You first then," I snapped. "Why don't you tell me about my dad? Why don't you explain why we never talk about *him*? He can't have been a bad guy because you keep his picture up on the windowsill downstairs. But whenever I mention his name there's always some excuse to avoid the subject. So what's going on, eh, Mum? What's the big mystery?"

I'd chosen the subject deliberately. It was my mum's one weak point. I was hurting badly and wanted to hurt in return. It makes me sick to think of it now.

Mum had shaken her head and turned back down the hall, slippers shushing on the carpet. "Goodnight, love, sleep well."

So no, it's not Mum opening the front door and padding softly up the stairs. There's only two people it could be. They've both had their own house keys since for ever, basically because they're family. Or they were. Now? I don't know what we are to each other. Everything is so jumbled and confused in my mind. All I'm certain of in this moment is that it isn't Morgan tapping at my door.

"Sparky? You awake?"

I sigh and move over to the door, resting my head against the wood. "What are you doing here, Cas?"

"I wanted to check you were okay," he says. "That's all."

"It's past midnight," I mutter back. "Why didn't you just call or message me?"

"I don't know. I felt like I should see you. And… Look, can I come in? I won't stay long."

I pull up the front of my T-shirt, use it to wipe my eyes. Then I open the door and let him in. He looks tired, as if he hasn't slept in days. We exchange muted "Hey"s and he goes to stand at the diorama table while I return to the bed, pressing my hands between my knees. I can see him out of the corner of my eye, gripping the table edge, his gaze playing across all those miniature movie scenes we constructed together.

"So I heard Louis asked Caleb out on a date," he says.

"Really?" I fall back onto the bed. "Good for Louis."

"Jesse, come on." He sighs.

"Cas, don't."

"I know you like him."

"And I know you know," I say, trying to keep the edge out of my voice. "That was what you were arguing about with Morgan in the club tonight, wasn't it? And why you've been so weird with him ever since he arrived. It wasn't only because you think his side of the family looks down on yours. It's because you saw that comment he left on your Instagram. The one under my photo. *Looking good, Emerald Eyes.*" I can't help laughing. "It's just his way, Cas. He's a nice guy and he likes to make people feel good about themselves. Despite what you might think, that's not a bad thing. But it didn't mean anything. I know that now."

"Jesse, just listen…" he begins.

But I'm not in a listening mood. I want to tell Cas what I think and then I want him to fuck right off.

"*Stop trying to interfere, Cas. I won't sit back and watch you ruin this for him.* That's what Morgan said tonight, and finally it makes sense. You wanted to ruin things between me and Louis. That's why you've been so negative about him all this time. Because you and me were drifting apart and you were jealous of the friendship I was developing with your cousin." I shake my head. "Well, I guess I can understand that. For years it's been the three of us, right? You, me and Morgs, facing the world together. It worried me too, that one of us would get left behind one day. But you know what? Your anxiety over Louis taking your best buddy spot isn't my fault. It's yours. Yours and Morgan's."

"Sparky, please."

"No, Cas. No. I'm done. You made me promise to stop asking questions about all this fucking weirdness that's been going on since prom, and I've respected that. But that promise comes with consequences. Things have changed between us, really changed, I see that now. And I don't think they will ever change back."

I sit up and look at him. In the light thrown by the streetlamp outside, I can see misery stamped on his face.

"What is it, Cas?" I say, hoping against hope that he will tell me. Finally, just tell me. "What happened to us?"

He opens his mouth, swallows, closes it again.

"Well then," I say. "I think we should call it a night. I'm really tired and we've got a big day tomorrow."

"Our last shooting day." He nods, and turns towards the door. He pauses there, his back to me. "He doesn't deserve you, Jess."

"Really? So is that why you were in his room tonight?" I ask. "Reading his notebook? Trying to find something to use against him? To prove that he's unworthy of me? So go on, what did you find?"

"I wasn't…" He takes a breath. "Nothing."

"Doesn't deserve me." I laugh. "Louis is so far beyond what I deserve it isn't even funny."

"Don't say that," he murmurs. "Don't ever."

"Why not? It's true." I can feel the anger surging through me, a rage so bright it obliterates any pity I might feel for him. "Cas, do you even know what you've tried to ruin for me? Do you have any idea?"

When he shakes his head, I go to my desk, rummaging in a drawer and pulling out Dr Myers's third sketch. The incision diagram.

"Ever since I found out about my surgery, I knew this was coming." I pass him the sketch. "Gonna look pretty, isn't it?"

He takes a look, folds the paper, hands it back to me. "It'll still be you."

"Don't be so naïve." I almost sneer. "Morgan was right in what she said tonight. Everyone judges by appearance, that's the way the world is. And I can't dig that little voice out of my head any more than she can. The only difference is, Morgan *is* beautiful. She always has been and she always will be. But do you *seriously* think any boy will look twice at me after I go through *this*?" I open the drawing again, make him look at it. "Can you see what this is, Cas? Can you imagine it? They're going to saw open my chest and then wire me back together again. They're going to cut me and stitch me and mutilate me to save my life. Do you think anyone will want to touch me after that? To be with me? To kiss me, hold me, have sex with me when they see how I've been left? This monster they've made me into." I throw the drawing into his face. "This ugliness."

"Yes," he says simply. "Of course they will."

But I'm not listening any more. "That's why I wanted to get close to Louis. To try. To just *try* and see if I could make a connection before it was too late. And you, my best friend, with all your hostility, you did your best to stop that from happening."

He's crying, one hand grasping the front of his shirt as if he might reach inside and pull out his own heart. "I'm so sorry, Jesse. I'm so sorry. I didn't know what else to do. If I could, I'd go back and do it all differently. If I could. If I…"

I want to comfort him. He's been my friend since for ever.

My soulmate. My Cas. But he's been so secretive, so closed off, and I can't. Not any more.

It's too late now.

After tomorrow, we're done.

34

"The world is ending. We know that now, all of us. We have fought hard, tried to deny the reality closing in around us, but everything we've known and loved and cherished is being ripped away. There's nothing left. Nothing to hope for. Nothing to cling onto. Except maybe…"

I look up onto the porch of the old Lester house, to the two figures standing there, side by side, strong and defiant.

"Each other."

Cas snaps the clapperboard in front of the camera.

"*Zombie Honeymoon*, scene one hundred and ninety-six. Take one. And… Action."

As if on cue, thunder rumbles through the neon-pink clouds that lower over the old house. The first spots of rain we've seen in weeks begin to patter at the boarded windows as the wind picks up, raking ancient autumn leaves out of the gutters and scattering them at the feet of our zombies. Brianna the wife takes Morgan the hitchhiker's hand. Together, they raise their makeshift junkyard weapons into the air. They were nameless in the script but this is how I think of my characters now, imbued with the spirit of the actors who have brought them to life. They share a glance, a look of fateful understanding. They know their time is up. They cannot win against the relentless monsters that surround them. They have both sacrificed so much, and in those shared sacrifices they have come to know each other.

"Ready?" asks the hitchhiker.

The wife smiles. "Ready."

Their hands part. They scream their defiance to the storm. And rush to meet their fate.

We see the undead horde swarm around them, a frenzy of rotten limbs. But no blood, no violence, no screams of pain. Only a curtain of silver rain closing over our heroes.

"Cut!" I shout. "Thank you, everybody. That is a wrap on *Zombie Honeymoon*."

It isn't like that triumphant moment after we captured the escape scene at the junkyard. Even though these closing shots couldn't have worked out better if we'd planned the storm, the end of all our hard work feels more like a funeral than a celebration. While Cas throws plastic sheets over the equipment and Morgan and Brianna disappear back into the house with Róisín to have their make-up removed, I double-check that Stan is happy with the sound.

"A-okay," the Cans Man says, taking off his headphones and beginning to pack up his gear. "Once you've got an early edit together, I can start mixing the track. Just ping it over when you're ready. Which I suppose won't be until after your surgery now?"

I nod, looking over at Cas. I've already told him that I want to work on the edit alone. He didn't object, didn't try to persuade me otherwise, hasn't even mentioned what happened between us last night. He just nodded and said he'd download all the footage onto a hard drive so that I could work on it when I felt able.

"It'll be a month or two," I tell Stan. "But hey, before you head off, I want to say thank you. It's been a pleasure."

He shakes my hand. "I'll do my best work on this one, I promise. This little film of yours, Jesse? I think it could really take you places. Just a pity it's all ending like this."

Stan glances at the squally heavens, but we both know he's not talking about the weather. Everyone has picked up on the mood, right from the first rehearsal run-through this morning. There's none of that jittery, giddy excitement you usually find on the final day of a shoot. Instead the atmosphere has been as bleak and solemn as the tumbledown house standing before us.

Most of the cast and crew were at Hinchcliffes last night, so even if they don't know the full details, they're aware that something upset Morgan. As for Morgs herself, I tried to speak to her privately before we got started this morning. I wanted to say that she wasn't alone in hearing

329

that nasty little voice, and maybe try one last time to get her to tell me what has really been going on since prom. All she'd say was that I should go speak to Cas. When I told her that wasn't going to happen and the reason why, her face had crumpled.

"It wasn't like that, not exactly. He wasn't trying to ruin things for you. He's been an idiot, but…" She sighed. "Please, Jesse, for my sake, try again with him. This is breaking my heart."

I don't know why, but hearing those words sparked a flash of irritation. "Mine too," I said. "But you were the one who told me Cas wasn't perfect, remember? You're the one who's been sniping and snapping at him for weeks, not me. So don't start defending him now. Or if you are going to, at least tell me the truth about all these secrets you've been keeping."

"I can't," she said slowly. "It isn't that simple."

"Oh, but it never is with you guys, is it?"

She didn't say another word, only brushed my arm with her fingertips and then went off to rehearse the scene with Brianna. It's only now that I realize I didn't tell her about the fears we share. And suddenly it seems too late.

I drift aimlessly through the crowd of zombie extras, patting backs, shaking hands, saying thank yous. They ask about any ideas I might have for a grand premiere. I say I'll get back to them. What on earth would a premiere even look like? Friends and family packed into the local community hall, plastic chairs, the smell of damp coats. Cold tea and warm orange juice being served through a hatch in the wall by the old ladies who run the kitchen. The director and cinematographer sitting together in the front row, barely speaking as their last project flickers onto some grimy old projector screen.

I wander up the steps and through the front door of the Lester house. My fingers play across tattered wallpaper. We've captured some real magic here. Scenes that sing, mostly because of Cas's incredible eye for the perfect shot. I move out of the hallway into the parlour, remembering the night we stumbled into this place together. His prank with the rocking chair and then him hugging me, holding me tight, worried that he'd hurt my heart.

"Hey, maestro! Congratulations!"

Louis comes striding into the room. He's smiling his typical Louis smile, the only one among us today who seems immune to the gloom. He takes my hands as the first burst of lightning flashes through gaps in the boarded window. It reminds me of the strobing lights on the dancefloor, of a chance missed.

"You did it," he says. "I knew you would."

"Thanks." I nod, dredging up my own smile. "And you were brilliant, Louis. We couldn't have done it without you."

"Oh, you'd have found someone else if I hadn't shown up,"

he says. "But I'm so glad I did. I got to be part of this wonderful project and through it, I met my cutie. First date tonight! Can you believe it? Oh, let me show you some pics I took of us after the gig."

I feel my soul sinking through the rotten floorboards as he takes out his phone and shares it between us.

"It's okay," I say. "Maybe later? I should really…"

He glances up at the sound of Brianna's voice echoing from the floor above. "Is that Bree? Is she with Morgan? Oh, Jess, I really should go and tell them how incredible they were in that last scene. Is that okay?"

That's more than okay, I think, as he closes the most adorable photo of him and Caleb, tongues poking out, faces squished together. He's almost at the parlour door when he pauses.

"Oh, and when I get back maybe we can talk about my play? No worries if you haven't made much progress yet, but I'd love to get some first impressions. Be back soon!"

Oh God, his play. With everything else that's happened in the past few hours I completely forgot about it. Maybe I've time to skim-read a few pages before he returns. Pulling out my phone, I bring up his message from yesterday containing the PDF and open the document.

I start to read.

My breath catches in my throat. "What the fu…?" My eyes skip ahead, plunging from speech to speech, action to action. My hand tightens around the phone until the casing squeaks. "What the actual fuck?"

It's the story of two brothers abandoned in childhood, brought up by a grandmother who has now, in the words of the script, "lost her marbles". A sweet old woman who is more comic relief than a living, breathing human being. The elder brother is the villain of the piece. A one-dimensional caricature without a single redeeming feature. A bully, nothing more. And the younger sibling? I feel rage burning inside me. A pathetic loser with obsessive hygiene issues and dreams he will never fulfil.

I close the document. Stare at the screen. Feel the floor tilt under my feet. A fresh rumble of thunder seems to shake the house. My hands shake with it.

"Jesse, is everything all right?"

Louis in the doorway, smiling his smile. Only in the flicker of lightning, his beauty is gone. It looks like a mask now, pale, fixed, inhuman.

"I've read your play," I say.

"Oh, that's great! What did you think?"

He comes forward, beaming, full of excitement.

"So all your research is finished, is it?" I ask, fingers flexing around my phone. "No more insights to be gained from your stay in Ferrivale? No more little notes to make? You know, Cas couldn't work out why you wanted to come and stay after all these years of no contact. Because they were the black sheep of the family, weren't they? The Loomises no one wanted to talk about? But still they opened their home to you, made you welcome."

He licks his lips, shrugs. "If you call that being made welcome. Cas made it pretty clear from the start he didn't want me around."

"Cas is a good judge of character," I say. "Always has been. Maybe he got a vibe off you right from the start?"

"Jesse." He laughs. "I don't understand what the problem is."

Another shard of lightning. His skin looks as cold as marble.

"You wouldn't." I nod. "It's funny, but I think anyone else might have thought twice before giving me this to read. But you're too self-involved, aren't you? Too arrogant, too oblivious to realize what you've done."

"All I've *done* is represent what I saw," Louis says, a waspish tone entering his voice. "I haven't lied. I actually thought I'd portrayed the three of them pretty sympathetically. Anyway, it's art, Jess; I thought you'd understand that."

"Whatever it takes, eh, Louis?" I shake my head. "You have to claw your way up onto that stage and, once you're there, make sure you stay there. Even if it means throwing your own family to the wolves."

"Family?" He laughs. "I barely know them. Come on, you're a writer. We need material, don't we? Things to actually write about. I can't believe you're just standing there claiming you don't understand." He sounds both angry and defensive. "So yes, I was going through this creative dry patch when I heard my parents talking about our 'unfortunate' cousins. If I'm honest, I could hardly remember them. But their lives – their challenges, their scramble to survive – you have to admit, that's dramatic gold. So I did what any conscientious writer should do. I packed up my bag and set out to do my research."

"And that was always the most important thing, wasn't it?" I ask. "The chance to observe your 'characters' close up. You thought you could do that at the flat, but a lot of the time Dean was out working and you'd already discovered that Cas was going to be making the movie. Hence the compliment about my photo on his Instagram, trying to ingratiate yourself before you arrived. If you were going to study Cas you had to get a part in *ZomHon*."

"Not that Cas made it easy," Louis admits. "Telling me the wrong time for the auditions and then continually giving me the cold shoulder. Oh, don't look so angry, Jess. You got a great deal out of it too. I gave you the best performance I could, pulled out all the stops."

"Don't pretend you give a fuck about me or this movie," I snap back. "That day I asked you to come to the hospital with me? Dean didn't come back late to the market stall, did he? You forgot."

"It was nothing personal," he soothes. "I promise. I hardly ever got to see Dean one-on-one. I couldn't pass up the opportunity of going to work with him. And I did come to see you in the end, didn't I?"

I give a bitter laugh. I can hardly look at him. "You betrayed them. Dean, Cas, Nanna. Their lives aren't some kind of kitchen sink drama for you to make a career out of." When I finally lift my gaze, I think Louis sees something in my eyes. He takes a step back. "I want you gone."

"Jess, listen—"

"Now. Or I swear to God, I'll call Dean and tell him what you've done."

I take a huge, shuddery breath, trying to absorb the shock of Louis's betrayal. That this person I had cared so much for could do something so cruel, so heartless. And that I was so blind I couldn't see him for who he really was. I watch him leave the room, scurrying away without a backward glance.

Then I feel my hands tighten into fists. My legs are suddenly weak, my fingers tingling. I gasp. There's this rising, blooming, horrible pressure inside my head. The wind screams. The sky booms.

Something is wrong.

35

I'm in the hallway. The front door is flung wide open and I can see Louis hurrying for the shelter of the trees. He glances back once over his shoulder, the look of a coward whose only concern is for his own skin. I dig out my phone and pretend to scroll through my contacts. When I look again, there's no sign of him. I take a ragged breath and slide the phone back into my pocket. I won't tell Dean. I wouldn't want Louis's deceitful, treacherous blood on my conscience.

My legs tremble. I snatch at the wall for support.

I'm trying to hold it together, but something is definitely wrong.

My heart seems to pound inside my skull. My vision shatters for a moment and it's like I'm seeing broken fragments of the house and the storm outside. A swatch of mouldy wallpaper floating among the trees; a knotted branch stabbing inside the doorway; the stone porch lapping into the rain like a long grey tongue. Then it settles again, everything sliding back into place.

At the sound of voices, I turn and look into the gloomy sitting room that stands directly opposite the parlour. Cas and Brianna are huddled together in a corner. She has her hand on his elbow, their eyes are locked.

"Thank you," she says, her voice only a whisper against the thunder. "You don't know what this has meant to me. I'm only sorry we did it this way. If I could go back..."

"But you can't," Cas says sadly. "Neither of us can. It's too late. Everything's ruined now."

I try to focus. Try to see the expression on their faces but my vision swims again.

"What do you mean?" Bree asks. "If this is about Matilda, I already told you how bad I feel. When she's back from her holiday, I'll explain what happened, apologize, beg her to forgive me."

"You should," Cas mutters. "And I will too. Jesus, Bree, what the fuck have we allowed ourselves to become?"

I can feel the pulse thudding in my neck, in my wrists, in my temples, like my skin can't contain the blood surging through my veins. I snatch down another breath. It feels like breathing through a straw.

"I'm sorry." She covers her face with her hands. "I am. I've learned so much these past few weeks. I'm not the same person who started all of this, I promise. Just being here with you, being part of this group, like a family. All working together on something positive. I've never had that before. At home, at school, it was only about how I looked, how I dressed, how I was seen. Now none of that seems to matter."

"But it did," Cas says. "It mattered enough for us to destroy the one good thing in my life."

"Don't say that," she pleads. "I was angry, okay? I had a right to be. But I didn't mean for it to hurt you like this. Not you, not Morgan, not Jess."

"I don't blame you, Bree." He sighs. "It's my fault. My stupidity, my weakness. I just wish I'd told him and then maybe we could have..." Cas has turned towards the hall, where he catches sight of me leaning against the doorframe. "Sparky? What's happening? Are you okay?"

I shake my head, try to bring him into focus. "I know what you've been hiding from me," I say. My tongue feels thick in my mouth, my words eeling around it. "You kept it secret."

He races over, grips my arm, exchanges a look with Brianna. "How did you—?"

"You didn't want to say anything because you knew how important the movie was to me. And if I knew what Louis was doing, how he'd betrayed you, there's no way I'd have him in our film. I'd rather trash the whole thing. Burn the footage. You... You saw it in his notebook, right?"

The notebook, Cas hunched over it. All that research, all those scribbled ideas for Louis's one-man play. Cas looks confused for a minute, maybe thinking that I was talking about his conversation with Bree. Something I don't yet understand.

"I wasn't searching for things to use against him," Cas says. "Honestly, Jess. I overheard him talking about it on the phone to one of his drama mates and I had to know what he'd written about us. I almost told you last night. I wanted to. But I knew if I did then you'd can the whole project. Because you'd hate him for what he did."

Brianna looks between us. "What are you talking about? What has Louis done?"

"But you only found the notebook last night," I say, the words slurry in my ears. "You didn't know before then what he was really like. You still tried to get between us, Cas. You still…"

"We can talk about it later," he says. "Jess, you're not well. We need to get you to—"

Blades of blinding light blaze through the open doorway. I feel Cas's hand tighten on my arm as I shiver. A bottle-green VW Beetle is screeching to a halt on the weed-cracked forecourt of the old Lester house. The headlights die and a moment later, Ethan Murray springs out from the driver's door like a demonic jack-in-the-box. Triumphant face gleaming in the downpour, he bellows over the thunder.

"I told you I'd get you back, you fucking losers!" He laughs, slamming a fist against the roof of the car. "And I did!"

At first, I wonder if he's come here to physically threaten us again, but he makes no move towards the house. Instead, his head turns to the avenue of trees through which he's just sped and a pulse of blue light washes across the forecourt. A police car rumbles to a silent standstill, parking up beside the Beetle.

"You thought I was some kind of moron, didn't you?" Ethan cackles. "Thought you were oh-so-funny, trying to humiliate me at that junkyard the other night? Well, I'm smarter than you think. Smarter than *anyone* thinks."

"What's going on?" Morgan says, joining us at the doorway. She looks from Ethan to the police car to Cas, who is still gripping my arm. Then her gaze turns to me and she lays her palm against my face. "Jess, are you all right? Oh God, he's shaking. Bree, call an ambulance. Now."

The police officers are out of the car and approaching the house. One of them calls to Ethan, telling him to get back into his own car and not to cause any trouble. I recognize this man – PC Bradstreet. The officer who interviewed us after we accidentally traumatized that motorist on our first day filming. The horror fan who wanted to come to our opening night. The friend who regularly plays poker with Mr Prentice. The rain is in his eyes, so I'm not sure PC Bradstreet can see us clearly as he starts up the front steps. But I can see him. Even as I struggle for my next breath and my vision clouds, I see an expression of sorrow rather than anger.

"Mr Spark, Mr Loomis, Miss Adeyemi-Perera. I'm really sorry it's come to this," he says. "But we have received information that you have been using the property of Ferrivale High School without permission. That you effectively broke into the school and stole equipment worth thousands of pounds. Now, I'll need you all to come with me to the station to answer a few questions, but first, I'm afraid that all illegally obtained equipment will need to be handed over."

Ethan must have overheard Brianna saying something about the equipment. Maybe heard her talking about the Lester house too. Reported us to the police. Did I say this out loud? I'm not sure. All I can hear is the sound of my heart.

Ba-doom. Ba-doom. Ba-doom.

I clutch at Cas's arm. "The film. The footage. All on the hard drives."

"Shhh, Jess," Cas says, holding me fast. "It'll be okay, I promise."

I let out a short, sharp breath.

Ba-doom. Ba-doom. Ba-doom.

Wait. Am I on the floor? Why am I on the floor? Did someone knock me over? Did I fall? Why is Brianna screaming? Why is Morgan crying and shaking my arm? Is that my arm she's holding? Must be. I can't feel it. I can only feel my heart.

Ba-doom. Ba-doom. Ba-doom.

Why is PC Bradstreet standing over me, talking into his walkie-talkie? Why can't I feel the wind on my face? Why can't I feel Cas's arms around me, holding me so tight, like he'll never let me go? Why can't I hear the words he's whispering while the tears stream down his face?

I can't hear them.

Ba-doom.

Ba-doom.

But maybe.

If I focus hard.

Ba-doom.

I can understand.

Jesse. Please. Jesse. Please, stay with me.

Ba-doom.

Jesse, I need you…

I sit on a plastic chair in the shower, watching pink bubbles skate down my skin. My few wisps of chest hair have been shaved and now the last thing I need to do is wash off this weird antibacterial soap. The canula running into the vein in my wrist makes my movements awkward, but the nurse who fitted it was very gentle and it doesn't hurt all that much. Apparently the anaesthetist will use it to administer all the drugs I'll need over the next three hours of surgery.

"Well, young man, we didn't expect to see you so soon," Dr Myers had said, coming into the side room and blinking at us through his thick glasses. "So it appears you had a very high spike in blood pressure this morning. We've managed to get that stabilized to a reasonable level, but I am concerned this is a warning that the aortic valve is in failure. And so, with your permission, I would like to bring the surgery forward."

Sitting at my bedside, Mum had gripped my hand. "How soon?"

"This afternoon. In the next couple of hours, in fact. Is that all right with you, Jesse?"

I had nodded. "Had to happen. Sooner or later. Right?"

Dr Myers blinked at me over his glasses. "Good lad. We'll see you in theatre."

Giving my mum a reassuring nod, he'd then slipped out of the room.

I remember my hands feeling very cold and Mum rubbing them between hers.

"I'm sorry," I murmured.

She'd glanced up at me. "What on earth are you sorry about, Jesse bear?"

Good question. I think I must have briefly passed out at the Lester house. I remember only fragments of what happened next – PC Bradstreet helping to lift me onto the paramedics' trolley; Morgan sheltering me from the rain with her coat as they trundled me across the forecourt to the back of the waiting ambulance; a glimpse of Brianna in floods of tears being comforted by Róisín – no performance now, no acting the part – a good friend in genuine distress; and Cas, arguing with the paramedics, insisting on coming with me, saying he wouldn't leave me. And he didn't. He held my hand all the way to the hospital and only let go when my mum arrived.

Finally, it came back to me. "The film equipment. The police. Mum, I swear we weren't going to keep it.

As soon as the movie was done, we were going to take it all back."

She reached up and brushed a tumble of hair from my forehead. "Don't worry about any of that silliness," she said. "It's not important."

"But if Cas and Morgan and the others get in trouble?"

"We'll see to all of that once you're better. *I'll* see to it, I promise. No one will get in trouble. And the film, well—"

"I don't care about the film," I had told her. And I don't. Not any more. We had created something really special with *ZomHon* – the dramatic opening scene on the forest road, the escape from the junkyard, the sacrifice of the husband, that bleak, beautiful final shot of the wife and hitchhiker accepting their fate. But after what I learned about Louis today, all of it feels tainted. Like his betrayal of the Loomises has infected every frame, polluting the soul of the movie as surely as any zombie bite. Cas was right. I'd rather it didn't exist at all.

Mum didn't try to argue. She just reassured me again that everything would be all right.

Now I turn off the shower and pull myself to my feet using the handrail. I take a little gasp of air. Dr Myers explained that my valve is struggling so much I'm not absorbing enough oxygen into my bloodstream. Still, I don't feel as bad as I did back at the Lester house, though my legs are weak as I drag myself over to the sink. I hold onto the basin, reach for the towel on the hook. After an exhausting eternity drying myself, I stare at my reflection in the bathroom mirror. A mess of damp curls, frightened green eyes. I let my fingers trail across my still unmarked skin. This is the last time I will see myself this way, whole and unblemished, and for once, I don't care. Oh, I'm sure that after it's all done, that nasty little voice will come back to me, stronger than ever. *Ugly, ugly, ugly.* But for now all I want to do is survive.

Survive and see my friends again.

Screw secrets. Screw lies. Screw this drifting between us. I need them. I always have.

Very slowly, working hard for every breath, I pull on the hospital gown that's been left for me on a stool by the door. Then I say goodbye to my reflection and clutch at the door handle, panting as I come back into the little side room.

Have I passed out again? Am I imagining things? Or are they here, sitting with my mum, their eyes shining back at me?

Morgan speaks first. "Jess. Don't you ever scare me like that again."

Then Cas, "There he is. Looking good, Sparky. Looking—"

Mum jumps to her feet but Cas is there first, catching me as I stumble, guiding me back to the bed. "He's all right. He's all right." He helps to lift my legs and pull the blankets back over me. "Just hogging all the attention, like usual."

But his smile trembles and he has to turn away, making a fuss of repositioning his chair. I see Morgan reach out to him and he grips her hand in response, nodding that he's okay. I pull down a tortured breath. I don't know what has happened between the two of them, maybe I never will, but if me passing out like a total drama queen has helped reforge their friendship then it's worth it.

"What are you smiling about?" Mum asks gently.

"Nothing," I say, gripping the bedsheets as I struggle between breaths. "Just. All this started. With me. Collapsing. At prom. And here we are. Again. Circle of life. Or circle of my. Weird. Life. Anyway."

Cas and Morgan exchange a look.

A beat.

"Please, Cas," she whispers. "Tell him."

He looks at me, looks down, shakes his head.

"Go on," Morgan implores. "It's time."

"What's going on?" Mum asks.

"I can't," Cas says quietly.

Morgan leans over to him, wraps an arm around his shoulder, murmurs in his ear. Like a parent reassuring a child that everything will be all right. But still he keeps his head down.

"I can't. I—"

"Jesse Spark, is it?" A hospital porter appears at the

door, wheeling in a chair. "Dr Myers and the team are ready for you now."

Mum comes forward and helps me out of the bed, settling me in the chair, kissing my forehead, telling me that she'll be there when I wake up. I nod. Feel numb. Not scared any more, not apprehensive, not anything really. Although maybe that isn't quite true. I'm curious about Cas. Worried about him. As the porter wheels me around to the door and I wheeze out a breathless goodbye, Morgan turns to Cas again.

"*Tell him.*" Her voice is breaking. "Please, Cas. *Please.*"

The door swings shut behind us. I can't hear them any more. I can't even ask the porter to take me back for a moment so that we can talk. We're already halfway down the long hospital corridor, the glazed entrance to the surgical theatres bearing down on us. I grip the arms of the chair, try to concentrate on my breathing. There's nothing I can do about Cas. Not now.

The porter swipes his security card and the glass doors slide open. Ahead, I can see another gleaming white corridor punctuated with more doors. We're moving again, rolling relentlessly onwards. A nurse in surgical gown and mask pops her head into the hallway and waves. The porter waves back. Almost there.

Almost.

"Jesse! Jess!"

I turn around in the chair. Cas stands with his palm pressed against the doors we've just passed through. He's saying something but we're now too far away for me to make out the words. All I can see is the desperation in his eyes, the sorrow, the apology. And then he's gone.

We've passed into the operating theatre and I'm being asked if I can stand and make my way over to the bed. It's so bright in here, so cold. This room is much bigger than the angiogram theatre and I feel very small, lost in all this vast, clinical whiteness. Someone helps me up onto the bed, tells me things that are about to happen. Says it all in a kindly, matter-of-fact voice, as if I'm a little kid at their first dental appointment. Everyone seems busy, checking computer screens, checking equipment. One nurse hooks up my canula to a long tube that threads away to a point behind my head.

And then Dr Myers is at my side. "How are we doing, Mr Spark?"

I snatch a breath. The air feels painfully cold in my throat. "Bit. Terrified."

"No need to be. Not with me as your surgeon." He pats my arm with a gloved hand. "I'm going to be with you every step of the way, I promise. And you're going to get through this. Know why?"

I shake my head.

"Because I want a free ticket to this new movie of yours."

He turns to his team. "All right then, people. Let's get Jesse started on the anaesthetic. Full concentration today. We have a very special young man in our care. Now then," he refocuses on me, "just so I know the anaesthetic is taking effect, I want you to start counting backwards from ten, all right?"

"Out loud?" I ask.

He smiles with his eyes. "Yes, Jesse, out loud or I won't be able to hear you."

"Okay." I touch my chest one last time, feel the thump of my heart. "Ten…"

I try to shut out the noise and bustle around me.

"Nine…"

Try not to think of what will happen when the darkness comes.

"Eight…"

Try not to think of what it will be like when I wake up.

"Seven…"

What I will be like.

"Six…"

Look like.

"Five…"

If I wake up.

"Four…"

I think instead of Cas.

Cas standing at that glass door, his hand pressed against

the pane. Words on his lips. Words Morgan had pleaded with him to speak. Are those words the cause of all the lies and secrets? Are they the reason we have been drifting these past months? What words could have that power?

"Th-th-three."

Three words?

But that makes no sense.

It can't be true.

Except it is.

I know it is.

I know

Darkness.

Nothingness.

No beginning.

No end.

No time. No space. No shape. No sound. No pain. Nothing to hate. Nothing to fear. Nothing to love. Nothing to cling to. Nothing to lose. Nothing to fight for.

Nothing.

Only.

Three words.

"Open your eyes. Jesse, can you hear me? Open your eyes if you can hear my voice."

I come gradually out of the dark. Sound first, the voice. Calm, coaxing. Then light. Brilliant. Blinding. Shapes moving against it, outlines of people. A room. Fuzzy, indistinct. Smell next. The hard, sharp, clinical smell of the hospital. Ugly but solid. Something real I can grab hold of. Now sensation. Damp sweat between my shoulders and the sheets, my hand pawing weakly at my side. And suddenly panic. I imagine arching my back to fight against it, but my body is slow, heavy, deadened.

There is something monstrous inside my throat. Something that shouldn't be there. Something harsh and artificial. It is plunging down into what feels like the pit of my stomach, choking the life out of me. Tears slide from the corners of my eyes. I try to lift my hand, to rip the thing out of my airway, but all I can manage is a flutter of my fingers. There isn't much pain but still it feels like I'm being suffocated, every scrap of air squeezed out of my body. Why won't anyone help me? Why won't anyone—

"Jesse, my name is Maria. I'm one of the nurses in Intensive Care. The operation was a success and you're now out of surgery. There's still a lot of anaesthetic in your system, so for the time being we need to keep a breathing tube in place. We'll be able to take it out once your lungs are strong enough to take over. It shouldn't be long now, but please try not to fight against the tube. Just relax as much as you can."

I manage to blink away the tears. Although I can understand what Maria is saying, still my instinct is to pull this awful thing out of my throat. I know it's helping me breathe but it feels like it's choking me too.

"It's all right, love. I'm here. Can you feel my hand?"

Turning my head is the hardest thing in the world, but

eventually my mum swims into view. She's sitting beside the bed. She looks happy but so, so tired. I try to speak and make only this tiny whistling sound.

"You're okay," she says, leaning forward to kiss my cheek. "You're okay, my baby. It went well. Very well, didn't it?" She looks at the nurse, who smiles and nods. "Dr Myers spoke to me and he's very pleased. You'll be home soon and back on your feet and driving me mad and making more films with Cas and Morgan. They're both outside in the waiting room. Been here for hours. Wouldn't go home until they knew you were safe. They send their love…"

I close my eyes, choke a little. I can't breathe. I can't.

I *can't*.

"Jesse? Jesse, look at me," Maria says. "I know it's distressing, and I'll remove the tube as soon as I can, but please try to stay calm. Think of something else, okay? Anything at all."

She glances at my mum, who draws closer to my bed.

"Listen, Jesse," she says, stroking the side of my face. "You know how I always say how goofy and ridiculous you and Cas can be?" She shakes her head, rubbing her eyes with her free hand and laughing a little. "Well, me and your dad? We were the king and queen of ridiculous. It's true. Like the time I said I'd love to go on a luxury cruise one day when we were older. You know, the whole five-star deal with a butler and a string quartet on deck, playing just for us? Well, the next morning I wake up and your granddad is going crazy because there's this random rowing boat sitting in our back garden, complete with one of your dad's best friends dressed up in a tuxedo, waiting to serve us canapés. And some kids from the school band are there, standing in the front of the boat, all in suits and ball gowns, playing show tunes. And there's your dad, lounging in the back, waving an oar at me and grinning from ear to ear." She brushes gentle fingers through my hair. "He was so much like you. Serious and silly and earnest and infuriating and so kind."

She holds my gaze for a long time and I can see the pain behind her eyes. The reason why she doesn't talk about my dad. Because she loved him so much that it hurts.

"I'm sorry, Jesse. I will tell you more stories about him. I will…"

I look down at our hands, and although I'm still weak, I try my hardest to give hers a gentle squeeze.

"We'll be brave, together."

Maria puts a hand on my mum's shoulder. "If you're ready now, Jesse, I think maybe you're strong enough to breathe again."

38

There's a stranger sitting in the chair opposite me. He's a boy of seventeen but his skin looks old and grey, his cheeks hollow, his lips drawn tight in anticipation of pain. He sits like a frightened old man, his movements slow and timid. He lifts a tissue to his mouth and his eyes narrow. He braces himself, ready for the agony of a simple cough. Then his hand flies open, the tissue falls, and he whimpers, feeling the healing bones of his sternum grind together.

I blink and the boy blinks back at me from the hospital room window. It's been forty-eight hours since my surgery. Early days, so Dr Myers says, though he's pleased with my progress. The new aortic valve is functioning well and all I need to do now is rest and recover. I might even be able to go home at the weekend. *If* I start eating properly. Strong painkillers have taken away my appetite and sometimes they make my brain foggy and forgetful, but still it hurts whenever I cough or move too quickly. I reach cautiously for the table beside my chair, using both hands to lift a small glass of water. A sip is enough for the dry bowl of my stomach.

Replacing the glass, I see my reflection again in the window. My dressing gown has parted a little and the beginning of something ugly is visible at the centre of my chest, starting just below my collarbone. Despite the twist of pain, I rush to cover it.

I haven't looked at the wound. Not properly. Even when showering, I'm careful to only catch glimpses of it. But what I have seen out of the corner of my eye has confirmed all my worst fears. A horrible scream of red; a nightmare that lies patiently waiting. It isn't going anywhere, it has all the time in the world, it *will* be seen. The nurses tell me it's "very neat" and that Dr Myers has done a "remarkable job" and that it "will heal beautifully". I nod and thank them and keep staring dead ahead.

A knock at the door. I straighten myself in the chair, summon the best smile I can. Apart from Mum, Dr Myers and the nurses, I haven't had any visitors since my surgery. All yesterday I was too exhausted to even lift my head from the pillow. The most I could manage was a group text saying that I felt okay (big lie) and that I was looking forward to seeing them as soon as possible (very true). Something happened right before I was taken into theatre, but the anaesthesia seems to have obliterated most of it. Only fragments come back to me, puzzle pieces trying to fit themselves together. Cas standing at a glass door, palm on the pane.

Three words.

I shake my head. "Come in."

They enter like scared kids, eyes round with worry. Cas is holding a shopping bag filled with treats, his grip so tight his knuckles stand out. Morgan trails a helium balloon with *Our Brave Little Soldier* written in big glittery letters. They come forward as if they're approaching a priceless vase that might shatter at any moment.

"Sorry about the balloon," Morgs says. "It was the only vaguely appropriate one in the shop."

"It's cute," I say as she ties it to the end of my bed. "Thank you."

They both pull up chairs quite a distance away from me and Cas starts unpacking his bag, describing the selection of sweets and drinks he's brought as if I've never heard of them before. Once he's arranged them all on my table, he draws back and retakes his seat.

"The weather's turned brutal," he says, glancing out the window. "Hasn't stopped raining since the last day of film— Well, since you went into hospital. Oh, Nanna sends her love, by the way. She's asked about you constantly. And Dean told me to say hi too."

"My mum asked if you'd been mobilizing yet?" Morgan rolls her eyes. "I said, give him a bloody chance, he's only just come out of major surgery. But you know what Mum's like…" She trails off. "Anyway, Jess, you seem really…"

"Guys?" I sigh. "Don't look so frightened. It's me. I'm okay, I promise."

Suddenly Morgan bursts into tears. She covers her face with her hands and her shoulders tremble. If I could, I'd jump to my feet right now and catch her in the biggest hug. But Cas steps in, wrapping his arm around her and flashing me a smile over her shoulder. There are tears in his eyes too. And although it hurts my heart that they're both upset, the sight of my two best friends comforting each other is the best treat they could have brought me.

"What's happened?" I ask them softly. "What did I miss?"

Morgan exchanges a look with Cas, and when he nods, she gets to her feet.

"Wait, what's going on?" I say. "You're not leaving already?"

"I'm going to grab a coffee downstairs." She comes over to me, kneels beside my chair. "I'm so glad you're okay, Jesse. I'll see you soon."

With a parting touch of Cas's shoulder, she's gone, leaving us alone.

We sit for a handful of eternal seconds. Then, very slowly, Cas gets up and takes a sheet of paper from his pocket.

"I drew this one day after school," he says, looking down at the neatly torn page from his sketchbook. "I was sitting at my desk at home, doodling a few ideas for *ZomHon*. This was weeks ago. You hadn't got your diagnosis yet, hadn't even started writing the script. We'd been throwing around storyboard ideas at lunchtime, and then walking home I suddenly felt this…" He struggles for the word. "Not anger. Frustration? Resentment? I don't know. A need to express myself, to be seen. To be honest, maybe. Anyway, this is one of the things I drew."

He hands me the paper.

It's Cas. The wavy hair, the big chocolate drop eyes, the cute Disney critter expression. He's standing beside what looks like the lake in the forest, looking back over his shoulder at the viewer. And his expression is so joyful. But he isn't alone. There's a boy standing next to him, holding his hand.

"Cas, what does this mean?"

"It means…" He closes his eyes. "I'm gay, Jesse."

I stare at him. I'm stunned; I don't know what to think, what to say. "Oh…wow. What…I mean, when did you realize?"

"A long time ago. This." He indicates the sketch. "This is me, as I am."

And suddenly everything makes sense. And nothing makes sense. And I'm happy for my friend and annoyed with him and I want to hug him and shout at him and all I can say is, "Why didn't you tell me?"

"You know why," he says, dropping heavily onto my bed. "Dean?"

He nods. "And other stuff. I suppose I knew right around the same time you knew. Maybe even a bit before. I was building myself up to it, getting ready to tell him, and then I saw how he started treating you after you came out. I love my brother, Jess. I know you think I'm an idiot for putting up with him, and maybe I am. But you have to understand, after Mum left us, he and Nanna were all I had. You have no idea what he's given up for my sake, to look after me, to keep a roof over our head. And I know that doesn't mean I owe him my soul and my truth and my identity, but still I couldn't stand the idea of him thinking less of me. It's fucked up, I get that. But it's—"

"It's family." I nod. "But you could've come out to me and Morgan."

Cas shakes his head. "Coming out isn't a fairy tale, Jesse. For a lot of kids, it's still hard and scary. We don't all have mums like yours. Of course, I knew I could trust you, but once the truth is spoken it has a way of leaking out. And growing up with Dean, absorbing all that bullshit machismo? I don't know. They call it internalized homophobia, right? You don't even acknowledge it, not consciously, but it's there, like acid eating away at you."

"Oh, Cas," I murmur. "I'm sorry. So all of this, is it connected to what's been happening with you lately?"

He nods. "It was the week before prom. Brianna was over at the flat going through some of Nanna's old fashion magazines, trying to get ideas for the perfect retro dress. Dean was at work and Nanna was out with her carer for the afternoon. Bree was so excited, showing me all these gown ideas, going on and on about how we were bound to be elected prom king and queen and I just…" He draws a huge breath. "I couldn't take it any more. I sat there on the couch and burst into tears. She asked what was wrong, started comforting me, and it all came pouring out."

"How did she take it?"

"She was hurt," he says. "She had every reason to be. I hadn't been honest with her. In fact, I'd used her. She's changed a lot these past couple of weeks. Being on-set with us all, mucking in, being part of the team. But she was never the selfish, vain airhead people liked to think. Even then, when I'd hurt her so badly, she cared about me. She said I should…" He closes his eyes. "She said I should tell you. Be honest. But I couldn't."

"So what happened?"

"Because I couldn't be honest, Bree needed a way out of the relationship. She decided that I'd be cast as the cheating villain while she stepped into the limelight, getting all the sympathy and attention. I didn't mind. I *was* the villain. A coward who'd lied to her from the start. But the way she wanted it done? I argued with her, tried to make her see sense, but she insisted. She knew Matilda had a thing for me..."

"Oh, Cas."

"I know." He looks so ashamed. "Sometimes I can't believe I did that. I feel terrible about Matilda. But I was so scared that Bree might tell everyone the real reason we'd broken up, and so I played along with everything she wanted."

"Everything?"

"I'd been talking up our movie for weeks," he says. "Telling her how great your script was going to be, what amazing ideas we had for the characters and action sequences. Well, now she said she'd really like a part, and not just a walk-on or a cameo either, but *the* central role. She never actually demanded anything, it wasn't blackmail, but I was scared about what might happen if I didn't at least try to get her what she wanted. It was impossible, though. I knew she couldn't get the part on merit. Not without help."

Suddenly it clicks. "Brianna's parents didn't pay for acting lessons, did they?" I say. "You told Morgan what was going on."

"She didn't want to do it," he says miserably. "She agreed with Bree. Said I should tell you. But I pleaded with her until finally she agreed to coach Bree until she was good enough to audition."

"She did an amazing job," I say. "And that's why you didn't back Morgan for the part of the wife? And why she insisted on only playing the hitchhiker?"

"I hated not supporting her," he says. "But I couldn't see any other way."

A jumble of memories swarm in on me all at once – Morgan defending Brianna's acting skills, telling me that "she's a better performer than you think"; Brianna at the club, asking us not to think too badly of her, whatever we later discovered, and that she really had tried to earn her place in the movie; Louis saying that something about Bree's performance seemed artificial, "as if the rehearsal itself has been carefully rehearsed".

"Morgan felt terrible for not telling you," Cas says. "And she resented me for making her lie to you. The weirdness you've felt between the three of us? The distance? That was all my fault. All of it caused by my lies, my fear, my stupidity."

"But I don't understand," I say. "Cas, why didn't you tell *me*? Never mind about coming out to everyone, surely you knew I'd be okay with it? That I'd never tell anyone if you didn't want me to." He hesitates. "Come on." I reach out as far as I can so that I can take his hand. "We've been friends since for ever. You know whatever it is, I'll be here for you."

"Friends." He nods. "Promise we'll always be that, Jess. Best friends. Because you…"

With his free hand, he reaches into his pocket and brings out a second torn piece of paper.

"You mean the world to me. You always have."

He passes me the drawing.

At first I can't understand what I'm looking at. The two boys again, hand in hand, this time face-on to the viewer, the lake rippling behind them, a dying sun throwing their long shadows on the ground. Their eyes are locked and the joy in one is reflected by the joy in the other. I run my fingertips over the page. I know this second boy is supposed to be me, but it's hard to recognize myself. My briar mop of hair is a tumble of cute curls, my dull green eyes are shining, my ridiculous face maybe not so ridiculous after all. Maybe even beautiful.

And suddenly I'm remembering that night in the woods, just before we arrived at the Lester house. A breathless moment when I brushed back Cas's hair and noticed how gorgeous his eyes were in the moonlight.

"Jess. The truth is…"

Three words spoken behind a glass door.

Cas speaks them again now.

"I love you."

39

I can't take my eyes from the drawing. I want to speak, want to reassure him, want to tell Cas how all this makes me feel. But do I even know? The pages of our history are flicking through my head, a blur of images, like a film being run too fast through an old-fashioned projector. And with each frame, an explosion of sight and sound and memory, each linked to an emotion that ties our lives together. We have been Cas and Jesse for so long. The best of friends. And now, with this single drawing, I'm being asked to look at everything from a new perspective.

It is a new perspective, isn't it? Perhaps not. I think back to that old unspoken crush I once had on my best friend. Perhaps deep down I've always known that he cared too. Perhaps I was just waiting for the opportunity to see things as they really are.

"You don't have to say anything," he says, a hitch in his voice. "I don't expect you to feel the sa—" He stands and goes to the window, pressing his palm against the glass.

"I don't expect anything. I just needed to say it. And to say I'm sorry for all the secrets and that I hope we can still be friends."

I shake my head, my eyes still on the drawing. "Did Morgan know?"

He sighs. "It's how this all started, in a way. Remember *Little Shop of Horrors*? Us two in the front row, cheering Morgs on as usual?"

I wince, sitting up a little straighter in the chair. I always knew it began the night of the Easter show.

"It was at the after-show party at Argento's when Morgs told me what she'd seen," Cas continues. "Whenever she was onstage performing and happened to glance down at us? Only you were looking back at her. Every time she looked at me, I was just sitting there, stealing glances at the boy I loved. In the dark, with everyone else concentrating on the stage, finally I could look at you. Really look."

"Cas," I murmur.

In the reflection of the window, I see the tears rolling down his face, mirroring the rain.

"She challenged me about it at the party. Said she'd guessed ages ago and that I needed to tell you. She was so kind about it. So gentle." He shakes his head. "And I threw it all back in her face. I was angry, scared, denied everything. Said she was delusional and should mind her own business. And then Brianna descended on us, in a state because her parents had slammed her performance. And so what did I do?" He bangs his fist against the glass. "I used her. Pretended I fancied her. To prove Morgan wrong, maybe to even prove myself wrong. I'll never forgive myself for that."

"You were upset," I say. "Not thinking straight."

He shakes his head. "Please don't make excuses for me, Jess. I can't bear it."

And so I say nothing. The rain drums against the window and Cas keeps his back turned.

"After I confessed to Bree, I had to go back to Morgan and tell her she'd been right. About everything. When I said I needed her help to get Bree up to speed for the auditions because she wanted the wife role, I thought Morgs would tell me to go screw myself. She had every right. I knew she loved that part and was desperate to play it. Instead, she begged me again to be true to myself, even if that meant only telling you. But I couldn't."

"Why not?" I ask. "If you loved me…"

"Because I was scared," he says simply. "Scared of what telling you might mean for us. Because we've been best friends since for ever and telling you could change everything. I couldn't. Morgan said she understood, but still she hated the position I'd put her in. Things hadn't been the same between us since the Argento's party and now we started drifting even further apart. Funnily enough though, the more she coached Brianna, the closer the two of them became. I think it surprised her, that she started to see some of herself in Bree – the way Brianna's family treat her, the expectations she puts on herself."

I nod. If ever she was the villain in our story, she isn't any longer. Brianna is our friend. My friend.

"That's why you and Morgan were so relaxed about the finances for the film," I say slowly. "You already knew Bree's dad would come through with the cash."

"But we couldn't tell you." He nods.

"And why Brianna mysteriously forgave both you and Matilda so quickly for betraying her." I shake my head. "Right from the beginning I had this feeling that I was being manipulated. But there's something I still don't understand. You only found out why Louis was in Ferrivale the night before the final day of shooting. Up until then you couldn't have guessed what he was really up to, but you were hostile to him from the start, getting me out of the flat before he arrived, telling him the wrong time for the auditions. Why?"

"Can't you guess?" Cas sighs. "It's what Morgan accused me of in the club."

My thoughts fly back to Hinchcliffes and Morgan's part of the argument I overheard: *What you need to do is stop trying to interfere. I'm serious, Cas. You made your decision and now you have to live with it. I've done what I can to help you out, even though I still think you're a fucking idiot, but I won't sit back and watch you ruin this for him. I won't.*

"I wanted to keep the two of you apart as long as possible," Cas says. "Because I thought he'd fall for you. And yes, I saw that message he posted under your photo and I was jealous. Not because he might take my best friend away, but because—"

"Wait. Cas, look at me." When he finally turns around, I can't keep the disbelief out of my voice. "You thought he'd fall for *me*?"

"Of course."

I frown, close my eyes. "Hold on, hold on. You honestly thought a boy like that would like someone like me?"

He seems genuinely puzzled. "Jesse, why the hell wouldn't he? You're smart and funny and kind and, well." He blushes a little. "Gorgeous, obviously."

All I can do is stare at him. It's like he's talking a different language. And then my gaze drops to where my dressing gown has pulled open a little and that first trace of hideousness begins.

"Funny kind of gorgeous," I murmur.

And suddenly he's kneeling before me, gently taking my hand.

"My funny kind of gorgeous," he says. "And this? This scar? Don't you get it? To me, this is the most beautiful thing in the world. Because it means my Sparky is still here, with me. My best friend. Hey, it's all right. Jess. It is. I promise."

He reaches up and brushes the tears from my eyes.

"I hid so much from you, but you never have to hide anything from me," he whispers.

And so I take a breath, and part the folds of my dressing gown, and see the horror that has been torturing me all these weeks. See it fully, but now through different eyes. Not as a wound, not as a flaw, not as a shame to be denied and kept out of sight. No, this is the scar that I'll carry all my life, and I will bear it as a blazing mark of pride. It shouts to the world, *I am Jesse Spark, I am here, and I survived.* It took this new perspective to make me understand. It took the eyes of a boy who loves me.

The boy I have always loved in return.

"Cas?"

He looks up and smiles that Disney smile. "Jess?"

"Please may I kiss you?"

Two Months Later

"Who even invented these stupid things? Honestly, were they designed as a medieval torture device or something? Gah! I just can't!"

Cas rolls his eyes and comes to stand behind me, reaching over my shoulders and swiftly fixing the perfect bow tie. Then he pops his chin on my shoulder and we both smile at ourselves in the full-length mirror. Mum managed to find my dad's old tuxedo hidden away somewhere in the loft. It's almost good as new and fits pretty much perfectly. She cried when I tried it on and spent the next hour telling me stories about their high school dance from a million years ago. We talk a lot about Dad now and it makes us both happy.

"Looking ultra-adorable, Sparky," Cas says, missing my cheek and accidentally kissing my ear.

"Looking very adorable yourself, mister."

And he does. One of Dean's contacts from the market owed him a favour and the result is this beautiful vintage dinner jacket with burgundy bow tie and shiny dress shoes.

"So," I puff out my cheeks, "shall we?"

He nods. "Your carriage awaits."

Before we leave the room, he places a gentle hand on my chest, his palm warm against the scar beneath my shirt. The wound has healed and the bones beneath are slowly knitting back together. Doc Myers says that within a year the scar will have faded into a long silver line. I know it will never vanish entirely and I'm glad. It is part of me now and I cherish it. After all, it marked so many new beginnings.

Mum is waiting for us at the bottom of the stairs. She looks amazing in this cute tulle evening dress with sequin beading. I think I can guess why she's made the extra effort, and it isn't only because of our special night. I shoot Cas a knowing look and he hitches an amused eyebrow in response.

My mum must have taken about a hundred pictures on her phone by the time we're halfway down the stairs, but then suddenly she stops and wipes her eyes. She's watching as Cas holds my arm, carefully helping me down each step. I'm loads stronger now but I'm still healing and stairs can be a chore.

"You two," she says softly. When we meet her, she wraps her arms around both of us and kisses our cheeks. "Come on then, let's get this show on the road."

The Thing of Evil greets us on the garden path with one of his customary snarls. Jacques is characteristically unfazed by the whole spectacle; even the gleaming limousine waiting at the kerb doesn't impress him all that much.

Our chauffeur taps a forefinger to the brim of his cap and opens the rear door for my mum.

"Can I just say, Miss Spark, you are looking absolutely—"

Mum shoots a warning glance. "Choose your next words very carefully, Dean Loomis."

He flashes back a cheeky grin. "Absolutely stunning. And the nerds don't scrub up too bad either, do they?"

"Thanks, Dean," I say, as he takes over from Cas and helps me into the back of the limo. "You're looking very smart too."

So yeah, funny how things work out. That little chat I had with Dean at the flat, the one where I told him how all his snide comments and homophobic jibes were primarily hurting his little brother? Well, it took him a few days, sitting with my words and his prejudices, debating inside his head, justifying himself, questioning himself, wrestling with his mistakes. He admitted to us both later that it hadn't been an easy process. He had shed tears, both out of anger and guilt. But when Cas came home from seeing me at the hospital, Dean was waiting. Before Cas could say anything, Dean pulled him into the biggest hug. He said he knew; that he'd pretty much always known, and that he was sorry. He said he couldn't explain why he'd been so hostile towards me, only that he wanted to protect Cas, mostly from people like himself. Stupid, intolerant bigots. He'd asked for Cas's forgiveness and promised to do better. And honestly? He is.

"How did you get hold of this car and that uniform?" my mum asks as our chauffeur takes his place behind the wheel.

He throws her a wink in the rear-view mirror. "Ask me no questions and I'll tell you no lies. Anyway, it was either this or my honey wagon."

Mum holds up her hands. "Just drive. And if we get stopped by the police, I'll do my best to talk us out of it."

He taps his cap again. "Yes, ma'am. Only, we've got one quick detour first."

I glance at Cas, who shrugs.

I'm not sure a limousine has hurtled through Ferrivale at quite such a pace before, but we manage to reach the far side of town in one piece. Here Dean slides back the huge sunroof and throws up his arm, waving at the Loomis flat. High up on the balcony, Nanna Laura and her carer let off party poppers and wave back at us. She looks very small and frail from this distance; the past couple of months haven't been kind. It breaks my heart but she can't quite remember my name any more, though she still knows that today is a special day.

We leave the town behind and start on the forest road.

The sun is beginning to dip behind the trees and all along the lane leading to the old Lester house, swags of fairy lights have been strung. I turn to Cas and grin.

"You did this?"

"Well," he says. "I might have had some help."

The limo sweeps into the forecourt of the old house, which has been garlanded with so many twinkling lights it looks like something from a fairy tale. I'm so mesmerized by the sight that it isn't until Cas helps me out of the car that I realize just how many people are here. A huge crowd gathered at the side of the house lets out this deafening cheer. Phones are held up like lamps, flashes going off in the gathering gloom. And then a dozen or so people break away and come rushing up to us. Róisín and Stan, the zombie extras, Tiny in the most enormous tuxedo I've ever seen, all shaking my hand and clapping me (very gently) on the back.

Finally I see the two people I want to speak to most.

Brianna is wearing a gorgeous red evening gown, her hair twisted up into a fiery spiral.

"This is your night, Jesse," she says, kissing me on both cheeks. "I'm so happy for you."

I shake my head. "Tonight belongs to all of us, Bree. And I can't wait for everyone to see how brilliant you are."

She glances between me and Cas before lowering her eyes. "That's very sweet of you, and more than I deserve. I only wish I hadn't—"

"Enough," Cas says gently. "No more apologies. Friends, right?"

She smiles and nods. "Always." Then she lays her head on Morgan's shoulder. "Best friends."

Morgs rolls her eyes, but in an indulgent way. "Who am I to argue with the queen of Ferrivale High? Especially after your dad forked out for all this." She glances around at the scene. "How did you persuade him, by the way?"

"I told him that my big screen debut had almost been ruined by my dumbass twin brother. Oh, and that unless he made tonight extra special, I might just send an anonymous email to the taxman, revealing the details of certain offshore bank accounts. I was joking, of course, but he doesn't have to know that." She shrugs. "Yeah, okay, maybe a little of the old Brianna Murray is still alive and kicking."

We continue chatting in our group while the other guests mill around us, waiting for the big announcement. At one point, Mum comes over on the arm of PC Bradstreet, or Hank, as he's now known to us. He looks a lot less intimidating in his dinner jacket and cummerbund. I tip Cas a knowing wink. Although they're pretty much mortal enemies professionally (according to Mum anyway), they seem to have bonded when Hank turned up at the hospital after his shift and sat with Mum throughout the long hours of my surgery. Since then they've been on half a dozen dates and things seem to be going well.

"Looking forward to the big event, Jesse." Hank grins. "Although I'm still not entirely convinced you guys didn't pull a fast one on me over that film equipment. What do you say, Toby? Did these young mobsters intimidate you into changing your story? You can tell me."

Hearing his name, Mr Prentice comes jogging over. Tonight the drama teacher is dressed in a crushed velvet suit with a striped orange bow tie. Classic Prentice attire.

"Are my ears burning?" He grins.

"I was just saying, that equipment. What was the real story there?" Hank asks.

Prentice purses his lips.

So here's the real story – while I was unconscious in the operating theatre, Cas was busy on his laptop – the only piece of tech the police hadn't seized – cutting together some very rough *ZomHon* footage he had saved in the Cloud. It was a desperate gamble, but it was also our only shot. After an hour of editing, he was satisfied enough to ping over a couple of scenes to Mr Prentice's school email, hoping against hope that he'd check it during the holidays. Luckily, it was also the email Prentice was using to communicate with Hank about the case.

"If I've told you once I've told you a thousand times." Mr Prentice sighs. "I gave the boys very clear permission to use any equipment they liked to shoot their remarkable movie. It isn't my fault if that idiot boy got his wires crossed. No offence, Miss Murray." He gives Brianna this strange little bow. "But your brother really is the most dull-witted student I've ever taught."

Bree nods. "I think that's more than fair. My dad definitely thinks Ethan's a moron. After he got that caution for wasting police time, Dad's had him down at one of our farms as punishment, mucking out the pigs until Christmas."

We all grin, and then Mr Prentice comes forward to shake mine and Cas's hands.

"A good job it *is* such a remarkable film," he murmurs. "Otherwise I might have remembered that conversation a little differently."

"Thanks, sir," we both whisper back.

"No thanks required. However, please remember our deal – one whole year helping out at junior film club every Thursday after school. Yes?"

We nod and blush.

Then suddenly the wail of an electric guitar cuts through the night. We all turn to the stage set up in the clearing beside the house, the canopy of a huge movie screen towering above it. Silhouetted against the screen is a boy in a sparkling black leather coat that reaches down to his ankles.

"Ladies and gentlemen," he croons into a big old-fashioned microphone. "If you could all begin to take your seats, our main feature is about to start."

Bree jumps up and down on the spot, clapping her hands. "Isn't he gorgeous?"

The boy on the stage catches sight of her and waves. Naturally Caleb Rush is our master of ceremonies. He'll also be performing with Dancing for the Super Worm after the film. Oh yes, and he is *also* Brianna's new boyfriend.

"Excuse me," she squeaks, and starts to skip away from us. "I just want to wish him luck for the concert later."

"She's something, that girl." Morgan smiles, shaking her head. "And I guess they make a cute couple. Better than him and Fuck-face anyway."

Fuck-face is Morgs's none-too-subtle nickname for Louis. Who has *not* been invited to tonight's premiere. Once I'd regained my strength a little, Cas had brought over his laptop to the hospital and, bit by bit, managed to reawaken my excitement in the project. I remember him perched next to me on the bed, showing me the rough-cut he'd sent to Mr Prentice. I had to admit, the movie really worked. And as Cas said – "*Yes, Louis betrayed us, but that doesn't diminish what we've all made together. ZomHom belongs to all of us. It's our journey, not his.*" Or as Morgs ever so delicately put it, "*Screw Fuck-face.*"

And so, after two months of hard work, here we all are, walking down the red carpet, the trees gently swaying around us, the stars just beginning to spark against the black. As we move down the central aisle of seats, Cas nudges my arm and nods over to where Signora Argento and her son Dario are excitedly waving back at us. Tonight the infamous diner owner is in a blue gingham gown and appears to have come as Dorothy Gale from *The Wizard of Oz*.

"Best wave back, Cas," I tease. "Remember, you're a friend of Dorothy now."

He laughs and tells me to shush.

And then suddenly a small, sniffly man in an immaculate dinner jacket, and with thick glasses perched at the end of his nose, steps out in front of us.

"I shan't detain you, Mr Spark," says Dr Myers. "I just wanted to say congratulations on your big night and to thank you for sending the complimentary ticket to my off— *Ooofff!*"

Cas has launched himself at the heart surgeon, throwing his arms around the little man and hugging him tight. "Sorry, sorry," he says, pulling back and brushing down the doctor's jacket. "It's just, I never got to thank you. For saving him."

Dr Myers sniffs. And then beams at both of us. "It was very much my pleasure, young man."

Cas slips his hand into mine and we walk together to our seats. Mum and Hank are to one side of us, Dean and Brianna on the other. But there's one seat empty as the lights go down and the huge screen in front of us glows white. My head flips around, trying to locate my other best friend. And then a spotlight hits the stage and Morgan steps into it. Caleb comes forward to adjust the microphone to her height and she thanks him before fixing me with her gaze.

"Good evening, ladies and gentlemen. My name is Morgan Adeyemi-Perera and I am so honoured, not only to introduce the incredible film you are about to see, but also to have played a small part in it."

"Yes!" Bree shouts, jumping to her feet and applauding. "And you absolutely smashed it, you gorgeous babe, you! And FYI, looking stunning tonight too!"

Morgan smiles at her, her whole face lighting up as we all start to applaud. "Thank you, Bree. And you know what?" She strikes a pose. "I *am* looking especially gorgeous tonight."

So yeah, Morgs has found a lot of confidence in herself lately. It isn't only from that sprinkling of positivity she received, and has now largely come to accept, from Bree, but from long conversations she and I have shared during my recovery. We've talked. And talked. And talked. Talked in a way we never have before. Perhaps because, for the first time in our friendship, we could truly understand each other's vulnerabilities. And so, being open and honest with each other, we've finally begun to face our fears head on. It hasn't been easy, and we're both still on a journey to accepting ourselves. We have a long, long way to go, we know that, but we're now making our way down that road.

Oh, and one other thing that has given Morgan a boost – there had been an agent present at her audition for the *Marsha Rivera Chronicles*. A smart guy who saw what those other idiots did not – Morgan's incredible gifts. Anyway, my friend is now all signed up to one of the biggest talent agencies in the business and auditions are flooding in!

When the clapping dies down, Morgan looks back at me and Cas. There are tears in her eyes. She lets them fall.

I reach for my boyfriend's hand. He takes it. My heart is full.

"We are here tonight because of the dream of two very special people," Morgan says. "I first met them when I was seven years old. A silly, bossy, lonely, scared little girl who was looking for someone to be her friend. Well, I lucked out that day. I didn't find a friend. I found my soulmates. My Jess and my Cas. And look at us now, ready to start new adventures. I love you, guys. This one's for you."

Cas and I exchange puzzled looks while at the side of the stage, Caleb begins to play the opening chords of our movie's theme. Meanwhile Morgan grips the microphone with both hands, her gaze still fixed on us, a smile on her lips. And then she starts to sing.

"*It's only love; Not the end of all things; Not a world torn apart;*

Only love; Like a tide drawing in; A complete work of art;
Only love; And what's love, after all?
For two undying hearts?"

Cas leans in. He whispers, "I love you, Sparky."

And under the stars, as our movie starts to play, I tell my best friend that I love him too.

Author note

Dear Reader,

Jesse Spark's story comes directly from my heart.

Pretty much literally!

A couple of years ago, I was diagnosed with a congenital heart defect known as a "bicuspid aortic valve" – not an ideal situation, as our hero discovers in the story! I was told that major open-heart surgery would be required one day to correct it. Well, that day finally arrived for me in October 2019. Despite the wonderful surgical team at the Royal Papworth Hospital, led by the amazing Mr Ravi De Silva, the operation was still a daunting prospect and my recovery wasn't a walk in the park either.

In fact, my first walk in the park after I finally got out of hospital wasn't a "walk" at all. More a hesitant shuffle around the duck pond with lots of pained grimaces and stops to catch my breath. An old lady of about eighty also paused at one point to ask if I needed help to get to the nearest bench. She ended up almost carrying me, bless her heart!

But here's the thing: I survived the op! I was alive! And I knew I'd eventually get back to full strength! Hurrah! Now all I needed to do was come to terms with what had happened to me. Because, you see, I hadn't just clawed my way back from the jaws of almost certain death (hey, it was open-heart surgery, I'm allowed to be a little melodramatic!) but I now had the mother of all scars to prove it. A great big angry red blemish (as I saw it then) tearing its way down my chest. In the early weeks of my recovery, I was super self-conscious about this monstrous thing.

I didn't want anyone to see it. Because it was ugly, right? Something to be hidden away at all costs.

And then slowly, very slowly, I began to think about my scar differently. This was my battle wound. My signal to the world that I'd faced something seriously scary and survived to tell the tale. It wasn't ugly. It was part of me. And you know what, I have lots of faults – like Jesse, I'm horribly klutzy and I sometimes let my mouth run away before my brain can catch up – but one thing my scar proved to me: I'm pretty bloody brave! And so I started to see it in a new light. My scar was a badge of pride, something positive.

And it was beautiful.

A lot of culture screams at us that we must be "pretty" – whatever that means. Some small and fairly toxic aspects of gay culture do this too. They insist that there is an "ideal" for boys like Jesse: the perfect toned body, the impossible abs, the flawless skin. To my mind, this is horribly corrosive and just plain WRONG.

And it's why I wrote *Broken Hearts and Zombie Parts*.

Surgical scars like mine and Jesse's aren't unmentionable horrors to be hidden away and ashamed of. They are to be embraced and celebrated as part of our journey through this joyous, tricky, surprising, upsetting, wondrous, scary, fabulous thing called life. Because you know something? None of us come through it without a scar or two, real or metaphorical. That is the journey I went on writing this book – exploring with Jesse all the feelings and nuances that arise from a serious health condition and the legacy – physical and emotional – such a huge thing leaves us with.

Pretty much everything in *Broken Hearts* comes from a real place. Things I lost sleep over, things I came to terms with, things that made me cry my eyes out and things that made me laugh myself silly. I've taken some very small liberties with the timing of certain medical procedures, that is all. This is far and away the most personal book I have ever written and it feels right that, although it tackles some serious subjects, it is a comedy. Because laughs aren't just to be found in the good times – they are there, waiting for us even in our darkest hour.

And perhaps that's when we need them most.

Your friend,
William

Acknowledgements

As already highlighted in the dedication for this book and in the Author Note, I owe undying (quite literally!) gratitude to Mr Ravi De Silva, Dr Stephen Hoole, Alison Ames, Suzanne Ward and the whole team at the Royal Papworth Hospital for saving my life and for looking after me with such care and dedication. Who knew that a book would come out of it too!

I would also like to thank my fellow heart disease warrior (and one of the bravest people I know) Kerrie Kent for all her insights and help with the initial stages of this book. Kerrie has faced some incredible health challenges with the kind of courage and humour you can hopefully see reflected throughout *Broken Hearts and Zombie Parts*. You can find her own gorgeous, life-affirming work on Instagram at @goldheartedclub.

My thanks, as always, to my agent Veronique Baxter of David Higham Associates. This is our first romcom and she has been as wise, supportive and encouraging as always. Thank you, V! My foreign rights and media agents Allison Cole and Clare Israel have also been brilliant on this quite different journey – everybody lives in this one! Hurrah!

Editor extraordinaire Stephanie King has been with me since *Hideous Beauty* and was so enthusiastic about "JESSE", as we originally referred to this book. Her early edits on the manuscript were typically incisive and big-hearted. Taking over from Stephanie for the later stages, I have been blessed by the equally kind and laser-focused editorial eye of the wonderful Sarah Stewart. My thanks also to Deirdre Power, copyeditor Hannah Featherstone and our sensitivity reader Helen Gould. Gratitude too is due to brilliant cover designer Will Steele and cover illustrator Ricardo Bessa, text designer Sarah Cronin and the fabulous marketing and publicity team of Jacob Dow and Jessica Feichtlbauer.

Debbie Scarrow and Dawn Andrew are my eternal readers of first draft and I owe them not only my thanks but a ton of cake. Thanks also to my old friends Kasun and Dina Perera for loaning Morgan their surname.

Love and gratitude as ever to my family: Dad, Carly, Jamie, Jackson, Charly, Georgia, Jon, Johnny and Lyla. And always to Mum – we miss you so much.

And thank you to my darling Chris. For making a silly old broken heart whole again x

About the author

William Hussey is an award-winning author of over a dozen novels. From thrillers for young adults to gripping whodunnits for grown-ups, he has written in almost every genre of fiction. His latest books include the acclaimed political thriller for teens *THE OUTRAGE* and LGBTQ+ love story *HIDEOUS BEAUTY*. William lives in the seaside town of Skegness with his faithful dog Bucky and a vivid imagination.

🐦 @WHusseyAuthor
williamhussey.co.uk
#BrokenHearts

Turn the page to discover more unputdownable YA stories from William Hussey

"Stunning...a gorgeous, twisty, gem of a book"
Simon James Green
HIDEOUS
Beauty
WILLIAM HUSSEY

How well do you really know the people you love?

Dylan falls for Ellis the moment he meets him – he's funny and fearless and makes living in a small town like Ferrivale more bearable. Dylan is head over heels in love, although deep down he sometimes wonders if Ellis is keeping secrets from him.

When a tragic accident rips them apart, Dylan begins to discover just how little he knows about the boy he loves, and that Ellis isn't the only person in Ferrivale who's been keeping secrets...

Powerful, page-turning and perfect for fans of Adam Silvera and Karen McManus.

THE
OUTRAGE

WILLIAM HUSSEY

Welcome to England, where the Protectorate enforces rules for everything: what to say, what to wear, what to do, what to think, who to hate and who to love.

Gabriel is a natural born rule-breaker. And his biggest crime of all? Being gay.

Gabriel knows his sexuality must be kept secret from all but his closest friends, not only to protect himself, but his boyfriend too. Because Eric isn't just the boy who has stolen Gabriel's heart. He's the son of the Protectorate's chief inspector – the man who poses the single biggest threat to Gabriel's life.

And the Protectorate are experts at exposing secrets.

"Disturbing, heartbreaking and terrifyingly believable – this is dystopia at its absolute best. A timely and important novel."
Reading Zone

Love this book? Love Usborne YA

Follow us online and sign up to the Usborne YA
newsletter for the latest YA books,
news and competitions:

usborne.com/yanewsletter

 @UsborneYA

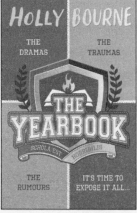
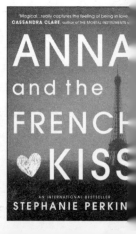